TENDER PREY

TENDER PREY

PATRICIA ROBERTS

CHATTO & WINDUS

THE HOGARTH PRESS

LONDON

Published in 1983 by
Chatto & Windus · The Hogarth Press
40 William IV St, London WC2N 4DF

British Library Cataloguing in Publication Data

Roberts, Patricia
    Tender prey.
    I. Title
    823'914 F   PR6068 o
    ISBN 0–7011–2730–9

Printed in Great Britain by
Redwood Burn Limited
Trowbridge, Wiltshire

for Harvey

TENDER PREY

1

I bother only with widows.

Solitude leaves widows more pliant than it does old maids, which perhaps is why the old maids are what they are to start with: neither use nor ornament. Actions speak louder than words, and while the spinsters fall into the right language sooner—by the second letter the fast ones are already calling you naughty boy and such—it is the widows who are more apt to turn words into deeds. There are those who will tell you the exact opposite, of course, but it has been my experience that, one sniff of a suitor and, abracadabra, the spinsters turn skittish as Cinderella's sisters. Sly as young girls, they treat you to this comedy of respectability and remorse—all for your benefit, you think, until you work out that through the crocodile tears, they are keeping a sharp eye on Prince Charming's true intentions. Give me the forthright lies of widows any day of the week. Life is too short to placate the long suspicions of old maids.

Or of rich widows, if it comes to that. Money makes the rich ones arrogant. With their accounts in the bank and their telephones in the front hall, they can afford to be carefree on the surface but, as I was fated to discover—and the price of that knowledge came high to me—it is a studied spontaneity that is both demanding and dangerous.

I was God's own gift to widows until I fell foul of a rich one. It was sheer bad luck that I got caught, for I had my pick of several responses—just as an ad, say, for Napoleon's sidearms will turn up such and such number of the faithful, so can you count on a certain number of widows to answer a personal. Spinsters in the main prefer to be the ones placing the ads, thereby attracting those types whose judgment is on a level with their enterprise; which is as the old maids want it, I don't doubt.

Luck was with me in the timing at least. If this had happened a couple of years earlier, before I had filed for citizenship under the immigration amnesty in '29, I would have risked deportation like a common Sicilian. It would have been back to Belfast for me, and if you think the work situation is bad over here, you should only know what's going on in Belfast: walls rubbed smooth at shoulder height from the jobless lounging against them. Protestant men, at that. Besides, the police over there are like elephants. They never forget; and who wants to be brought face to face with the ghosts of yesteryear?

This time I got caught with my hand in the till, more or less; the details aren't important. The long and short of it is, I was sentenced to one-to-ten in Sing Sing on a grand larceny two. It was my own Black Thursday, let me tell you, that day in December—December '31—when I was sent packing up the river. But I learned my lesson, as the judge who tried me was fond of repeating. Never again would I lock horns with a rich widow. Never again would I spend Christmas in jail—though that second vow was not quite to be.

December is an unlucky month for me.

I have spent three Christmases in jail; the two in Sing Sing and the last one in the prison ward at Bellevue. The doctors there said I was abnormal, on account of my use of language of a lewd and indecent nature. I've got a mania for swearing is what they meant, and that's a pretty mild way of being abnormal when you consider it; a misdemeanor and no harm done. The doctors must have thought so, too, for they let me go at the end of three weeks, though not before they had used some of their own kind of language on me. Constitutional psychopathy, they said, and put their John Hancocks to it. With strong obsessive trends, they said. I saw the report.

It was a prank had me in Bellevue in the first place. I was living in New York City when I got this job upstate as an attendant at the Rockland State Hospital for the Insane, which is something to smile about when you think of me in the other position in Bellevue. I am a shipwright by trade, but there's not much going on in that line of work nowadays and Roosevelt left us out of his WPA schemes, so I take any job I can get. I have been a sexton and a janitor in my time, but working in a lunatic asylum is not so hard on the back as digging graves or hauling garbage, and it's got other rewards besides. You never have to buy food, for one thing, and you can pick up free bedding, too, if you know enough to be careful about where it's been. My first week at Rockland I found a skeleton that one of the doctors in Admin had thrown out, and nothing wrong with it that I could see but a broken rib. Just propped in a can.

It was having a parochial school opposite me that got me into trouble. I had rented a little place outside New City, and I had been working at Rockland for about a month when all this happened. That's when I was rotated to the night shift, and my new schedule found me wide awake at three in the afternoon, just in time to watch a parade of girlish innocence making its way to the bus stop a few yards past my house. I got the idea of standing back in the shadow of the door and calling things out to the girls as they waited, their faces half hidden by those funny hats the nuns make them wear. One of the girls must have reported me to the sisters, and nuns have no sense of humor, they're well known for it, and they called in the police. The coppers caught up with me at Amsterdam Avenue, where I had gone for a weekend of relaxation. I expected them to take me back to Rockland County for questioning, but my New York address was listed as my perma-

nent one, so they carted me off to Bellevue instead. Funds must
have been low in the county that month. Or maybe Mother Superior bribed the police. Those types stick together.

While I was working nights at Rockland State, I would pass
the time making lists of ideas, themes you might call them, on
what I would say to the girls the next day. If I showed you the
kind of things I wrote, you would see it was all meant as a joke,
man-of-the-world stuff, nothing serious enough to get put away
for, especially if you saw the loons I was cast in with at Bellevue.
Not that most of them were not harmless, mind; just men who
had tried to kill themselves or who went around pretending they
were Napoleon or the Kaiser—more Kaisers than you would expect after all this time—but there were a couple of sorts there the
doctors did well to label abnormal.

My second night inside, Harrison was brought up. He had
come to Bellevue of his own accord and hidden himself in a lava-
tory until everyone had left. Then he tied an elastic band around
his private parts and cut them off. The rubber band was so he
wouldn't bleed to death. He did it in Bellevue because he knew
he would need medical care afterward, but his scheme almost
went awry. He passed out from the shock, and if a nurse had not
come in and caught sight of Harrison on the floor and his privates
in the sink, it would have been too late to save him.

"How did you do it, Harrison?" I said when he was well
enough to talk to. "Did you have one band around the whole
thing, or did you tie up each bit by itself?" I was enthralled by
the way he had planned everything, right down to timing the visiting hours.

"I just did it," he would say, not answering me directly. "I always wanted to get rid of that garbage, and now I've done it."
Cold sober he was, too, when he did it.

I never did get to see what he looked like down there. He
was kept swaddled the whole time I was in Bellevue, and even
when he was well enough to walk around, he still did his business
in a bedpan behind screens.

The only person Harrison would sit with was this Byron
Something-or-other, one of those long Greek names, who talked
all the time. The day before the police pulled me in, Byron had

got himself arrested on a drunk-and-disorderly and was thrown in a cell to sober up. Sometime in the middle of the night, the police put some bum in with Byron, and the Greek claims he woke up with the man's member in his mouth. More or less by reflex, Byron says, he bit it off. The bum lay there screaming, but nobody came, and in the morning the police found him in a heap on the floor. He had bled to death in the night. The coppers looked high and low for the missing part, but they couldn't find it anywhere, and when they roused Byron, he was still too drunk to remember what he had done with it. That's why they sent him to Bellevue.

You can understand at this point Harrison's fascination with Byron, though no one but me seemed to see the humor in the coincidence. When I tried to talk to Harrison about it, he cried and had me turned away. My interest was not wholesome, the attendant said. More doctor language.

The night before he was to be transferred, Byron got hold of a pork-chop bone. He must have had it smuggled in from another ward: All our meals were chopped up for us, and we ate them with wooden spoons that were counted up at the end of the day. Woe betide us, too, if one was missing, for we were not allowed to go to bed until it was found. Anyway, Byron spent his last night with us sharpening the bone on the windowsill, and by the time he was finished, it was good as any knife. The next morning, on his way to the Tombs in the Black Maria, he killed himself with it. That long-winded Greek was a great one for embarrassing the police.

This all took place on Christmas Eve, the day visitors were supposed to stay longer, in honor of the season. When news reached us about Byron, though, everyone got into such a state the extra hour had to be canceled, and Harrison was put into isolation under twenty-four-hour watch. The ward was a bear garden the rest of the day, a proper bedlam, and a lot of turkey went to waste in the visitors' hall.

You have to understand about the visitors. They did not come to see their father or their son or whoever. Armed with great bundles of food, they came to eat. By the time the prisoner was brought to the hall, the family had spread their wares all over the table: bread slabs thick as doorsteps and fruit enough to cater a wake. None of them said a word until everything was eaten, and not much afterward. Just a lot of sighing and burping, with the visitors trying not to notice that their fathers or sons or whoever were likely as not playing with themselves. The room was at right angles to the ward, and I could see it all through the window. I swear, if I had not known beforehand which were the prisoners and which the visitors, I would have been hard-pressed to tell one group from the other. Every time one of the Napoleons opened his mouth, for instance, his wife or whatever she was would pop a candy in, then slap her knee and cackle. Every time. She knew that she had stopped him, for the moment at least, from telling her yet again how an attack of piles or some such had cost him Waterloo. Which is what I heard all day.

I had no visitors. My wife, Emma, had left me in '22, taking Robbie with her. Robbie was two and christened John when I met Emma, but we changed his name to mine after we were married. I suppose he is back to being John again, since that's the name of the man she ended up with. Mrs. John Muller, she was calling herself last time I heard, though they are not properly married. How could they be? She is still my wife in the eyes of the law.

Wallace is a Scottish name. I was born in Belfast, Northern Ireland, like my father before me. His father had come over from Argyll, Scotland, I was told, so I guess I could have called myself Scots-Irish if I had known the term. We didn't have such fashionable hybrids back then. I thought of myself as Irish, of Scottish descent, and after all these years I still smile when I hear talk that the Ulster Protestants are not true Irishmen. I can't speak for the cockneys of Londonderry, of course, but everyone knows, should know, that the Scots came from Ireland to begin with. Everyone should know, too, that Protestants have been to the fore in most of the Free Ireland nonsense. Tone was a Protestant; so was Parnell—Charles Stewart Parnell—though that fact was only remembered, in typical Irish fashion, after his disgrace. If they are good for nothing else, the Irish can be counted on to turn the ashes of yesterday into the fuel of today, and let de Valera—and a real Irishman he sounds—put that in his pipe and smoke it.

I was born on March 26, 1885, the same year the Mussulmen of Khartoum sliced off Chinese Gordon's head—and whatever else besides, if you read between the lines. There's nothing like religious fervor to bring out the devil in a man, and the appetite of Allah's disciples is every bit as catholic as those of Christ in that particular respect.

Two years after my birth, my sister, Margaret, came along, and my father, with a growing family to feed and no work in Antrim, crossed to Scotland to work on the Firth of Forth bridge. A great marvel in its day, that bridge. A few months before it was finished, my father fell off it and died—or so it was explained in the black-edged letter that accompanied the death certificate. That was the only thing included with the certificate. This was 1890, remember, and there was no thought of compensation in those days. Anyway, the upshot was that my mother found herself penniless, and I, at the age of five, found myself in the Royal Ulster Orphanage. Maggie, who was a touch feebleminded, was sent elsewhere.

I wet the bed almost every night my first two years in the orphanage, and every morning Matron would drape the bed linen around my shoulders and march me up and down the dormitory until the sheets were dry. If a night did pass when I showed self-restraint, Willie McKee in the next bed would be sure to pee over mine for me, and none too careful in his aim, either, making the others laugh as Matron pinned his still-warm sin to my body. Willie was one of the worst, a true foundling named for the night watchman who had brought him in. He had been abandoned in a basket at the gates of a mill; like Moses, said Matron, who did not know him. She knew a lot more about the Bible than she did about boys. Under Scottish law, Matron told us, the souls of orphan boys slept no more quietly than their bodies, which—like those of hanged men and suicides—could be used after death for medical research. A predestinating Calvinist, she took our lack of grace for granted, and so, after a while, did we. Might as well be hanged for a sheep as a lamb, Willie used to say, though it was the lambs he always picked on. Perhaps, after all, Matron understood us better than we knew.

At the beginning of my third year at the Royal Ulster, my

mother married again and moved to Ballycastle, in the north of Antrim. She had been coming to see me once a month, on Visiting Sundays, but she broke the news of her wedding by letter. In the opening sentence she let me know that the new husband did not want the old one's children around, and though she promised to send for me as soon as he changed his mind, I did not believe her. Neither did Matron, who was reading the letter to me—everything sent to us was opened first in the office—and our suspicions were justified. First my mother stopped visiting me: Ballycastle was a long way off, she said; and then she stopped writing as well. I was left to rot for three years.

Predictably, my life at the orphanage became easier from that time on. Now truly abandoned, I joined the ranks of the have-nots; it became my turn to torment. In an orphanage, in any institution for that matter—jail, school, the poorhouse—those who get anything extra, a new pair of bootlaces, a second potato on the plate, are picked on in terrible ways by those who get nothing. Mr. Bennet, who taught Reading and Scripture and who, unlike Matron, knew us better than he should, had this little trick of showing favor to a new boy just to make sure the rest of us would give him no mercy. Afterward, the old hypocrite, and he a deacon in the Church of Ireland, would rush forth to comfort the victim. A new arrival, therefore, meant some excitement for us, and—though this was not Mr. Bennet's intent—the result was educational, even kind in a way. One week into slavery, as we jokingly called our situation, and the youngest boy understood. (The girls, too, I suppose, but they were held in the building across the yard, and all we saw of them was their laundry.) Lads of five in the Royal Ulster were quick as boys twice their age on the outside. And in spite of their fear of the torture that partiality brought with it, it was my experience then, and has been my observation since, that the favored preferred abuse to deprivation.

I waited five months for a letter from Ballycastle before I gave up hope; before Matron told me about Jamie. My mother, Matron said (and this explained the look on her face when she had read me the wedding letter), my mother, just before she married my father, had put another son, my older half brother, into the orphanage. Jamie had been incarcerated there for eight years, six of them without word from my mother, who had been living in Belfast the whole time. Two years seems to have been her tolerance for the role of visitor. Nine months before I arrived at the orphanage, Jamie had turned eleven and signed up in the Navy. His imprisonment in the Royal Ulster had bought me what little family life I had known; and I had not been aware of his existence.

With all this in mind, then, it came as a surprise when my mother showed up at the Royal Ulster in the August of '95. I was ten and full of thoughts of joining, maybe meeting, Jamie on the seven seas, but my mother had other plans. Her new husband—who, it turned out, had been old—had died on her; but this one, instead of saddling her with children whom she would undoubtedly have scattered among Antrim's institutions like so many more worthless seeds, had left her some money. With her dower, she explained, she intended to open a pastry shop in Belfast. This is where I came in. She knew from Matron's reports that I was handy in woodwork class and, in return for taking me back, she set me to building shelves and putting up the counter and the partition that divided the shop from the back part. Everything was bought on tick, of course.

From the day she opened it, the place did well. My mother was a first-rate pastrycook, and we were the only such shop on Clifton Park Avenue, which was a good section then, though I hear it has turned Catholic and gone downhill since. The customers did not know it, but most of the cooking was done in advance upstairs, where we lived. She baked only a few pies in the rear, for the smell. She was a woman who took great pleasure in petty deceptions.

Well, I take great pleasure in petty deceptions, too. I was the delivery boy and bookkeeper, and within a few weeks I was putting by not only my tips but some of the profits as well. From that time on, I never again wore shoes too small for me—I lay all my later troubles with my feet to those years when I had to squeeze into other people's castoffs; whatever else we lacked, we orphans always had shoes—and from that time on, I never again trusted women with money. For it is a fact that my mother, with all her self-serving guile in other areas, did not once bother to examine the books. When we finally did fall out, it was over Jamie, not the money. I had cached that in the cellar and kept it safe with my talk of mice. I nicked my finger and showed it to her. "Either it was a rat," I said, "or we have the largest mouse in Christendom living down there."

She denied Jamie. Even when I threatened to bring Matron to the house, she continued to disown him. She was on the point of denying Maggie, too, but she caught herself in time. She gave us so little thought, is my belief, that she had our ages confused. It must have been the expression on my face that warned her I was the older child. At any rate, she changed her story. Maggie, she said, had died in an epidemic that carried off half the backward children in Antrim. But who knows?

I was tired of playing her fool, that much I knew. I collected my satchel from the cellar that night and, four years after entering her house, I left for good. I never saw her again.

She is dead now. Not too long ago I ran into someone who had known the shop. He told me that she had become R.C., like the neighborhood, before she died. There's no accounting for the actions of a woman without character, and to this day I don't know if she turned so that she would fit in better—she was a great believer in accommodation, when it suited her—or if she did indeed get the Papist call. Perhaps she did. She had the kind of ruthlessness that converts with age to sentimentality.

I was fourteen when I ran away from her. Was that the end of my childhood? the doctors at Bellevue wanted to know—and me having just finished telling them how I worked like a man from the age of ten. Orphans don't have childhoods, I told them. If you define childhood as that period when, in return for protection, a boy submits his will to the whims of his elders, then my childhood ended when I was five, when I entered the Royal Ulster. There, where the rules were like piecrusts, made to be broken, I lived in a state of rigid anarchy. The tighter the discipline, the slacker the morality, if Mr. Bennet's old-smelling bed is the model. And when, too, a child is denied the simple freedoms of family life, when he can't go to the toilet as he needs to and in private, but must go on the hour with an army of boys jeering at his parts, then will that child turn inward and dream of more extravagant liberties. Except in his dreams, there is no sanctuary for orphans. "You can't have a childhood without a family," I told the doctors, but they were too protected, too privileged to see such an obvious truth.

In 1899, the year I ran away, the Boer War had just broken out. The Royal Navy was screaming for volunteers, but by then I had lost any inclination to drown for England. I crossed to Liverpool, the first city in the world to have a society for the prevention of cruelty to children, what a laugh, and joined the merchant marine as an apprentice shipwright. I spent the next three years sailing to every port on the Continent, carrying cotton mostly, and to some in North Africa. It was not until 1902 that I made my first run to New York; and felt as though I had come home. The expressions on the faces of the people here were as familiar to me as my own nose. Fear, humility and cunning: the three-tined survival kit of the world's unwanted, as identifiable and as irradicable as a birthmark. Long before a man opens his mouth, I can tell by the way he holds himself, by the posture he adopts when he is about to speak, that he is an immigrant. I know from the way a woman sneaks ahead in a line that she does not speak English, that she's trying to get ahead in the only way open to her. New York was a city of orphans, all trying to get a little bit more than the next one. It had no rules to daunt the likes of me.

I jumped ship on my second run, and stayed. I spoke English, of course. Yet my sense of craft was European, or so I played it, and I got work denied to others.

You can tell from the kind of life I have led that I am an independent sort. I can take people or leave them. The doctors at Bellevue tried to make a fuss out of Emma running off, but the truth is, I missed Robbie a lot more than I missed Emma. Like Maggie and Jamie, Robbie, too, is lost to me. Today he is a man of twenty-three who probably answers to the name of John. There is nothing left of the ten-year-old boy I last saw.

We were living at the better end of Astoria Boulevard in Queens when they left me. I had never been happier. Around the corner from where we lived was this old Dutch Reformed church —I always dwell close to God, it seems. The church has a new altar screen, which I designed and carved when I was sexton there, and I did the inscription that's cut into the dado below it. The dado was part of the original church, and the wood—old oak—was the hardest I ever worked on. Later, even after I had gone to work at a proper job, the minister called me in to make a new arm for the big Christ over the altar. The hand had to be carved at an angle, just so, to fit the crucifix, and the elbow had that awkward crook in it, yet I did the whole thing from one piece of pine and aged it so well that you could not tell the new arm from the old. You can see I took great pride in my handiwork until Emma ruined everything.

What made it all so unfair was that Emma had seemed calmer than she had been the year before. That was when Robbie fell ill with the consumption and had to be put in hospital. I took on a second job to pay the bills and fill his parcels with toys, while Emma saw fit only to stand at his bed and cry. Robbie came home after ten months, and there was no more talk of consumption, a diagnosis in which I had put no faith in the first place. No blood came up that I ever saw. As I said, I was never happier. I was renovating some warehouses in New Jersey at the time, staying over there during the week and coming home weekends, and what with the extra money coming in from my sculpturing, we were luckier than most those days. This was 1922, and while it may have taken seven more years for the Crash to make poverty official, most of the world had known about it a long time before that. With the poor and meek and lowly, Lived on earth Our Saviour holy: Jesus would have felt right at home among New York's immigrants.

I got back to Astoria earlier than usual that Saturday. The house was empty. I thought my premature arrival accounted for the mess—Emma was a lackadaisical housekeeper at best, and I knew it was her custom to do a hurried cleanup just before I was due. At any minute I expected her and Robbie to walk through the door, and an hour had passed before I grew uneasy.

It was beginning to get dark when there was a knock on the door. A neighbor, Mrs. Bing, stood on the welcome mat, and right away I knew something was wrong. Mrs. Bing used to steal the cream from the top of our milk as it stood on the doorstep:

Emma, up early for a change, had caught the woman in the act, and they had not spoken in months. Even if that had not been the situation between them, I would have guessed from Mrs. Bing's brightness of eye, of mouth quivering to inform, that whatever she had on her mind was giving her too much pleasure for it to be anything but bad news for the Wallaces. And so it proved. Talking so fast I could scarcely make out the words, Mrs. Bing told me that she had seen Emma and Robbie walking off, dragging a couple of suitcases apiece. A bare half hour before I showed up.

My first thought was that Emma must be out of her mind to burden Robbie so. He had been home from hospital less than two months. It was only after I had spent fifteen minutes going through everything with a fine-tooth comb that the full significance of the news hit me. Everything small—the china teacups I had brought with me to America, the cuckoo clock I had given Emma when we were courting—was missing. All her clothing was gone, and the sheets, too. She had even stripped the bed. Worse, she had taken my clothes as well, including my good shoes. The puppy I had given Robbie as a coming-home present had also vanished, but the little wooden dog I had made for him when he was ill was still on the mantelpiece, next to my mouth organ, which he loved to play.

Two things grew clear to me as I tabulated my loss. Emma wanted Robbie to forget me, to have nothing that would remind him of me. She had always been jealous of us. And she had taken my clothes to her new man. For I saw at once that there had to be a man. It's a rare woman who will walk out like that without having someone to go to, someone she's been going to for some time, if the truth be known, who will pay the rent and put food on the table. And keep the bed warm.

I went nearly mad that night, trying to think what to do. It was one thing for Emma to take a lover behind my back, but quite another to steal off with Robbie—and half my worldly goods into the bargain—and disrupt our lives in this way. You can see that I had not yet grasped that they had gone for good.

The next day, too, passed in a daze. I cleaned up the place, which was bogging, and at one point decided to go buy some eggs and convince myself that the outside world was going on as usual in spite of my catastrophe. But the neighbors were out in force that day, loitering with intent, it seemed to me, and I retreated inside. Early Monday morning, after two days in a kitchen as bare as Mother Hubbard's and two nights on a bed without sheets, I was glad to get back to my job in Jersey City. I still had no clear idea of what I should do.

The following Saturday I was back in Astoria, waiting to question the mailman, with half the neighborhood as audience. When the mailman came, he proved rude and uncooperative. Something he said made me think he knew that I was not Robbie's natural father, and it dawned on me that Emma could have taken more than one lover. Long before I had gone to work in New Jersey, there had been all those days when she was away, visiting Robbie. She could as easily have been bouncing on some mail sack in the depot.

It was the milkman, a married man with children, who told me where she was. She had, he said, transferred her milk order to Francis Lewis Boulevard in Bayside; an action quite out of character for Emma, who looked ahead about as often as did Sam, our puppy—until I remembered her feud with Mrs. Bing. Emma was not the kind to leave bottles around to be raided by her enemy. It meant, too, that she had known in advance not only that she was leaving but where she was going.

Mrs. Bing and I had become almost friendly by this time, for a man deserted by his family is less than the equal of a woman caught stealing milk. Throwing pride to the wind, I asked her if Emma had been in the habit of receiving visitors while I was away. "Only the minister," Mrs. Bing said. "Robbie's tutor." Tall and dark. Not bad-looking, she said, smirking.

I was Robbie's tutor. Most of the time that he was in hospital and part of every Sunday since he had been home, I had been helping him with his reading and his sums, and considering that he had missed a year of schooling, he was hardly behind at all. I have a better-than-average vocabulary, and what I lack in formal education I have more than compensated for by a program of private study. Nobody could mistake me for one of those foreigners flapping his arms about to fill in the gaps in his English.

Robbie had said nothing about another tutor. Neither had Emma, who had no money to pay for one. If I had believed for one minute in the minister-tutor, I would have asked at the church or the school. But I could think of no one at either place who answered Mrs. Bing's description, and I had no desire to shame myself that way. Instead I took a ride to Francis Lewis Boulevard. I had been waiting less than fifteen minutes—I knew the block but not the house number; it was off the milkman's route—when our dog came out of a door. I crossed and knocked on it.

Emma was surprised to see me. She did not invite me in. Just stood there, her face growing red and angry. I pushed past her, but there was no sign of Robbie.

"He's at the movies," she said, by way of greeting. She was wearing her hair differently, looser, and it made her face look fatter.

"I'll wait," I said. There were lumps in the sugar bowl, as if she were expecting company. Sam, who had followed me inside, began barking and leaping at the sight of me.

"You keep that thing quiet, or I'll strangle it," came a voice through the door Emma was standing next to—guarding, I now realized. I shoved her aside. I had it open in a trice, and there on the bed, on my sheets, no doubt, lay a man naked to the waist. He was long and thin, with a nice head of hair on him.

"Who are you?" I said, very poised considering the shock of finding a stranger in my wife's bed.

He leaped up when I spoke, but I was ready for him. I had come armed with a walking stick, and I smashed him on the head with it, sending him reeling. I grabbed him and yanked him through the door, and with one arm around his throat and the cane threaded through his suspenders, I half marched and half pushed him into place in front of Emma. He had smooth-looking arms, strong like a prizefighter's, and he was younger than I by a good ten years. Without the cane I would not have felt so jaunty. He was taller, too, and hipless, and I saw that, while my shirts might fit him, Emma could have left me my trousers and my good shoes. He did not look to me like either a minister or a tutor, but Mrs. Bing was right in one respect: In spite of the large egg swelling on his forehead, he was a good-looking lad.

"Who are you?" I said again, cane at the ready.

"He's John Muller, and he's been staying here a few days," said Emma, bold as brass.

"And a few nights, too, I shouldn't wonder," I said. I wasn't angry. Surprised to catch him so easy, of course; and interested. The truth is, I became quite excited at the idea of what he and Emma had been up to in that house. I had been married for eight years, and a man needs a change of scenery, and he who denies it is a liar, which we all are from time to time, being human. I have had my share of thoughts about such things, and it crossed my mind that we three might have a pleasurable evening together if I could set the right mood. "Maybe we should sit down and have a little talk about this situation," I said to him.

But he was suspicious and not the right sort, and he ran for the door. I grabbed the bread knife—I had been eyeing it in case something of that nature occurred to him—and I managed to gash his arm before he galloped off, leaving behind him a generous amount of blood on the doorframe.

"Look," I said to Emma, putting down the knife to show her she had nothing to fear. "Your fancy man has left us his crimson calling card." The thought of Muller—who, for all his German name, had a chest hairless as an Englishman's—running bloody and half naked through the streets of Queens suddenly struck me as funny. I began to laugh.

Emma became very agitated.

"You're dangerous," she said, and backed out the front door. "If you're not out of here in five minutes, I'm going to get the police, and by the time I'm through telling them the kind of things you get up to, they'll lock you up and throw away the key."

"There's blood on your sleeve," I called after her, but she was gone.

I did not wait for Robbie to get back. Emma probably had plans to intercept him anyway. I stayed long enough to find my shoes, then left. Although I did not believe that Emma would really go to the police, I did not go straight home, just in case. After all, I had not anticipated her leaving me either.

The next day I returned to Bayside, and discovered that Emma had pulled another vanishing trick. She and Muller had moved out right after I walked away, or so the woman on the stoop next door told me; a widow lady. That's when I learned that Emma was expecting the first of the two bastards she had by her fancy man. I looked no further after that, but it was a bleak way for us to end.

I had met her in the summer of '13. I had been doing some work outside Princeton, and I was walking back to town when a dog came running out from nowhere and bit me on the leg. I had learned at the Royal Ulster to attack first and question later, so I kicked the dog with my good leg and was about to bring my workbag down on its head when this girl came running up.

"Please, sir, he's only a puppy, please don't hurt him," she said, or words to that effect, and she scooped up the dog in her arms. There was blood trickling down both her legs, and I thought the animal had attacked her, too.

"Give it to me," I yelled. "I'll kill it, the savage brute." But she turned and ran like greased lightning to this house off the road. I followed, limping.

That was Emma. Strange, how dogs have played such a part in our lives: A dog helped to bring us together, and a dog helped to separate us.

She locked the beast inside the house, then brought out some water and began to clean my leg. She looked about twelve with her blond hair loose and her skirts hitched up, but she told me she was sixteen. I realized after a while that she was not hurt; she was bleeding because her courses were on her, and she was letting them run free. A dead fox lay under the porch where we sat, and rats or something were moving through the garbage that was high as a hill against one side of the house, a shack really. The stench of it all was enough to turn a stomach—this was August— yet it was the sight of Emma kneeling at my feet, washing my naked leg and unaware of any shame in her own condition, that stays with me still. The dog snuffling behind the door was the only sound. I asked her if she was alone in the house.

"Papa is asleep upstairs," she said, and giggled.

Papa, it turned out, spent most of his time in bed. In eight years of married life, I never set eyes on the man, not even at the wedding. He could not have been asleep all the time, however. Emma was one of eight—actually, she was one of seven, but at the time of my original count I thought that Robbie was Emma's brother—and a sorry life she led until I rescued her; a fact she would not be too anxious to be reminded of today.

I began to drop in on Emma and her family on my way home from work. I mended the sagging porch and painted the side of the house that faced the road, and before the ground got too hard I buried the fox and the worst of the garbage. After a couple of months of hard work and sweet-talking, I sounded out Emma's mother on the idea of my marrying her daughter. I was twenty-eight, temperate and employed, and you would have thought I'd've been a welcome presence in that shiftless house. Mrs. Anderson, though, urged on no doubt by the layabed upstairs, kept putting off her decision, saying how Emma was a child still, and what a loss Emma would be to her and all. Meanwhile, Emma, who by this time was baring more than her soul, as they say, was whispering that her mother would not miss her except as a servant to cook and clean, but not too much of the latter that I could see. Anyway, I caught on to what was expected and offered compensation. "For the loss of Emma's company," I said. We all knew what it was, really.

Until the money changed hands, Mrs. Anderson let not one word slip about Robbie—who was still called John at this point. Then, taking me aside one evening, she presumed to tell me the story of his birth. Emma, so her tale ran, had been seduced by a traveling man the family had good-heartedly befriended. I had already heard about it from Emma, though the rape part got lost and sundry other details were added in Emma's version. I had early on noticed Emma's attachment to the child, and when I questioned her about him, she did not bother to lie. I should have guessed then that she did not love me.

It is to Emma's credit that she did not want to leave the boy with her mother; and for her part Mrs. Anderson, while pretending reluctance at losing him, clearly had no intention of keeping him. The upshot was that, after a three-day honeymoon, Emma and I picked up Robbie—Emma had agreed to the name change —and we set up house as a threesome. The Andersons must have thought me a rare muggins.

We were married on my birthday, March 26, 1914, at Calvary Episcopal on Madison Avenue in New York City. Afterward, I took Emma for a ride on a trolley. I had planned to show her the city on foot, but she was too chilled. With all that I had given to Mrs. Anderson, the woman had not seen fit to provide Emma with a warm winter coat.

I had to show Emma how to tear old sheets into squares, the way the girls in the Royal Ulster did at their time of the month. At first Emma only made use of this knowledge when she went out, or to bed. I had grown fond of a clean bed to sleep in. The rest of the time I would wipe up after her, and pleased to, until Robbie got too old. "It's a lot easier than grease spots," I used to tell her, and she would giggle.

I was teacher as well as husband to Emma in those early years; and father to her son, whom I loved as my own. Robbie was a frail, small-boned boy, but I didn't mind that. It made him look more like me. He had a quickness of mind that he must have inherited from the fast-talking traveler, and none of the Andersons' low cunning. He could read by the time he was four, and I had him doing sums at five. Simple sums that he would add up on his fingers, giggling like Emma. He lacked for nothing. Watching him at his schoolwork, I would feel almost holy. Suffer little children, Jesus says in Matthew. Jeremiah was my first favorite, but Matthew 18 and 19 I like best of all. For of such is the Kingdom of Heaven, Jesus says. Nothing about grace or orphans there.

Robbie filled my life, and when he and Emma left, there was a void such as I had never known. Submitting myself to the neighbors' gossip, I stayed on in Astoria for six more months, in the hope that Robbie and Emma would return. Or better, that Muller would tire of the role of stepfather and would make Emma send Robbie back to me. That way I would have a chance to undo the damage Emma had caused by getting Robbie to lie to me about the tutor. When it finally became clear that Robbie was not going to return, I moved away; though I was careful to leave a forwarding address the first couple of years.

Time heals, as they say, and so does hard work. Until the Crash I was never without a job, traveling as far as Ohio in one case. And since all work and no play makes Jack a dull boy, I balanced my life with a few pastimes. I was a free man and nobody to stop me. I went fishing in the personals and landed my fair share of widows. I even did a little sculpturing.

2

"'Now the hungry lion roars, And the wolf behowls the moon,'" Ali chanted, carrying the plates to the table.

"Four," her mother said, and handed her another plate. "It's rude, your forgetting."

"'Whilst the heavy ploughman snores, All with weary task fordone,'" Ali said. She sidestepped over a box, stretching on tip-toe to avoid the lid that was slowly opening. She was small for thirteen, and her legs, sheathed in green tights, looked shorter than they were because of the thin green skirt that came halfway down her thighs. On her head was a dark green sock that hid most of her brown hair. The toe dangled against her shoulder

"What did I do with the salt, Ali? Did I pack it?"

"I already put it on the table, Mama."

"We mustn't forget it," Mary James said. "That top's real silver, you know."

"We won't, Mama," Ali said, straightening a knife. Mother

and daughter, they would glean the trash one last time. " 'Now the wasted brands do glow'—"

"That's enough, Ali. It's time to cut the bread."

"I cut it now, it'll be dry by the time they get here," Ali said reasonably.

"They'll be back around seven," Mary James said. "We mustn't forget the clock."

"We won't." The clock worked only when it was on its face, and Ali tilted it to see the time. "They'll be another half hour, easy." She sat at the kitchen table and opened a book.

"Aren't you hot in that sock, Ali? You remember when Junie had ringworm and they shaved her head? And I was so worried her hair wouldn't grow back, remember? I made her a little cap."

"More like a bonnet," Ali said without looking up.

"A pretty piece of lace on it, remember? Junie wants me to throw it out, but I packed it anyway. For the lace. Though for the life of me I couldn't tell you where." Mary James walked over to the boxes stacked against the long wall, and her lips moved as she began to count them. "Thirteen," she whispered, and went through the open door into the middle room. Ali could hear her murmuring.

"Twenty-three," Mary James called triumphantly. "I never knew we had so much stuff."

The excitement of the game had left her flushed, and as she came back through the doorway, the light to the side of her, Ali could see the resemblance to Junie that everybody talked about.

"I'll cut the bread now, if you like," Ali said, closing her book. She and Junie had counted twenty-two.

"The tomato, too. It won't last the night," her mother said. "I wonder what kind of fish he'll bring back. I wonder what kind of fish they get up there." She sat in Ali's chair and watched as Ali cut the bread. "Not like that, you'll cut your thumb off." Then: "You gonna look like that in front of all those people? Wearing those stockings and all?"

"I'll have a real hat by then," Ali said. "But I'll be wearing the tights. They're part of the costume." She put down the knife and with an appeasing gesture removed the sock. The bobbed hair underneath was matted with sweat.

"Maybe you should wait with the tomato," Mary James said, and Ali carried the breadboard to the table. Leaning forward and tugging at the skirt, her mother went on, "Can't you pull it down a bit?"

"I'm a sprite in tights," Ali said, skipping away. "I play tricks with this magic juice, and I mix everybody up, but it all comes out right in the end. I know it all but the last bit."

She came back and joined her mother at the table, and they sat facing each other, like guests too early at the feast.

"They're late," Ali said, without consulting the clock.

"It must be the train," her mother answered absently, but by eight o'clock she had begun to fidget.

Ali brought her a glass of water and covered the bread with a plate. "By the time they get here, it'll be too late to cook anything," she said. "Why don't I boil a couple of eggs?"

"It's those big trains. How can they see where they're going with all that smoke?" Mary James fretted. She leaned forward into the light and aged twenty years. Ali looked away quickly.

"I don't think I want anything," Mary James said after a pause. "I think I'll go out for some air."

Ali put on two eggs anyway, and lowered the flame the way she had been taught. Junie might have had an accident, might be lying dead somewhere, knocked down by a car or fallen off the train platform. He would have run away, ashamed, and the police would not know who Junie was and there would be no one to claim her. Ali shuddered and checked the clock. It was eight-thirty.

She had eaten her egg and more than her share of the bread by the time her mother came back in at nine. The other egg, cold, lay on the plate in front of her mother's chair.

"Maybe they had an accident?" Mary James said.

"If they did, the cops would've let us know by now. He's got our address on him," Ali said. "She could've been took sick, though. The train ride could've upset her."

"Like the time on the trolley, remember," Mary James said, nodding to herself. "She must've been took sick, and he decided to stay the night. At least we know the house is ready."

By ten o'clock, however, they were both fidgeting. Mary

James turned with a start every time footsteps approached the front window, and slumped back when they passed on. She had eaten the egg, and the shattered shell lay between them until Ali, her chest lurching, took it out to the garbage.

"Maybe we should go to the police," Ali said finally.

"With my luck," Mary James said, "he'll meet us on the way and be angry and maybe leave for good. No. He's a busy man. He'll be back soon as Junie's fit to travel."

"What if—" Ali began, and stopped. She was trying to hold on to the image of Junie smiling as she left. Fear kept dissolving the image; it grew fainter each time Ali tried to recall it until panic overwhelmed her, settling in her bowels, and she ran to the toilet. She sat there in the dark, fingering the rosary she and Junie had hung over the stack of newsprint that served as toilet paper. She began to shake with the effort of not thinking, of keeping down the shutter that raised itself briefly in her mind. "St. Anthony, bring her back," she said aloud, and pulled the chain to cover the words.

They went to bed hours after their usual time, and even then Ali lay sleepless, staring at the ceiling. They had left the little lamp burning, just in case he brought Junie back in the middle of the night, and by its glow Ali watched a water roach run up the wall and vanish into the framework of the window. Any minute now, she thought, another one will follow; they always go in pairs. That was the worst of living in a basement, you could never get rid of the roaches. Junie had once wakened to find one on the pillow, and from then on they had kept a light going next to the bed. It had seemed to help, though Ali worried about fire.

She awoke to the sound of a voice. It was her mother, standing in the doorway.

"He should've sent a wire," her mother was saying, and Ali could not tell if her voice was shaking with fear or anger. "He could've phoned the police, and they would've let us know. Or Sol or somebody. Why didn't he send a wire?"

"Maybe he couldn't. Maybe he's the one sick. There'll be a reason, something we haven't thought of," Ali said, and swallowed quickly, tasting egg. Breathing through her mouth, she swallowed again, and the nausea passed. She shifted over to

Junie's side and patted the warm spot she had vacated. "Come to bed, Mama."

"I should never have let her go," Mary James said, climbing in beside Ali. She began to cry softly. "She's never been strong, and the excitement was too much for her, and God only knows what's happened to them."

"We'll go to the police soon as it's light," Ali said, to soothe her.

"Oh, Ali," Mary James whispered, rolling away. "This wouldn't have happened if you'd gone, would it?"

Pray for us sinners now and at the hour of our death amen, Ali breathed, and wept soundlessly into the pillow.

They waited until ten the next morning, to give him and Junie time to get back on an early train, then Mary James and Ali went to the Tenth Precinct on West Twentieth Street and reported them missing. Ali had been there before, with Junie, to pick up the free coal and flour that Mayor La Guardia had given away in the cold spell, and she led her mother, stooped and hesitant, to the desk. The room, which had been so warm in January, was like an iceberg.

"Speak up," the sergeant said loudly. "I can't hear you."

Ali could not be sure, she was squinting in the painful light, but she thought the sergeant winked at her. She tried closing her eyes to rest them and found herself swaying, clutching at the desk.

Her mother began again.

Her husband and daughter, Mary James said, still whispering, had gone to City Island yesterday, Sunday, and had not come home last night. She feared an accident. Did the police know of an accident? A train crash?

As the sergeant wrote down the time, 10:15, Ali saw that the date at the top of the ledger was written backwards: 27/5/35.

Name? the sergeant said.

Mr. John James. And Frances June.

Your name, I mean, the sergeant said.

Mary Margaret James.

Address?

Her mother stopped in mid-breath, and her head jerked round. The face she turned to Ali was frozen with shock. She's beginning to realize, Ali thought. A house by the ocean blue.

"409 West Seventeenth Street," Ali said.

"Now I write down their names," the sergeant informed, not unkindly. "How old is Mr. James?"

Her mother lowered her eyes. She does not know how old he is, Ali thought helplessly.

"Forty-five," Mary James said softly, turning her back on Ali. "But he looks older."

And Frances June?

Ten next month. That's why they called her June.

Where had Mr. James and June gone to in City Island?

"She's worn out," Ali said. "Can I get her a chair?"

"Here." The younger cop standing next to the sergeant brought a chair from behind the desk.

The address in City Island, the sergeant said again.

Mary James sat down heavily.

Her husband, she began after a pause, owned a house up there. And a store. They were planning to move up there this coming weekend, and her husband and daughter had gone up to see if everything was ready.

And the address?

"I don't know the exact address, I haven't been up there yet," Mary James said. "But it's right near the boats."

"You just bought it?"

"Oh no," she said, stung. "My husband has owned it for years."

There was a silence. The sergeant, his eyebrows raised, turned to Ali.

"They've been married a month," Ali said.

"April 26," Mary James said. "That's why we haven't been up there yet." Comforted by the reasonableness of the statement, she went on with growing confidence, "The girls' name is still Stephens, but my husband has registered them in their new school up there as James. It's all legal. He's going to adopt them as his own."

The sergeant, his face expressionless, nodded at the younger cop, who went into the office next to the desk. Blinking to keep her eyes in focus, Ali watched him through the glass window as he made the call. The two other cops in the office turned to look at her and her mother, then looked away as they saw her staring. When the cop came back out, he took her mother's arm.

"Her, too," the sergeant said, tilting his head toward Ali, and the cop, like a priest at a funeral, guided them upstairs to the squad room. The eight or ten men in the room stopped to stare and did not look away, and it occurred to Ali, feeling as though she were making an entrance onstage, that she would never learn the last bit now. Connie Costello with her funny voice would get to do the part now. With her fat legs in tights.

"Get another chair over here somebody," a thin, angry-sounding man said as he approached them. "I'm Detective Long."

He was a short, intense man with no eyebrows to speak of. Their function had been taken over by his forehead, which did the scowling and the frowning and the registering of surprise that punctuated his every word. Perhaps it was Long's restless face that caused Ali and Mary James to look away so consistently, or perhaps it was his deep bellow that built a wall of sound behind which they could hide. Whatever. Jim Hackett, watching through the glass door, from the beginning saw them more clearly. If it was true that at first Hackett thought Ali younger than her years and her mother older, it was also true that at thirty feet he saw the movement, the collapse in Ali's spine as she began accepting the facts and the stiffening in Mary James's when she began fighting them. The exchange in their postures led him to guess at their relationship and, unable to hear a word they said, he knew that Long was asking the wrong questions of the wrong person. The girl, rousing herself at this point, looked up and saw him watching them. She turned away quickly, but not before Hackett noted that, even tear-filled, her eyes were wary.

Long, distracted by the girl's wandering glance, gave up the pretense that Hackett was invisible.

"Mary Stupid James," he said, taking Hackett aside reluctantly. "Why'd she have to wait all this time to come to us, huh?"

Waste all this time, he meant. The first twenty-four hours were crucial in a kidnapping case; after that, the odds got worse with every passing hour. After that, too, the local precinct had to call in the Missing Persons Bureau—Hackett, in this event. Because of Mary James's delay in alerting the police, Long had not only lost precious time, he had lost his initial exclusivity in the case. Smelling death in the wind, he resented what he saw as Hackett's useless intrusion. With some justice, Hackett conceded: Only one in three thousand missing person cases was a homicide, and Hackett by no stretch of the imagination could be thought of as a seasoned authority on murder. Still; Long might have kept his impatience to himself. But then, he wouldn't be Long if he did that. Hackett had worked with him before, and both respected and disliked him. They were bound by mutual rancor.

"What they don't know about John James would fill a fucking prayer book," Long was saying. "And most of what they do know is probably lies. Sometime at the end of March, the mother answered a lonelyhearts ad in the *Police Gazette*, you know the kind of shit they run. Widower with own business interested in meeting widow with view to matrimony, blah, blah, blah. Anyway, she wrote and he wrote, and they ended up meeting in Grand Central for coffee. That's when she told him about the girls, and he clammed up. Look at the woman. He would've seen right off she wasn't the type goes in for his kind of shenanigans, am I right? It's safe to assume the bastard was after the girls, or one of the girls, from the start. Anyway, after that she didn't hear from him for a week, and just as she's figuring she's lost him, she gets another letter. We got that one. The mother had dabbed it with perfume and put it in her missal, and the kid there, the sister, she remembered to bring it along. Nothing useful in the way of prints, far as I can see, but you'll get it checked. The mother didn't save the first letter or the envelopes—though Ryan, who's over at the house now, says she seems to have saved everything else since the Flood. The sister, she's twelve, no, thirteen, says they were both mailed in the city."

Through the glass, Hackett looked at them. The mother was crying, and from the girl's unnatural stillness, it could be thought that she was listening to the sound, as to music. The girl stirred. As if she knew he was watching, she again glanced at him, again turned away. Alice Stephens, Long had named her.

"They were married downtown on their fifth date," Long said, "and he moved in. Just until his house was ready, he said. He was out a lot, buying supplies for the store, he told the mother. She doesn't know what kind of store. A bit of everything, she thinks. A week ago he volunteered to take both girls to see their new home, but it was raining and Junie had a cold, and the mother didn't want her to go. He didn't force the issue. He just got angry and marched out. He didn't come back that night."

Long stopped to light a cigarette. "That's as far as we got," he said. "And you? You got news or history?"

Hackett ticked off the points on his fingers. "No, no and no," he said.

"No, no and no," Long repeated. "That's news?" And he turned and hurried ahead into the room. He never walked next to a taller man if he could help it, and he was sitting down by the time Hackett reached the desk.

"I'm Detective Hackett," Hackett began, clearing his throat. "From the Missing Persons Bureau."

Mary James stopped crying to look up at him. She had been unaware of Long's absence, Hackett realized, and his own appearance in front of her had startled her. Alice Stephens, not looking, shifted her chair closer to her mother's.

No accident, Hackett said, trying not to stare at Mary James's swollen face, no accident had been reported on a big train. And anyway, no big train went to City Island. You got there by subway and bus. No one by the name of James owned a store or a house in City Island. No girls by the name of either James or Stephens had been entered in any of the area's public schools.

"John James is probably not his real name either," Long said brutally, and set her off crying again.

What's in a name, Hackett wondered as he handed her his

handkerchief; except all her plans and the fate of a child. He waited for Long to hit her with the bigamy line.

But it was Alice Stephens, pretending there had been no interruption in her mother's story, pretending that Hackett had not entered and said all those things, who spoke next.

"He came back about eight-thirty on Monday morning," she said, looking at nothing in general and avoiding Hackett in particular. "Full of smiles. He had a bottle of scent for Mama, a doll for Junie, and a necklace like emeralds for me to wear in the play. The play I'm in, in school. He said he'd got upset because he'd bought some wallpaper for our rooms, and he'd wanted us to choose one. So he could have our rooms ready before Mama saw them, he said."

Listening to her low, well-modulated voice—though that could just have been the contrast with Long's—Hackett nodded, his guess confirmed. Mama was the third child in the family, the one who got the best surprises, and James, of course, had played on that. As if she had read his thoughts, the girl shifted her chair again, this time away from her mother.

"He said he just wanted to see me happy," Mary James said suddenly. She lowered the handkerchief and her face, that of a brooding Pietà, brooded at them. "A week ago today this all was. Seems like months now. Anyway, he said he could take the girls this weekend, and when it turned out that Ali had to practice for her play, I let Junie go without her. I didn't have the heart to disappoint him again."

Frances June was Junie to her family; Alice was Ali.

"He said he'd bring back some fresh fish, and me and Junie could stay up, and we'd all have a late supper together," Ali added, and her mouth twisted.

Later, when Mary James had been led away—ostensibly to get a cup of coffee, but in reality to answer Moylan's questions about James's bedtime habits; Moylan with his collar turned, he had the right sad look—Ali, alone with Hackett, looked at him straight on and said, "He liked Junie a lot better than he liked me. She called him Papa."

Hackett, taking care not to echo her change of tense, kept his voice soft and his face still.

"You don't like him?" he was saying, when Long barged back in and ruined it.

"You still here?" Long said, picking up his jacket. Getting ready for the press. "Kids that age," he went on, his back to both of them, "they talk to make themselves interesting."

Ali closed her eyes, and Hackett, silent with recognition, knew that she was sealing herself against them, him and Long; a flower folding against the night.

"Moylan," Long said from the door, "says she ain't coming clean about the dirt. Pretty cute, huh?"

3

Publicly, Hackett hoped, it had been a standoff with Long, and perhaps it had been. Long, ruthless in his own bailiwick, had ordered the neighborhood search, dominated the press, then ceremoniously conducted mother and daughter home. In between, he had ignored Ali and, knight to squire, had called over his shoulder to Hackett a series of commands: Canvass the neighbors. Question the friends. Search the files. Standard procedure, but coming from Long's mouth, it had sounded like shit work. As he had meant it to. Hackett, shielding himself as well as Ali, had taunted Long, drawing his wrath with sentences of convoluted structure that left his forehead furrowed and his face distorted in the photographs that appeared in the afternoon editions. It had seemed important to Hackett to disassociate himself from Long in front of the girl.

Avoiding what he knew would be a circus on West Seventeenth Street, Hackett instead went looking for the ad. But too much time had elapsed, a young man with no front teeth explained at the *Gazette* offices on West Thirty-fourth Street. The originals were thrown out once the ads were paid for and had appeared in print. Besides, lots of the personals were phoned in these days.

"No wonder," Hackett said. John James's relatively sedate come-on was wedged between an offer of twelve unusual photographs, guaranteed French models, and a recipe, also guaranteed, for curing social disease in the privacy of one's home.

"Heaven and health at a dollar a throw," Hackett said, flipping through the photographs, the kind Vice got paid to look at. "You send this stuff through the mails?"

"It's art," the clerk said with an old-man smile. "They're not as good as last month's batch. Wanna see?"

"Another time," Hackett said, and wondered how Mary James had come to read such a rag.

"Me and Junie found it in the trash," Ali told him. She was alone in the apartment and had pretended not to recognize him in the gloom. "The men in 3B get it all the time. Me and Junie cut it up for the toilet."

After me and Junie have read it, Hackett thought, walking in uninvited.

"You should ask who it is before you open the door," he said. Neither she nor her mother seemed to realize that, but for the play rehearsal, Ali too might be dead. Nearly thirty hours had passed since James had walked off with Junie, and by now Hackett had no doubt that the child would not be found alive. "It could've been the reporters back," he said. Who would relish pointing out, if they hadn't already, the luck of Ali's escape.

"Mama says if he sees Junie's picture in the paper, he'll know we're worried, and he'll bring her back." She was mumbling, not looking at him.

Hackett sat at the kitchen table and studied his chipped nails. He made a show of not noticing the rest of the apartment. Long's men had left the place in unlovely chaos; the contents of the spilled cartons were strewn all over. Through the connecting door he caught sight of an unmade bed piled with what appeared to be kids' clothing. A sweet sight for the mother, if so, though it was hard to tell in the unlit room. Just so no one should forget it was a basement, the walls had been painted a brilliant blue that effectively soaked up any light penetrating the high, barred windows.

"You think that, too?" he asked.

"I dunno," she said, like a longshoreman.

He had timed his visit to catch her alone, and much good it was doing him. Mary James, the lone cop outside had told him, was still upstairs, resting at a neighbor's. Hackett tried again.

"This morning, your mother said maybe he's the one got sick, and Junie's staying with him to take care of him. Junie old enough to do something like that?"

"I dunno," she said a second time, but her eyes had moved to his hands.

"You mentioned," he said, moving a book from the path of a seeping tomato, "this morning, that he liked Junie better than he liked you. Why did you say that?"

"Because Junie's prettier than me. And she smiles all the time. People like kids who smile a lot," she said, and Hackett heard the shuddering sigh she tried to turn into a cough.

She was staring at him, defying him to find her ugly. Her nose was too broad in her narrow, peaked face, but her eyes, blue and almond-shaped, were intelligent. It was strange, he reflected, how much more clearly he could see her here than in the station house's blinding light. She would have made a better-looking boy; she must take after her father. The picture of Junie, smiling, showed a fair-haired child, a younger version of the mother.

"You don't think Junie would have run off somewhere?" he said, as much to give Ali a chance to anchor herself as to get the question out of the way.

"Oh, no," she said, calmer, and the lack of emphasis in her voice was extraordinarily convincing; if he had needed convincing. "Junie loved the idea of moving to a house by the sea and getting presents and all. Going on boat rides and all. She's never been on a boat. She didn't run away."

Part of John James's bounty was hanging from the wall: a light blue coat, larger than but otherwise identical to the one

Junie had been wearing when last seen. Ali's spring coat, and never worn. The $4 price tag still dangled from a front button.

Ali's eyes followed Hackett's to the coat.

"He watched her when he thought nobody was looking," she said without prompting. "He never looked her in the eye. He never looked me in the eye, either, but that was different. That was because he didn't know I was there most of the time. All I'm trying to say, I guess, is he didn't offer to take me on the trip when Junie was sick, but he didn't even think about not taking Junie when I couldn't go. And I knew that's what would happen. That he would take her, I mean. Not that he wouldn't bring her back."

"You tell your mother any of this?" Hackett asked quietly.

"Oh, no. She knew he liked Junie better. She was pleased with Junie. Pleased with herself, too."

"Where did he take her?" Hackett said after a while. "You got any ideas about that?"

"Boston?" she said. "He sounds like Connie Costello, and she comes from Boston."

"Boston?" he repeated stupidly. It was the first he had heard of an accent. "You mean 'the car park is far,' stuff like that?"

"More like the way President Roosevelt says 'can't,'" she said, smiling at his effort. "And he says things like 'I shan't be long' instead of 'I won't be long,' stuff like that."

"You do that very well," Hackett said, meaning it, and her eyes filled with tears.

"I knew there was something wrong with him. But I didn't know he was one of them," she said, pointing to the *Gazette* in Hackett's hand. "I would've said something if I'd known."

"What d'you mean, there was something wrong with him?" he said roughly.

Her face, a half-moon in the fading light, retreated into shadow.

"For one thing," she said slowly, "he lied. Silly things. One time he was telling us about a famous mountain near his house, and when I asked him what its name was, his eyes stopped moving, the way they do when people are lying, and he said it was a hill really, and didn't have a name. Then he started telling us a

funny story about Sam who helped him in the store, but I know
he was just trying to change the subject. I didn't believe he had a
store at all, at first. I kept waiting for him to come in and say it
had burned down or something and we wouldn't be able to move
after all. But when he began saying me and Junie should go up
with him and get the house ready for Mama, then I believed
him."

For one thing, she had said. She who had told her mother
nothing. Hackett went back to studying his nails.

"Anything else?" he said.

"I don't know," she whispered. "I don't know that it wasn't
me. You know, imagining things. Because I felt left out."

She stopped, embarrassed or humiliated, and Hackett held
himself still. His fingers, upturned, grew cramped.

"When Mama married him," she said finally, "she moved
the big bed into the front room. The day after he'd been out all
night, last Monday, he went to bed early. Me and Junie sleep in
the middle room, and when we went in, I noticed that the door
to the front room was open. I couldn't see him, but I knew he
was standing there. I thought he was listening to us, waiting to
hear if we were gonna talk about him coming back, maybe, but
now I wonder if he wasn't watching us. You know, get undressed.
The lamp was lit. When Mama came through, I saw the door
close."

A truck outside thundered in the total silence. Hackett flexed
his fingers.

"That happened just the once?"

"That I know of," she said.

"He never touched Junie? That you know of."

"He never touched her," she said, equally remote. "I was always around."

On purpose? he wanted to ask, but she was still too fragile.

It seemed to Hackett that the man had shown unusual restraint, if that was the right word. There should have been the
too frequent trips through their bedroom in the middle of the
night. Just on my way to the kitchen, he would say, if Ali woke to
find him standing over the bed. Just stopped to tuck in the blanket. There had been no stroking of Junie's hair for Ali to worry

over, no quick rush to the toilet, his fly open, oops, I didn't know you were in here. Three weeks he had waited, lying and looking, then another week, to get what he wanted; and in all that time there had been one indiscretion so subtle that Ali had not been sure. Ah, but she had been sure; had undressed beneath the sheets that night, he would bet on it. At thirteen you see and you know and are tongue-tied with shame. Unless you are lucky.

"You tell anyone, a friend, about this?" he asked.

"No." Said short. She thought he was doubting her.

"Talking helps sometimes, that's what words are for," he said, feeling foolish. "Some caveman worked out one time that a scream meant a wolf was around, but to talk about the fear of being eaten by the wolf, things like that, he found he needed words." Which broke the circuit to nightmare, sometimes.

"I read," she said after a pause, "that the Russians said wolves don't eat people. It was being poor killed the peasants."

"Just an old wolves' tale. They're a bunch of Bolshies, what do they know?" he said, standing up, and she almost smiled.

He walked through the middle room and into the front room.

"Like this?" he called.

"Not so much," she said from the other side of the door, startling him.

With the door open a crack and with the only light that from the oil lamp on the chair next to the bed, James would still have had a pretty clear view of the room. Ali began to pack the clothes on her bed into a chest of drawers.

"When's your birthday?" Hackett said, back in the middle room.

She stopped working to stare at him. "December the tenth."

"Mine's the ninth. We're practically twins, give or take a couple of decades. You know what it means, a December birthday? It means that when you fill out forms in the New Year, it looks as though you're a year older than you are."

"I never thought about it," she said, still staring.

"That's because you haven't filled out enough forms yet," he said comfortably, continuing through to the kitchen. He turned at the door. "Listen. I don't think I want to tell your mother about him watching you that night. Not right now, anyway. If that's okay with you."

Hackett learned nothing from the men in 3B. They did not know who John James was, they explained uneasily, looking to each other for comfort. They could not tell Ali and Junie apart. Their main concern was to rid themselves of his presence and, since it was obvious that—whatever their interest in the *Gazette* —it had nothing to do with little girls, Hackett left. The fat one with the black eye saw him to the door.

At 2A, Martha Butler would not let him in.

"She's just fallen asleep. Mary Stephens, Mary James, I don't know what to call her anymore," she said, settling on the stairs with a baby in her arms. "Sol sent over a draught."

Crouched on the step below, Hackett saw that she was a talker. Who would tell him about Sol who sent over a draught. About James who stole a child.

"I knew right off he was a wrong un," she said confidently. "Mister John James. I said so from the start. It was that business with the limp set me off." She stopped when she caught his frown. "You don't know about that?"

"No," he admitted. It would have to be added to the circular.

"I used to see him walking down the street, and he'd be limping, and then he'd get near the stoop and be all right. I asked Mary about it, but she said I was mistaken. But I wasn't. Ask Ali." She stopped to jiggle the baby, then went on. "He was just using her, that's what I said to Ed. What's a man with his own house doing down there? I said. They get rats." She shifted to face him, and Hackett moved, too, to avoid looking up her skirt. "I thought," she said threateningly, "it was against the law these days to live in that type basement. Ain't it?"

"I think so," he said weakly, cowed by her vigor. She was very young and shapely to be the mother of four. Twenty-five, maybe, and more than a match for the three kids who at that moment put their heads around the door.

"You take them back in and keep them quiet, Tessy, or I'll

know the reason why," she said to a child no more than six. All three kids nodded solemnly and retreated.

Turning to check that they had closed the door, she said softly, "Junie hated the rats. That's why she liked that man. Junie's the kind of kid, you could hit her with a bat and tell her it was her fault for getting in the way, she'd believe you. It's hard to think anyone could have hurt her, but that's what he's done, ain't it?"

"It's too soon—" he began, and paused. "Probably," he said, as quietly.

She was silent a moment, then: "She wouldn't have had a chance, would she?" She tucked the baby closer to her, and still sleeping, it turned to nuzzle. "Listen. I feel real bad I didn't say more when I could've. It might have made the difference."

"Everybody thinks that afterward," he said. "But he would've done it anyway. He would've caught on and moved sooner, changed his plans maybe, but he would've done it. That's why he was here." He would have to remember to tell Ali that, he thought: You weren't to know.

"It wouldn't have happened if there'd been any kind of man around," she said. "A brother, an uncle, somebody like that," and Hackett, surprised, nodded in agreement.

"About the basement," she added. "Somebody's got to do something about it. Mary can't, poor bitch, she doesn't have the brains she was born with. She tried, and look where it's got her. It'll all be back on Ali's shoulders again. She's the one gets Junie's toothaches taken care of and sees that the rats don't overrun the place."

"She's down there alone," he said.

"She ought to be in bed. When you go down, tell her to come up. I don't know where I'll put her, and that's a fact, but she shouldn't be alone. I don't know what Ed'll say, the both of them up here, and I haven't even begun supper yet."

Ed won't say anything. He wouldn't dare, Hackett promised himself as he went down the outside steps.

"It's me again," he called before he knocked.

"Yes," Ali said, opening the door at once. "I saw you pass the window."

So you did last time, he thought. Her eyes were redder than before and her face, if possible, was paler.

"You're to go upstairs to 2A," he said, trying to sound as firm as Martha Butler. "Your mother's asleep, and you should be, too."

"I can't leave the place like this," she said, her voice rising.

"You tell me where to put things," he heard himself say, "I could help." I used to clean up all the time when I was your age.

"No," she said venomously. "We've had all the help we can use, thank you." Weeping, she began to close the door on him.

He felt absurdly betrayed, staring at her. They're all like this, he thought. By the age of that kid upstairs, they're already nurturing grievances, hoarding them in some Pandora's box against the day—and the timetable, erratic, was secreted in their dark places—when they could let fly their monstrous angers.

"You never told me he limped," he accused. She closed the door in his face.

Going up, he stumbled on the steps, and for two weeks carried a bruise, like the badge of a schoolboy, on his shin.

Men hoard, too, he thought next, in his need to absolve her. But men hoard different things.

4

Hackett found Sol right where Martha Butler said he would be: behind the counter, flicking a towel; making it clear he was about to close.

"He only come in one time," Sol said hurriedly, pouring Hackett a cup of coffee. "With Junie. That's how I knew who he was. Epsom salts is what he wanted, that's all I know. He didn't say what for, and I didn't ask." He darted behind the other counter to fill a prescription, then darted back again.

"She was a nice little girl, Junie," he said, relenting. "Pretty as a picture. Ali delivers for me sometimes, and often as not, Junie goes along. She's not the brightest kid in the world, Junie, I wouldn't let her do it by herself. But a sunny kid, you know?"

Hackett nodded and closed his eyes. When he opened them again, Sol was peering at him.

"You look as if you could use something stronger than coffee," he said. He crossed to the door and locked it, flipping over the sign. Out of nowhere he produced a bottle.

"Jesus," Hackett said after the first sip, worrying about the lack of blinds.

"It's not good?"

"It's terrific," Hackett said simply. "Where'd you get it?"

"I got a whole case back there. For services rendered. So feel free."

"How come?" Hackett said, feeling free on his third. Neither of them had spoken in the last five minutes, and his voice was loud in the silence. "How come, you got a whole case, you don't know it's good?"

"Never touch the stuff," Sol said, pouring himself more coffee.

Shaking his head at Sol's innocence, Hackett carried his drink to the phone.

"Hi," he said when Ceil picked up.

"Why, Maureen," Ceil said quickly. "Your ears must be burning. We were just talking about you. I'm going to be late."

"Shit," Hackett said. "He still there?"

"I'm fine, thank you. Never better. It's Con. He was sick all weekend. A chill. But he's leaving any minute."

"Maybe he'll die."

She coughed. "Nothing that good," she said. "Let's stick with Schrafft's. It's cheaper, and the food's better."

"I'll call back," he said. "It works out, wear the black thing again, huh?"

"Why, Maureen O'Day," she said, and her laughter was throaty and unsafe. "I do believe you've had a drop or two."

She was one quick-witted lady, he thought, walking back to the counter; always at the ready to dodge fortune's slings and arrows. Her wits, and her sharp tongue, too, were part of the arsenal with which she faced a dangerous world. Though her tongue could be sweet and slow on occasion, he remembered, and, smiling, drained his glass.

"She been found?" Sol asked, mistaking Hackett's expression.

"No," he said, ashamed. Then: "I hear you sent something over for Mary James?"

"And for Ali, too. I marked them both clearly so's there couldn't be any mistake."

"Maybe tomorrow as well," Hackett said.

"You don't expect to find her then." It was a statement. "You know, this wouldn't have happened if there'd been a man around." (This one's for Mary, and this one's for Ali. Sol had been talking to Martha Butler.) "That poor woman," Sol added, blushing. "It's too bad, you know?"

"Yeah," Hackett said. At the door he turned so swiftly that Sol, off guard, retreated a step.

"No wonder they're all half nuts," Hackett said, low and angry. "Must be a strain, living with what they know. That we're a bunch of fucking animals."

Ceil wore the black dress that night, but in his deflated state, Hackett thought it made her look mournful, not enticing. He couldn't wait to take it off her.

"And where did this huge, hairy thing spring from? Ouch," she said, joking. She brought to their lovemaking a mixture of lust and levity that he, after six months, still found unsettling. She was more at ease in bed than he, more inventive; making it hard for him to accept that he was her first lover. He didn't count Con.

Making it hard, he thought, and grunted in the dark.

"You like that?" she said, and when he didn't answer, she laughed low and continued.

"Don't," he said when Ceil, naked, crossed the room and pulled open the curtains. As if she owned the place.

"It'll be cooler. Nobody can see in." She was ignorant of or ignoring his mood, it was hard to tell with her.

He got up without a word and reclosed the curtains.

"At least," she said after a silence, "let's turn on a light."

So that they could see each other, she meant. Watch each other. And afterward, when she cooked for him, she would not bother to cover herself either. She would use the heat to justify her lack of modesty, and he would stand furtive, eyeing her breasts as they brushed the doorjamb. He wondered, not for the first time, if she did it on purpose, this brushing things with her breasts.

But none of her stuff was working tonight. Her presence had

not distracted him from the memory of Long's snubs, nor
dispelled the misery that had flowed from the face of Ali
Stephens and gathered like an ugly thickening in his head. It was
chastening, too, that anger had taken precedence over pity in his
train of thought.

Unable to climax and holding it against Ceil, Hackett
stretched and switched on the lamp. The sight of her above and
astride him banished other visions, and he finished in a rush.

Holding it against her; the pun dawned. I'm beginning to
sound like her, he thought.

"Hungry?" Ceil asked. Her breast brushed his arm as she put
down the plate.

He wasn't, but he ate anyway. He wanted to be alone, but to
be rid of her entailed the long drive back to Brooklyn. As he
chewed, not looking at her, Hackett wondered that he had allowed her to encumber his life with ritual. The fucking, the feeding, the long drive home, they were all by her design. She intended to make life as difficult as possible for him when the time
came. To break off, she meant. She had told him so, she had no
pride. He was all she had in her life, she had told him that, too,
and when he was with her he believed her, and used the belief to
urge her to greater inventiveness. Not that she needed much urging, he told himself, then felt like a rat. But what more could she
expect from him? He had all too much in his life at the moment,
thank you.

Ceil, waiting to go, still looked severe in the black, and
Hackett was reminded of his first impression of her. The name
Ceil suited her, he had thought then, reeling from the shock that
she was Con of all people's wife. A cold name for a cold dame, he
had thought then, until she turned to stare at him. And so much
for first impressions, he had thought next, and had stolen her.
Right under Con's nose.

Heavy with nostalgia in the car, Hackett grew reluctant to
have her leave. It was something he'd been noticing lately and
trying not to: an apprehension when she walked from the car
that one day it would be his last view of her. His superstition,
that's all it was, was aggravated tonight by the knowledge that a
murderous bastard was about to intrude on their time together.

Anger rose again, and Hackett, almost verbatim, told her what he had written in his report. He explained about the time—the loss of time—and Ceil nodded, passive.

"Call me, at least," she said at her corner. "Listen," she added as if it were an afterthought. "Next time you have something like this on your mind, tell me about it before." Before bed. "Otherwise, you see, you leave me thinking it's something I've done wrong." She spoke quietly, but there was no mistaking the edge. After bed, she was less anxious to please, that was something else he'd been noticing lately, too.

He watched from the corner until she was inside. Inside a house that he would never enter, though at the beginning he had sneaked past it once or twice, curious to see where she lived. A light went on upstairs, that would be her bedroom; he remembered the other light, in his bedroom. He had been the one to turn it on. She knows altogether too much about me, he thought, and smiled. On a whim, he detoured through the old neighborhood, and not a soul in sight. In thin rain smelling of dogshit, ah, the scents of summer, Hackett rumbled across the Williamsburg Bridge into Manhattan.

5

It was said in the old neighborhood that Jim Hackett was a secretive boy grown to a solitary man. Other things were said, too, but on the quiet, for he had a nasty temper and, when roused, would drop the aloofness like a used sheet. He was a strong and vicious fighter.

"Lot of his father in that lad," John Murphy said the night Hackett half killed Con Lynch, and when he was told, Hackett smiled as at an accolade.

"A chip off the old block, even." Hackett spoke out of the side of his mouth that still moved. "Wordy little fart."

It was said in the old neighborhood that Jim Hackett liked the ladies, but when he turned seventeen he stopped dating the local girls, though he remained friendly with Kathy Philips next door. Kathy, a simple girl running to fat, had given her maidenhood to Jim—or to Bobby Brennan, she was not sure which, she had never worked out the technicality—and she was gratified by his loyalty. The rest of the girls thought it a shame he plowed other fields, and they protected themselves from the slight by laughing at his finicky ways. Behind the curtain he had hung across the kitchen, he bathed almost every night, heating the water himself and pouring it into the tin tub; and he was fussy as an old maid about his table manners. It was a joke on the block that you could put him off his feed by drooling. Still, it was a shame. He was tall and dark with a thin Mick mouth, and when he smiled he was quite good-looking.

Irishtown they called his part of Williamsburg, the section along the East River, though audacious Jews had already pressed across the bridge from New York (to Hackett, to any Brooklynite, Manhattan was New York) and infiltrated the territory. There was no privacy on the dreary streets, and it bothered Jim, growing up, that the people he ran into knew his business better than their own; people who, conditioned by a life between paperthin walls, spoke in murmurs even when they gathered on the corner. For the poverty was not yet so deep that it had erased concern for the neighbors' tongues. Voices, of course, might be raised on a Saturday night ("Drink brings out the devil in a man," the listening women would mutter), but the next morning the wives and children would show up at Mass as though nothing much had happened. And nothing much had happened. Once in a while, it was believed, a man must throw off the chains that bind him or, like Eddie Donahue, he might break loose and run, never to return.

Jim was an only child on a street where families routinely ran to six. He was seven when his father died—time enough, given the procreative cadence on the block, for his parents to have spawned five—and he was eight before he linked his mother's moodiness to gin. (Ignorance is innocence that goes on too long, he figured out afterward.) She was not a raucous public drinker. She sipped at night, in the kitchen, and the overhead cast a shadow over the cup, so that he could not tell what was in it or how much. Later, when she no longer cared that he knew, and there was no need of the peppermint drops and the cold teapot, a decoy at her elbow, she would still drink from a cup, her hand half covering the rim.

By the time he was ten he had heard the local gossip, or

most of it. His father—Kathy next door was the first to hint— might not have died from pneumonia after all. Hemming and hawing and scuffing their shoes, girls put things that way, he knew, to stir up mischief and escape the blame; and Jim, trapped by a fear stronger than his pride, was forced to question her. It was believed, Kathy said—though not necessarily by her, her tone implied—that after Jim was born, his mother had never again let his father near her. A broken heart, Kathy said. A different kind of chill, Jim thought. He had been so sure she was going to bring up the drinking that in gratitude he let her kiss him, though she was no oil painting, even then. He wondered if his mother had drunk while his father was alive; and if his father had known.

He began to fool around with Kathy when he was twelve, and it was on his return from one of these probings—still only his finger, but she was crumbling fast in the face of his threatened desertion—that he first found his mother sprawled on the kitchen floor. Uncertain of her sense of smell, for she revealed strange insights when she was drunk, he washed his hands before cleaning her up and putting her to bed. He stored the bottle where she kept it, behind the senna, medicinal. Neither of them mentioned it the next day; he was not sure how much she remembered. She continued to cook his meals and change his bed, but from then on he stopped thinking of her as his mother and, no longer stiff with shame, no longer counting each cup, could eavesdrop on her bitter soliloquies. After two cups (he did not have to count, he knew the stages) she would forget that he was there and would retreat into a world of accusation and accounting, of monologues with invisible characters whose roles she endlessly recast. He recognized his grandmother and his uncles, but she never raised her voice to call his father. The boarders, interlopers who had moved in when his father died, could overhear her on those nights when the despair reached a level denied her in sobriety; and in spite of the rupture between them, a dissolution caused less by her drinking than by the indifference to him that the drinking brought out in her (though he did not think of that until years later, either), Jim would pretend not to know the boarders when he met them on the street, even the one who wet his bed or the one who cried in the hall the day he got his pink slip.

The September before Jim turned thirteen, he changed schools. Sister Justina had called him from class in June and handed him an envelope. "You'll be going to St. Andrew's next year," she said, naming a Franciscan-run school infamous for its discipline. "Wear a white shirt and tie."

The first day at St. Andrew's, Brennan, fair-haired and stocky, had walked over to Hackett in the schoolyard.

"They've got dogs and paper routes. They eat store-bought cake," Brennan said, jerking his head toward the others. Nobody had told him about the white shirt and tie. "They think their shit don't stink." He did not include the Italians, a swarthy, prematurely aged group that moved as one through the school. It was a year before Hackett had them sorted out, but Brennan, early the politician, knew them all by name by the end of the first week. He was open-faced and close-mouthed, and within a month Hackett was introducing him to Kathy Philips.

"She says she will," Hackett said on the way over. "But she's got fat legs."

"It's all them potatoes." Brennan sleeked his hair in anticipation. "Listen, Jim, you can't be too fussy in this life. You take what's offered. Besides, it means she's got big tits."

"She has." Hackett didn't think he was too fussy.

But his mother had nearly ruined it by coming into the yard. He had been forced to introduce Brennan.

"You never told me your mother's a dipso," Brennan said, and pushed Jim into the shed where Kathy Philips, her legs wide, was waiting.

Slowly, his voice creaking like an old machine, Jim learned to share in other ways, too.

"You look at her blouse, you know every meal she's had the last week," he said of his mother. He knew Brennan had noticed.

"Could be worse," Brennan said. They were staring down at the river, which looked to Hackett like gleaming metal dulled in parts with scum. Only the sour smell gave up the secret that it was water.

"She ain't whoring around or beating up on you," Brennan said. "She feeds you, don't she? You got a bed to yourself. A room even." Brennan was one of a large brood. "The third or fourth, depending on whether you count the twins as one or two." He knew the privilege of privacy when he saw it.

Two french letters lay entwined like lovers in the water below. Brennan had spotted them; it was why they had paused. As they watched, the condoms untangled and drifted apart.

"You think girls know what they're for?" Brennan said, and Hackett gaped.

"Course they do," he said flatly.

"You're the first only child I've known," Brennan went on, as if he were describing some rare but benign disease. "And it's made you picky. You ought to change places with me sometime. I'd like to see you learning your Latin irregulars with eight kids screaming in your ears. Well, seven. 'Cause I'd be at your place, living the life of Riley."

But the truth was, Brennan did very little work. He was lashed more often with the knotted ropes that hung from the brothers' waists than any other boy in the school. Only in Brother Gregory's class was he safe, for Brother Gregory, too fat or too lazy, rarely bothered to hit anyone. Perhaps it was because of this leniency that the brother's classes were the one part of their schooling they remembered; Hackett clearly and Brennan with affection.

"Compare and contrast," Brother Gregory would begin, staring just above their heads into limbo, and on he would ramble about Cleopatra and Lady Macbeth; about Cleopatra and Juliet. He was in love with Cleopatra. Or again: "If it is true, as a clever Frenchman has written, that grief develops the powers of the mind, how think you, Jim Hackett, this applies to the Moor?" They were reading *Othello* that term.

"What does the Frenchman mean by the powers of the mind?" Jim asked, playing for time. "Is he talking about intelligence, Brother? Or does he mean feelings?" The French, dying in their scarlet uniforms along the Marne, must be a different breed from Eileen Buckley mourning the death of a son. "Because

Othello doesn't need grief to develop his feelings. They're already powerful enough." Stronger than his brains, which could have used a little help, from grief or anything else. Hackett thought Othello a fool. "Isn't that the point, Brother? That grief destroys Othello?"

"Like a diseased parrot," said Brother Gregory serenely, "you are regurgitating what you think I have fed you. But I call your attention—and that of the other three boys who appear to be listening, and that number does not include you, Bobby Brennan—to your use of the word 'destroy.' Let us not forget Iago's part in Othello's agony."

There was no forgetting Iago, Brother Gregory saw to that. And as he lingered over the envy, yea, the very essence of evil that was Iago, Jim worried uneasily that he was missing something. Iago would not have lasted two days on his block.

"But Iago's hate," he demurred, winking at Brennan, "isn't envy grown to evil. The envy's a sign of Iago's inferiority. The evil is part of his soul. You know that if he wasn't going after Othello, he'd be messing up somebody else's life. That's the way he is."

Brennan was seized by a fit of coughing.

"Aha," Brother Gregory pounced, and that was the end of *Othello* for the day. "And do you see any connection, say, between Iago's rage and that of the English in Ireland? Between Othello's passion and that of our boys in Dublin right now?" It was the week after the Easter Rising. Behind Hackett, the Italians groaned out loud.

All the brother's classes went like that. Shakespeare was the only Englishman Brother Gregory ever said anything good about, except for Sir Thomas More, who didn't count as English since he was certain to become a saint. Which could not be said for the archvillain, worse even than Iago, who had doomed More to martyrdom. "Did you ever stop to think that, but for the debauchery"—here the class perked up, but the brother was on a different tack—"the lechery of Henry VIII, America would be a Catholic country today? Every church in Brooklyn a Catholic church? That— What are you up to now, Brennan?"

"Nothing, Brother."

"Among your other sins, you are guilty of *suppressio veri*, and you will undoubtedly go blind," Brother Gregory said, but his tone was amiable enough. "Keep your hands where I can see them."

Yet he had made Hackett work out the dynastic dilemma of the second Tudor, had made him trace the clever Frenchman. "Quite the detective, aren't you, Jim," he said when Hackett produced the name, though Hackett had known right off that it would not be Voltaire. "'*C'est une pièce grossière et barbare . . . cet ouvrage est le fruit de l'imagination d'un sauvage ivre,*'" Brother Gregory had once read to the room of drowsing boys. "That bitter and shameless heretic wrote that of *Hamlet. Hamlet!*" And worried that God at the last minute might have relented and let Voltaire into Heaven. Drunken savage indeed.

"What did he mean, your sins?" Hackett had asked Brennan after class.

"Of emission?" Brennan punched him lightly on the arm. "It was all Greek to me."

And Jim had raced off to do his homework and make a copy for Brennan, forging Brennan's absurd script and throwing in a mistake or two to keep the brothers at bay; so that the evening would be free to absorb lessons not found in the school syllabus. "What's a brother know about life? Real life, I mean," he said on one of those nights. Brennan, intent on the two girls ahead, did not answer, and it was left to Hackett to work out later that his days, too, had held instruction beyond the curriculum.

In the weeks before Hackett quit school early, without his diploma (his mother's haphazard housekeeping had cost them their two best-paying boarders, though that was something he told only Brennan), Brother Gregory, distressed and disapproving, stopped calling on him in class. Later, remembering things past and seeing his school days as a time of achievement, Jim found his reminiscences marred by the brother's censuring face. Brother Gregory was still teaching—he must have been in his forties when Jim was thinking of him as a fat old man—and Brennan, of whom no one had had expectations, felt free to drop in on him whenever he liked. Hackett had never been back.

Hackett became a cop. Before that, though, there had been the job at his uncle's funeral home, where he had lasted three days; and a stint delivering for Walsh the florist. He was working at Abraham & Straus, he had started there as shipping clerk and had just been promoted to assistant buyer, when, bolstered by Brennan's encouragement, he had taken the exams for the Police and Fire Departments. The police appointment had come through first.

"It's a strange choice for a lad that don't like dirt," said old John Murphy, who took certain privileges unto himself since he, too, was a cop. This time, when he heard, Hackett did not smile.

He was still living at home. One by one the boarders had moved out, and at the end of four years, Jim was the last one left. It was assumed he would live there until he married—unless they were blessed with a calling, the children of Irishtown escaped only when they married and settled in a better part of the borough; Queens came later—and he found it hard to plot a bachelor move to Manhattan. The chance to leave—he was promoted to detective, transferred to Missing Persons—had come and gone a dozen times before he made the break.

"It's the birds," he said to his mother. She kept canaries and an aggressive mynah that Hackett had christened Onan ("Because he spills his seed," he told her), and the kitchen was festooned with their cages. She had inherited the first two when old Mrs. Moore died, then had added to their number in trips to the pet store as furtive as her liquor pickups. They were replacing the phalanx of relatives in her midnight monologues, and with unexpected diligence she had taught the mynah a tune. It surprised him because he had never heard her at it. "The birds make me sneeze," he said. Brennan had given him the idea, he had a sister-in-law so afflicted; and Hackett hoped that the urge to convince his mother of the lie would hold his attention long enough to get him through his apathy.

"Not apathy," said Brennan, who'd lived all his life within a half-mile radius of the block where he was born and who knew everything. "You're scared. Jesus, Jim, New York!" As if Hackett were moving to Paris. Hackett felt as if he were.

His mother had turned white at the news. Silent and sober, she helped him pack his bags. Twenty-one years had passed since the night he had first found her on the floor. He was thirty-three.

That had been a year ago.

You climb on a chair, Brennan had said then, and you can see the bums on the benches. The house on the far corner obstructed most of the view promised in the ad, but the shower had a glass door and five nozzles, and Hackett had taken the apartment anyway. It was on a quiet street off Central Park West, in a brownstone so sturdy the only sounds were occasional footsteps overhead. Hackett did not know if they were Steiner's or Browning's, the names on the doorbell.

A far cry from Williamsburg, Brennan had said, appraising the high ceilings and the elegant fireplace. But the hot-water supply turned out to be as erratic as any in the old neighborhood, and when Hackett complained, he was told to go back to Brooklyn where he came from.

He built closets in the bedroom and painted the walls white, adding brown trim in the living room as an afterthought. He hung opaque draperies across the yawning windows, high to match the ceilings, yet the place still had a spartan, unfinished look. The only color was in his books, and those he kept in the bedroom, partly because he had been taught that books do not belong in a front room; mainly to conceal them from the world.

His mother had visited once and felt uneasy.

"All this white, it looks like a kitchen. Or a hospital," she said, rubbing her hand across her lower lip. She had not been invited back.

"The bastard set them up, of course," Hackett reported to Cahill at the bureau Tuesday morning. "All we know for sure is around noon Sunday he took Junie Stephens' hand and led her to the Ninth Avenue el. Since then, nothing." Hackett ran his hand down the page. "Moylan. Everything normal in bed, the mother told Moylan, but who knows her standards? James talked a lot doing it, she says, and she was concerned the girls might hear. Said she couldn't remember what he said. Sweet nothings is Moylan's guess from the way she acted, embarrassed, but he got the numbers out of her at least. Twice a week for the first two weeks, then just once. Saving himself for something better by that time, Long said, and the kid, Ali, still in the room."

The alert went out over the eight-state teletype system and into Canada. Junie's picture was printed in the papers, and later that morning Hackett had to fight his way through the crowds on West Seventeenth Street. The tabloids took up the cause, and that first week photographs appeared daily of Mary James sitting alone in the kitchen (Ali in tears had rushed upstairs when she saw the photographers); of Mary James looking mournfully down the empty street (Hackett watched as the crowd moved obligingly to one side for that shot); of Mary James on Long's arm being helped into Headquarters to view the known sex offenders the police had rounded up.

"Rounded up?" Mary James said. Two days had passed since she had waved to Junie from the church steps, and her mood had changed. She was taking refuge in anger. Her rage at being duped by James—Judas, she called him to a reporter, who got a headline out of it—seemed to have overshadowed her grief at Junie's disappearance, and she elaborated to the press on the ways James had worked to gain her regard. Her cogency would have done credit to a trial lawyer. She left nothing out, Hackett noted, and why should she? It was the recital of her hopes in bitter reverse. "What do you mean, rounded up?" And Hackett caught the echo of Martha Butler. "What they doing running round the streets in the first place," she demanded, "if they're known sex offenders?"

"What was I supposed to say to that?" Long said, chewing on the inside of his mouth. "She's right. These goofs get sent a couple of months someplace and spend their time weeping over how wicked they been. Till the doctor says it's okay to let them out. Till the next time. They're never crazy, God, Father. No doctor in his right mind's gonna get caught using a word like that. Unbalanced is what these specimens are, abnormal, and they get to spend two easy months inside before even that's agreed on. Second you see one with his pants open in the playground, you know the fuck he's crazy. One second's all it takes, am I right?"

Every man walking with his daughter was suspect that first week, and the police were deluged with calls. Mary James, stunned, received dozens of crank letters and grew hysterical at sight of the mailman. Ali took to meeting him at the top of the steps and delivering the letters, unopened, to Long at the Tenth.

"Just as well," Hackett said, who had witnessed one of the scenes. Long, who hadn't, nodded; thinking Hackett was talking about fingerprints.

By Thursday, Hackett knew by heart the letter that James

had sent his future wife. The man had known just the right thing to say to convince the woman of his respectability. He was still calling her Mrs. Stephens, for a start, and the sincere tone, tempered later in the letter with the hint of future familiarity, never wavered. No taker of untoward liberties, this man. The letter began with an apology for his silence, and the diffident anxiety came through loud and clear as James explained that he had not been sure at first that he could become a good father at this stage of his life. Hackett nodded. Responsible and sensitive as well as solvent: What more could a mother ask for? But it was the final paragraph that most interested Hackett. With something of a repetitive flourish, James had concluded: "Hoping that, with your help and guidance, I may enjoy the pleasures of paternity as well as of spouse."

Sic, Hackett thought. The man wrote, he saw, with the pomposity of the self-taught; and while that was a hypothesis that fit his image of James, it was not, Hackett saw equally clearly, something he could hear himself telling Long.

The pleasures of paternity. Hackett read it again and shivered. Mocking bastard.

"Legible bastard, though," he said out loud as he sat up comparing James's even penmanship with the handwriting in each of the crank letters. Nothing matched, and Hackett added the letters to the file, bulging now with Junie's medical record, with the list of rooming houses Long's men had searched, and with the useless lab report on the pair of suspenders James had left behind. The only thing he had left behind. On the day he snatched Junie, James had said, plausibly enough, that the more he carried with him on this trip, the less they would have to worry about on Saturday. Mary James, hurrying to get to church, had stopped to help him hide his traces; had added to his suitcase some kitchen stuff.

"What kind of kitchen stuff?" Hackett wanted to know. He was beginning to feel like an incompetent dentist, prying out the decay bit by poisoned bit.

"Some china dishes. She wrapped them in his underwear," Ali said. No knives, her eyes said; answering the question in his.

Answering the impatience in Long's voice was something else.

"Just what you figured," Hackett told him on Friday afternoon. He was phoning from the Bureau of Criminal Identification, where, surly with self-pity, he had worked his way through files covering a ten-year period. Because he was prejudiced, he had begun with the psycho-wanted, proceeded through the out-of-town, and ended, stiff-backed and squinting, with the anatomical and age-group files. He had unthinkingly accepted as accurate Ali's estimate of James's age as fifty, and when he realized what he had done, had to go back and check Mary James's figure. Not that it made any difference.

"Nothing," he repeated to Long the prophet, who hung up on him. His nails were bitten to the quick.

7

The weather, said the radio, would continue unseasonably warm. The church smell was strong in the heat. Robbing the tiered candles of their dazzle, sunlight came dappling through the windows and what had been gaudy a moment before sparkled now with a kind of glamor. Hackett was standing and kneeling by rote. You can't beat the Catholics for class, he thought, and smiled with affection on the painted plaster Virgin and the Sacred Heart bleeding to his left. It was his first Mass in years, his first ever in New York; and he was surprised by the poor attendance. It might have been the hour. Brooklyn prayed later.

There was no sign of Mary James. Ali, as though caught short by the sun, was wearing a wrinkled blue dress and a black beret that gave her an incongruous sporty look. Watching her as she returned, eyes lowered, from the altar, Hackett wondered if the hat's color was a gesture of mourning. This church, where the blood of Christ flowed daily in redemption, would bury Junie if he found her. Bloating in the heat.

"Mama didn't feel like coming," Ali said. She had accepted without comment his presence in the rear, and they were descending together the steps on which Junie had last been seen.

Hackett nodded and waited until they had walked themselves free of the small crowd leaving the church. Then: "Did John James come to church with you on Sundays?" Deliberately formal, he used the full name to separate the man from Ali. To separate himself, too. He was feeling self-conscious, walking next to her.

"Three Sundays. The only time he missed was the day he got angry. He was very religious, it sounded like. He was always quoting Jesus and stuff. He was going to take instruction, he said."

"He wasn't Catholic?" Because of the churchgoing, Hackett had made the assumption.

"Oh, no. That was something he couldn't fool us about. That's why they couldn't get married in church. They were going to do that later."

They turned south onto Ninth Avenue. Sol's was closed.

"You know," Ali said, "that Sol is sweet on Mama? She should've married him. He'd have made a good father."

Interested in her definition, Hackett asked, "You remember your father?"

"Of course," she said, surprised. "I was nine when he died."

"Mine died when I was seven." And until he was ten, the only way he could spell it had been to put "fat" and "her" together.

"I can remember things about Papa from when I was five," she said, challenging him. She had picked something up in his tone. "I remember he had to walk to work one time because I dropped my ice cream, and I cried so much he had to use his fare to buy me another." She smiled and looked up at him. "Papa seemed so tall. Everyone seemed tall to me then. They still do."

Hackett considered and rejected the idea of holding her hand as they crossed Ninth. He considered and rejected the idea of mentioning Junie to her. He wondered if Ali thought of Junie as dead.

"He didn't like to go to church much," Ali said, still smiling. "But he showed up at my First Communion. To watch Mama cry, he said. He was mostly quiet, I guess, though he was pretty noisy about the rats." She blushed when she brought up the rats, and Hackett distracted her.

"My father was pretty quiet, too," he offered. They had reached her house.

"Is that why you don't remember him?" she said, frowning up at him from the steps.

Long was right, he thought, smiling to himself. Children should be seen and not heard.

Ali had switched to a sharp, adult voice, and the "don't" had come out sounding like "won't."

Monday morning, armed with Junie's dental chart, Hackett drove to the morgue. He dawdled all the way to Bellevue, stopping behind buses, timing himself to catch the red lights. I could do it tomorrow, he told himself, but persevered north anyway. With unhappy foresight he had called ahead, and Schnitzer was expecting him.

Larry Schnitzer was a Missing Persons Bureau detective assigned to more or less permanent duty at Bellevue. In spite of the fact that they were both MPB, Hackett and Schnitzer had barely known each other until the day Hackett, delivering an unidentified, found himself swaying from the smell.

"Let's get you out of here," the plump bald man had said without preamble, and led Hackett into the anteroom. But invisible bodies slept noisome in the sealed trays, and Hackett, taking shallow breaths, had allowed Schnitzer to walk him to a small office down the corridor.

"They assign me here," Hackett said when he felt safe, "and pension or no pension, I quit."

"Ah, you get used to it," said the man, a file clerk for the dead, fingering and measuring the grisly—disarticulated, they wrote mutely on the reports—remains. He carried the smell with him as he stood in the little room, and later, at Schnitzer's home even, Hackett would sometimes fancy that he caught a whiff of formaldehyde when Schnitzer passed. It was not anything he could confirm with Etta, Larry's wife, of course.

"Besides," Schnitzer had said at the elevator. "Anyone tries to give you my job, I'll tell them you're weak in the head."

Schnitzer was the only Jew Hackett had ever been friends with. He had tasted sweet butter (he had thought it rancid) and potato pancakes (he was amused there was a non-Irish variation) for the first time in the Schnitzer home, and he had helped move them to their new apartment in Bay Ridge when Etta became pregnant. He found Etta sexy and liked the idea that even when she was five months gone, she still looked shapely from the back.

"It suits her," Schnitzer said one night, patting her rump as she served the soup.

"You're drunk," Etta said, growing pink.

Schnitzer raised his glass. "It's the Mick presence."

"Drunk! You haven't finished your first yet." Hackett made it a protest and a sneer.

"Listen. While you were boozing on stoops, building up your intake, I was delivering *flanken* for my old man." Schnitzer's father had owned a kosher butcher store in Williamsburg; Hackett vaguely remembered the store, but not the family. ("I remember you, though," Schnitzer said. "Mean and stringy. We couldn't get over the fact that you went to St. Andrew's. Street fighters weren't supposed to be smart as us. We could never understand why you didn't come over to our block and beat the shit out of us, like the rest of your kind." "Not enough challenge," Hackett had answered.)

"My father can't read a word of English, you know that?" Schnitzer went on. "He walks around with a copy of the *Times* under his arm 'cause he's sensitive, and the only thing he could ever read in it was the stock prices that wiped him out. When I graduated high school, he learned my diploma by heart so he could impress the wholesalers, who couldn't read a word of English either. It was his way of sharing the glory."

"It's his way of being proud of you," Etta said, and kissed him good night. Because she was expecting, she went to bed right after dinner the whole summer, and Hackett and Schnitzer would sit around, drinking and talking.

"What about me, don't I get a kiss?" Hackett called after her. She waved in consolation.

"You keep your kisses to yourself," Schnitzer said complacently when she was gone. "Not that it'll do you any good. It takes a strong Jew or a weak *shaygets* to live with a woman like Etta. I'm the one, and you're not the other."

"That work the other way around?" asked Hackett, flattered. Brennan's youngest sister had just taken up with a red-haired Jew from Eastern Parkway.

"No, sir," Schnitzer said, lowering his voice. "And that's why your kind hates us. Not because we're Christ killers, but because we make your women cream. Because we're hairy and potent." He stroked his arm absently.

He was the hairiest bald man Hackett had ever seen. Hair grew all over his chest and his back and along his arms and legs. "He looks like a bear with the mange," Etta had said as together they watched Schnitzer emerge from the sea at Coney Island, sloughing off the water with comic, muscular shrugs; and briefly Hackett had envied him his matted pelt and his fond, fecund wife.

"Mother of God," Hackett said to provoke him, still caressing his arm. "From carcasses to corpses, sure what can the dear man know of women?"

The tiles shone clean, but the stench, a putrefying fog, enveloped Hackett as he entered the autopsy room. Schnitzer was watching Cassidy hose down an obese white woman, the river's flotsam still clinging to her. Cassidy always got the floaters. He was a holdover from the old coroner system—before Hackett's time—when the Brooklyn coroners, and Cassidy was a native son, had paid the rivermen to push the bodies over to their bank, for the autopsy fee. And grew swollen on the corpses, or so it was claimed: twenty thousand a year; dollars, not bodies. Police Commissioner Valentine drew $11,000, the *Daily News* said. Detective Second Grade Hackett made a fat $3,200.

Stretched out on the next table was a skeletal man, his body mottled with cherry-red blotches. Death by asphyxia, thought Hackett, playing doctor. Probably illuminating gas. Garrick was cutting him open as Hackett watched, and blood was spurting through the table slats and forming intricate pink spirals in the water-filled tub below. Hackett concentrated on the tub, the kind his mother had used when dyeing clothes, an early sideline, for the widows of Williamsburg. He would often recognize the stuff later, hanging in nearby yards, and would mentally file to no end the date when the private mourning was over, semaphored by a white petticoat or a pair of pink drawers fluttering among the black. Sometimes it took the full year.

Schnitzer was talking to him.

"You haven't found her?" he asked, taking deep breaths as if the air was ozone.

Hackett shook his head, and they walked to the office down the corridor.

"So what do I need this for?" Schnitzer said, tapping the dental chart Hackett had handed him.

"To make me feel better?" Hackett suggested.

As though Hackett's answer made perfect sense, Schnitzer nodded equably, and they sat side by side on a bench.

"Let's say we get lucky," Hackett said finally. "Let's say we find her. How long will it take you to know?"

Schnitzer stared at him a moment before answering. "To satisfy ourselves, an hour. Less," he said then. "To satisfy a jury? For that, we'd take an X ray, a lateral skull plate. With the processing and drying, say, a day."

But Hackett was no longer listening. He could see Ali looking up at him, talking, but the words were missing; like a balloon the cartoonist had left empty.

Some of the strain must have come through, for Schnitzer leaned forward, studying the floor.

"This can wait, Jim. You're doing this backwards."

Ass upwards is what he meant. It was a mystery to Hackett that his thoughts, the ones he knew about, could be so organized and his actions random, almost chaotic. It was as if the part of his brain that was supposed to let him know what he was going to do next did not bother to send all the messages, and only later would he work out the ellipses that had governed his decisions. Brother Gregory had been the first to point this out in him, on the subject of homework assignments, and Hackett knew that, despite the demands of his job, he was still too ready to count on the hidden signals to justify, belatedly, his seemingly unmotivated conduct.

"I don't know what the fuck I'm doing, to tell you the truth. This bastard James is bringing out the superstitious in me. Part of me thinks that if I act as if I'm gonna get him, then maybe I will."

"And another part of you is scared that you won't."

Hackett snorted. "You and Ceil. You've both got a real gift for clearing the head, you know that? Like too much pepper."

"We're salt of the earth," Schnitzer said, but he continued to stare quizzically at Hackett.

America was still on the move in 1935, and it made sense to assume that John James could be hiding among the drifters that rode the freights from city to city, squatting in jungles that scarred the landscape and the mind. Hackett had read somewhere that the population of a small town could triple when a train pulled in. It made sense, then, to alert the railroad bulls; to take Mary James (who never came alone but brought either Ali or Martha Butler along) through the shacks in Riverside Park and past the lines—shorter than last year's—waiting outside the Salvation Army; and Hackett did all those things, though it went against the grain.

"He's around here somewhere, I can feel it in my bones," he said to Ceil in bed one afternoon. Junie Stephens had been missing two weeks, and it was Hackett's first day off. "Not skulking around like a fugitive either. He's tucked away in some place he had all ready, and he's reading every pathetic plea the mother makes, following our every move in the papers. He's laughing at us. We're better than the funnies."

"Why do you never call Mary James by her name?" Ceil said as she eased off her stockings.

"Don't," he said, showing more of the strain.

The case was slipping from the headlines and the public's interest, or perhaps it was the other way round. Junie Stephens' disappearance could no longer compete with the excitement of Amelia Earhart's solo flight from Mexico, and Hackett saw that photographs of the smiling aviatrix, how they loved that word, had replaced the somber shots of Mary James on the front page of the tabloids. And Hackett had great faith in the tabloids.

"Don't give me that shit about truth. Or taste," he would say at Missing Persons to McCoy, who had 'literary pretensions and read only the *Times.* "Your paper says almost the same thing, but in smaller type and longer words. The *News* and the *Mirror,* now, they know what the public wants, what it feels. A little laughter, a few tears, they follow the swings of the pendulum. Their genius is in not losing touch."

"They pander," McCoy would say, rustling his paper. "They make a two-bit gunman sound like Robin Hood. Like a dog to shit is the *Mirror* to lies."

"Not lies," Hackett would say, grinning. "A different kind of truth."

But the truth was that Junie Stephens had become a paragraph on page four of the *Mirror;* and he was the only one still looking for Junie.

Long and his cohort at the Tenth, protective of their image, had withdrawn first from the press—and here the loss of Long's colorful rhetoric may have been a factor in the diminished coverage—and then from the case. Long had expected to find Junie's body in an adjacent warehouse or along the river ("It'll be within a mile of the house, you'll see," he had promised), and when his early optimism was thwarted, a disappointment compounded by the failure of his informers to produce, he had turned to other things.

Having nowhere else to turn, Hackett had tried to tap Long's sources, which were said to be legion. Informers, Hackett suggested to Long in Flaherty's, were not much use against an amateur, a murderous unknown whose motives could not be trusted. Against the established clientele, however, stoolies were worth their weight, and it was possible—Hackett had done his homework and the statistics made it more than probable—that their man, a presumed tyro at murder, had already compromised his place in Heaven by efforts in some other field of endeavor. In other words, said Hackett—and it was a premise that grew from this point on to become a conviction in his mind—their man's name, if only they knew his name, was probably lying right then in their files. Somewhere.

Under the pressure of Long's presence, Hackett could hear himself lapsing into Brother Gregory's delivery, false syllogism and all, and he cut himself short by ordering another round. When the whiskey arrived, he raised his glass in delicate salute and proposed that Long's informers be questioned again, from this angle.

But Long, tired of the unrewarding chase, had waved away the supplication.

"It's possible I already done all that," he snapped, slamming down his glass in rebuff. Hackett, caught out and seething, had been stuck with the check.

Yet in all fairness, Hackett thought unfairly as he studied Ceil's legs in the shadowed room, the cop had not been born to whom Long would entrust his snitches. As for Long, he knew in turn that Hackett would not give him the drippings from his nose. Though that did not excuse the old snotbag's arrogance.

"What's this?" Ceil asked, and touched his leg gently.

"I scraped my shin. On Ali Stephens' steps."

To him, as to Mary James, it seemed a long time ago.

On the day that Junie Stephens would have been ten, Mayor La Guardia's special committe announced that one-third of the city was on Home Relief, to the tune of twenty million dollars a month. If the middle class continued to collapse, half the city's population could be on the rolls by the end of the year.

Mary James, however, had removed herself from these gloomy numbers. Three weeks after Junie's disappearance—kidnapping, the police listed it—she had accepted Sol's offer of a part-time job at the soda fountain, meals thrown in, and she seemed to be making an effort to pull her shattered life together. She had already gone back to calling herself Mary Stephens.

"I never want to hear that name again," she said in quick anger to MacDonald of the *News* as she overcharged him for his eggs over light. "Except to learn that he's dead."

She clung to the hope, in public at least, that James had

taken Junie to bring up as his own, in California perhaps, somewhere golden and far off, from which Junie had been unable to find her way back. Even with Ali she did not discuss other possibilities.

"But I hear her crying nights," Ali told Hackett as he walked her home from Sol's one evening. She went to Sol's most afternoons to eat and to help her mother, who had no head for figures. "She's frightened to say out loud that Junie's gone; because then it'll be true. Like a curse, you know?"

The mood of the confessional must have been in the air that day, for Martha Butler cornered Hackett on the basement steps.

"Ali's not sleeping properly. The janitor was out in the yard the other night and caught her whispering through the window to the cat on the wall. She was talking about Junie, he said, and the cat seemed to be listening. Gave him a real scare, he said, and I can well believe it. I asked Mary about it, and she says Ali's got a lump in her throat that swells up nights, except the clinic can't find the lump. Whatever that means. I know they leave Junie's light on nights. For Ali, I mean. It's not safe."

Hackett, no stranger to nighttime fears, did nothing about the lamp, and instead bullied the janitor into adding a second lock.

"It's like bolting the barn door after the horse has fled," the man grumbled, but he complied.

Hackett could think of nothing else to do. Mary James, back to being Mary Stephens, had not recognized any of the drifting poor. Other authorities—Hackett had written or phoned contacts as far away as Boston and Washington—either had not come up with anything at all or had ignored his request entirely. The phone calls to the police had petered out, though an occasional letter still found its way to West Seventeenth.

"From one of your slower readers," Hackett told the *News's* crime reporter.

Ali learned to deliver the letters to the sergeant's desk. Long had stopped receiving her.

During the next four weeks Hackett retrieved, among others, an old woman lost by the river and returned her to her ungrateful daughter; found two brothers who had run away to join the circus, the Civilian Conservation Corps, anything, and when he took them home, Hackett could see why; and did not look for the men who had done simple skips. It was the middle of July before he went back to West Seventeenth and told Mary and Ali Stephens of his lack of progress. The faces, clean and shining, that they lifted to him out of the gloom made him feel as bad as he deserved. The rehearsed lines came out slowly, full of pauses, and he and Mary Stephens stared down at the empty cups while Ali's eyes flitted from one to the other, but she did not move or speak. The damp on the walls, violet splotches in the blue, gave off a rank odor, though it could have been the sweat slick in his armpits.

"More tea?" Mary Stephens asked.

"It's too hot, Mama," Ali answered for him.

"We could use some air, and that's a fact," Mary Stephens said absently. "Open a window, Ali."

Ali opened the kitchen door, and a slight breeze teased Hackett briefly, then died. The windows were already open. Sunday sounds—of children in their best clothes playing quiet, to avoid damage—drifted in from the street, softening the growing silence in the kitchen.

There had been no outburst at his confession of virtual failure, and Hackett began to see that, rather than being dismayed by his words, they were in fact reassured by his presence. As he sat there sweltering, it struck him that time moved differently, more slowly, for the poor. Ali was subsisting in an apartment that had no bathroom, no heat. Except that the icebox she used might leak less often, and the toilet was in the hall, not the yard, Ali, a generation later, was living the turn-of-the-century childhood of her mother. Poverty, he thought, fused the past with the present, giving to life a continuity that had nothing to do with tradition.

Time, of course, had been further arrested by the Crash, which had taken those people who, by ability or birth or good luck, had found a way to speed up life's pace, and had taught them the murderously slow rhythms of poverty; had taught them what the poor have always known: Without money, only bad things—sickness, unemployment, death—happen fast. In a strange way, it meant that life had become more equal, for the poor had more practice anticipating, perhaps evading, their lot. A bit like the hardened criminal in jail with the first offender, Hackett reasoned; but the metaphor offended against Ali, and he dropped it.

"Ali's going to a new school," Mary Stephens told him.

"Washington Irving High," Ali said after a while. "But not until September."

"They'll be teaching her all sorts of newfangled things there, the teacher told her."

"Latin," Ali said after another pause. She blushed. "Maybe French, too."

Besides, it was not only Ali's faulty sense of past continuity that was bothering Hackett. He knew that Ali believed, from seeing them above her, that airplanes existed. He knew that Ali believed, from seeing them in movies, that lovely ladies glided across bathrooms twice the size of her apartment. And he knew, too, that it was beyond Ali to care about the difference between the fact of an airplane and the fiction of a movie theme, for both were equally remote from her life. She must regard them in much the way her forebears looked on stained-glass windows: wondrous images that the lowly might behold but only the worthy could lay claim to. Once again, though, the thought offended, and again he corrected himself. It was, he decided finally, Ali's inability to foresee, let alone plan, any change in her life that would cripple her. Her unwitting communion with the past had robbed the future of promise, had turned it into the present conditional passive. A new Latin tense.

He got up to leave.

"I'll keep in touch," he said, and they nodded, believing him.

8

The mailman calculated afterward that it was just after eight in the morning when he knocked on the door.

"Too late for Thanksgiving and too early for Christmas," he said to Ali as he handed her the package. It was the size of a shoe box, wrapped in brown paper and tied with string.

Your common, garden-variety-type package, the mailman said later. Nothing special.

"Well, open it," Mary Stephens said, smiling.

Ali tugged at the door. "It's a mistake," she said, and would have been up the basement steps if her mother had not blocked the way.

"It's for me," Mary Stephens said. "That's my name on it. The other name." She took the package from Ali and began to untie it, one knot at a time. "There's no mistake," she added quietly.

The wrapping fell away. Underneath was a white box, plain except for the B. Altman name printed across the lid. Ali slitted her eyes, ready to close them fast. There was a brief, static pause, then Mary Stephens, breathing deeply, plucked off the lid.

When Ali opened her eyes she saw, nestled on a bed of white tissue, a wooden doll dressed in dark blue fabric. The doll's features were clustered together in the center of the finely carved face, giving it a prissy, old-fashioned look. The arms and legs were jointed. Pink lips smiled up at her.

"That's her dress," Ali said, and the words clung to the silence.

"Dress?" her mother said dazedly. "God forgive me, it's her hair."

I am a man of passion, and from the beginning Mary's dense-ness in that area was a hindrance. A stupid woman will cling with surprising stubbornness to the three thoughts in her head and will, with equal obstinacy, resist the addition of a fourth. And so it was with Mary.

When I first met her, I assumed she could be taught to take care of my needs. She had long hair, which is a woman's glory and to my liking, and the kind of timid grace that brings out the bully in lesser men. Proceeding on the theory that the shy ones have the most to hide—like all those tales of the vicar's daughter —I gave her silences the benefit of the doubt, though her clothes made me wonder. They were not merely shabby, but plain. Never trust a woman who does not adorn herself, especially one who is pretty, or who, like Mary, must have been so at one time. There is a direct connection between vanity and pleasure in a woman, and in spite of all my efforts, there was no pleasure in Mary.

On the other hand, however, you can never trust a woman

who adorns herself too much. Lurking behind the overpainted face is the arrogance the ill-favored develop when they have learned to improve upon the looks the good Lord gave them. Worse, the paint can hide a flaw much uglier than the arrogance: Plain women, ugly women, they know men all too well. Never having had the shield of beauty that protects pretty women from reality, they come armed with a vision denied their happier sisters. And there's no telling how far a woman without illusions can see.

Take my rich widow, for instance, the one who had me put away in Sing Sing. She was ugly as well as rich: a double threat. I should have known better. (I keep calling her "She." The fact is, I can't remember her name. "She" is the cat's mother, Matron used to scold when we failed to address her by her title. In the case of my rich widow, She was the dog's mother.) Indeed, I did know better. It was just that pride had made me blind to the danger. At the trial, though, that same pride put paid to any idea that she was the only one who could see clearly.

"Mutton dressed as lamb," I taunted her across the courtroom, and the look on her Jezebel face as she caught my meaning was ample compensation for the judge's reprimand. She had a good twelve-year edge on me, I knew. A good fifty pounds as well.

"You can't fatten a thoroughbred," I yelled during a pause. I was always more put off by her fullness of figure than by the powder caking in her wrinkles. In fact, it had taken two weeks of skirmishing on my part before I could get myself to move in for what she called a trial marriage. Even at that late date my scruples might have saved me had I not discovered that my old gray mare really did own a candy store—as I said, everyone lies in this game—and, what's more, kept a sizable chunk of its proceeds in the house.

I walked off with the cash, of course. My bride-to-be had taken the Long Island Rail Road into the city—only a wedding gown purchased in New York would satisfy her arrogance, not to mention her proportions—and I scarpered with the money as soon as the train was out of sight. But she must have found her tent of a dress more quickly than she deserved, for she had the law on my doorstep before I had finished packing. I was living on Amsterdam Avenue at the time.

"Don't wait for me," I jeered at the sentencing, as if that might be her intent—and who can tell with dark-haired women? "I'm not the man who wants to look in the glass and see beside him a face twice the size of his own. And twice as old." That way I let her know, whatever her second thoughts might be, that I would never pardon her. Forgiveness is a form of collusion, a way of condoning after the fact those who have trespassed against you. And I had no wish to collude in any way with her.

After all, it was on her account that I did eighteen months in Sing Sing.

I can say it today because time has restored my sense of humor, but it seemed to me while I was in jail that the electric chair would have been punishment above and beyond anything they might have needed to rid the world of my frail presence.

Eighteen months seems a long time when you are inside, and if it is true that a hungry man is not a free man, then I did double my term up the river. A few more months there and, honor bright, I would have starved to death—and this from someone brought up on orphan muck and seafaring swill. Bread hard as a rock was our daily fare, and the maggot-ridden meat, when we got meat, always ponged to high heaven. And for all that the food was so bad, it meant a knifing if fair division was not made of it. Nowhere is injustice felt so keenly as in prison, and I once saw two men die over a piece of spoiled meat. This was in Lawes's time, too—and you can imagine the jokes built around a warden with a name like that—when everything was supposed to have been improved; indeed, had been improved, if you listened to the lifers, which I did. Lifers are a prison's historians.

I was paroled, and none too soon, in June '33. I emerged a thinner if not a wiser man, and one free of the wrath and rumor of life inside. Prisons are as full of delusion as a Presbyterian's notion of Heaven.

The Depression was flourishing like a strong weed when I left Ossining, and that turned out to be not a bad thing for me. I joined the odd-job brigade, picking up work where I could, and no questions asked. I breathed dust for a while at a quarry in Vermont, a place crowded with drunken Scots and Irish—Roosevelt and Repeal having taken their places in the sun during my eclipse in Sing Sing. That was the town where I ran into the stonecutter from Belfast, the one who had known my mother's shop. By this time, anyway, the noise and the company were getting on my nerves, so I moved on to a pleasant interlude with a widow in Pittsburgh—a poor one, and not too plain, you can count on it. It was not until the autumn of '34 that I drifted back to the New York area, and even then I stayed only because the Rockland State job came my way, and with it the parochial-school girls.

After my little holiday in Bellevue—three square meals and diverting scenery—I found myself too fidgety to settle down in Rockland County. The house was too close to the schoolgirls. I began going down to New York so often that I finally took over my old room on Amsterdam Avenue, and went back to the county only twice after that. The house up there had been abandoned by the owner—he had gone West; Oregon, not Hell—and while that meant I could use the place for nothing, it also meant that there was no one to pay for the repair of the stove. Reared though I was on a cold island in the Irish Sea, a rural winter was no joke with improper heat as my only solace.

Until Mary. Which brings us once again to the monstrous regiment of women, as Dr. Knox has called them. I mean Matron's Calvinist, of course, not the grave robber; though they were both resurrectionists in their fashion.

I was full of careful smiles that first evening I met Mary. I made a point of mentioning my store in passing; just enough to whet her appetite. It was obvious from her bearing as well as her clothing that she was penniless (though rich with other assets, I learned. "Mary and her jewels," I said when she introduced me to them; I have a way with words), and my quiet talk of loneliness, with a hint or two of money to spare, caused the widow's heart to sing for joy.

While service with a smile remains my motto, I am more careful about the customers these days. I did not rush to set up a second meeting with Mary. Instead, I let a whole week go by before I wrote to her again. In between, I looked over the two remaining widows, both being typical of the kind of woman who answers personals, and no better than they should be. The first, too experienced for my taste anyway, did not stay to finish her coffee. The second was ugly as sin, and I, tolerant as a priest in such matters, left her to the dignity of unsullied mourning. She had made the mistake of showing me her insurance money, but you don't catch me stepping into the same trap twice. I did not show up for the second appointment.

It is the successful soldier who plans ahead, and besides, I knew my delay in communicating with Mary could only work in my favor. Time may heal, but desperation softens, and by the end of our second meeting, Mary was as putty in my hands. I knew by then, as sure as Paul is Saul, that I was reading this one right. Mary was poor enough and, in the matter of looks, passable. She was no threat. She was not one of those women—not for nothing had I served my term—whose stupidity was hiding other, more pernicious faults. In her case, the cover fit the book, and a slim volume at that. If her situation had not held promise of further reward, I would not have wasted the price of another carfare on her.

I was working three shifts a week those days at a lumberyard on New York's West Side. Even in a buyer's market, the boss there was glad to have me; he saw that I was a cut above those types who came to work in caps and took the full break to eat their sandwiches wrapped in newspaper. He offered me a fourth shift, and I could have used the money, life with Mary costing me more than I had budgeted for; but I had to refuse. I had moved in with her at this point, had married her; and the job, for all that it enabled the bridegroom to play benefactor to the bride, left me with the obligation of explaining my absences. Brushing myself for sawdust, I would hurry home from work and tell Mary that I had just come from a supplier, having spent another six hundred dollars on the store; that I had just come from my lawyer's office—after all, I wouldn't live forever. Everything I was doing, I was doing for Mary.

Now there's nothing wrong with the Irish that a little turn of Mr. Darwin's evolutionary wheel won't cure—and I mean all the Irish when I say that, for as anyone knows who has seen them both, there's little to choose between St. Patrick's Day in New York and the Orange Lodge parade in Belfast. And what is wrong with the Irish can be turned to good effect, if you know what's what. I counted on the fact that Mary, from the diffidence that drunken men seem to breed in their women, would not risk embarrassing me by asking too many questions; and I was right. Just to make sure, however, for I have learned to take nothing for granted, I forestalled any curiosity by giving her a log of my activities.

"Any day now, and we'll be ready," I said on the second Friday. "And once we move, your jewels will glow in the sun instead of in this dark place that dulls them."

She loved that kind of talk. Together with my money, it was all she did love about me, as anyone with half an eye could see.

It should be remembered that from the start Mary saw me as a meal ticket; her clumsy attempts at affection were barter for a full belly. As testament to her powers of self-deception, moreover, she managed to convince herself that, dried up and worn out as she was, she was yet the answer to a lonely man's prayers. She has only herself to blame if the contract came with fine print that she was too blind to read.

I will say this for her, though, for she was not without virtue: Mary was cleaner about her person than any woman I have known. And she kept the apartment spotless. I could even see where, in honor of my advent and perhaps to let me know how well she would take care of my home, she had tried to spruce up the place. Full of the form if not the content of a bride, she had gone out and bought new sheets; and I am sure she was the one who had thrown out the broken chair and the orange tea cozy I found in the yard. Tickled by the color, I retrieved the cozy.

I have lived in worse places. In defense of my moneyed background, however, I let Mary know that I was used to better circumstances. Sighing at the stockings on the kitchen line—Mary of course being too modest to hang her personal linen out back— I comforted her with the news that work had already begun on the new electrical system in my house. Anything of that nature was a mystery to Mary, and I made use of her ignorance to gain time. Until my plans were set, I needed to keep my arrangements as loose as the waistband in her panties, though the leg elastics were so tight they interfered with her circulation.

But like a pantomime horse, I'm wandering ahead of myself.

For our second meeting, I had volunteered by letter to call on Mary at her apartment. From the corner I watched her waiting at the top of the steps, looking flushed and as close to pretty as I was ever to see her. As I drew nearer, I realized that somebody was snooping at one of the upstairs windows, so, keeping my hands behind my back, I kissed her gently on the cheek. Claiming her, but courtly with it.

I can say without exaggeration that as we went downstairs— Mary apologizing the while for the state of the steps, which were crumbly and uneven and hard on my foot—a feeling came over me very like the one I had experienced when I first saw New York: that, without my knowing it, the years had been spent preparing me for this moment. Nothing is wasted.

I knew what they looked like before they opened the door. On my first date with Mary—though that sounds too light a word to use of our solemn appointment—she had brought along their photographs. I had memorized their features, but what I had not foreseen—the photos were of their heads only—was the similarity in height. Mary had told me that one was three years older than the other; yet there they stood, day and night of equal length.

It would be poetic at this point to say that I was speechless with excitement. The truth is, like most people, I tend to blurt under such circumstances. Knowing this about myself, then, and having no wish to stammer foolishly, I had prepared in advance a little speech. Jewels, I called them until I was sick of the word. "God bless the children," I went on, switching to surer ground and only just in time. One of God's blessed was showing signs of blasphemous impatience.

I turned the tide by bringing my hands from behind my back. I was bearing the first of many gifts to the trio, though these—first impressions being something I know the value of—I had chosen with special care. A mere suitor for the present, I had kept the presents small but select: scented soap for Mary, and a cross on a chain for each of the girls.

The girls.

Out of politeness, I had used the plural in complimenting them. In reality, as in the photographs, the younger one was the true jewel, a solitaire without facets. The other, an abrasive garnet, could have had only sentimental value. They were as unlike as two sisters could be.

Else my text sound too fanciful here, I am beholden, as the parsons say, to the Song of Solomon. But in the sun, Junie's hair really did gleam like gold, her eyes did shine like sapphires; and all her movements—and she was always in motion—were graceful. Tossing her hair around her long and shapely neck, she never stopped chattering and smiling. Even when she slept I would hear her murmuring, and next morning her hair would be tangled from all her turning in the night. The hair had a natural curl to it, like her mother's—though Mary hid hers in a tight bun and loosed it only in the dark, quickly pinning it up at first light—and on Sundays, before church, Junie would brush her hair into ringlets that were especially becoming. Truly there was no spot in her.

If she did have a blemish, it was that her sister's influence was too strong over her. As often as not when I got back from work, Junie would be out with Alice. If I was there first, waiting when they returned from school, Junie likely as not would vanish upstairs with Alice to a neighbor's. Lacking a father, Junie in effect had two mothers, and so happy was her disposition that she had no trouble obeying both, though one was a fool and the other a bully.

Dark women are offputting. They are harder on their men than fair women, and more sure of what they don't want. (I'm not alone in this. Look at history and Mary Queen of Scots, say, or Boadicea daubed in woad.) The very texture of their skin is tougher.

Alice, of course, was dark. And she had these strange, squinty eyes, and this ungainly way, when she looked sideways, of swiveling half her body. She needed glasses, is my guess. Perhaps that's why she stared too long and saw too much of the little within her range. And when she wasn't staring, she was reading, or pretending to. She would pick up a book whenever I entered the kitchen,

but she never turned the page. I could tell what she was up to by
the telltale shift of her body: Like nothing so much as a blue-
eyed Chinaman, she was watching me out of the corner of her
eye. From her very first yawn, I had known she was going to be
trouble.

None of this is to say, however, that I was looking a gift horse
in the mouth. Even though I found myself saddled with Alice's
arrogance and Mary's stupidity, I had no regrets. Indeed, Mary's
limitations in the bedroom became my protection outside it, for,
rather than being, as is supposed, at odds with reality, imagination in fact defines it. Mary, lacking the vision that either intelligence or ugliness would have brought her, was doubly blind. How
else could she have failed to realize that nobody in his right mind
and possessing property and cash would have settled down with a
drab woman and a meddling child?

I knew the answer, of course, for she was transparent as glass.
She believed that Junie would turn me into a father; would keep
me happy and with them. And I still wonder, had life gone the
way Mary hoped, how long it would have taken before her eyes
were opened to more than the sailboats that dot the City Island
seascape.

Be that as it may, and those are only fancies for a rainy
night, I still had to deal with Alice.

Using the mother as ally, I took it upon myself to spurn the
daughter. Mary, by acknowledging the differences between the
girls without knowing that she did so, made it easy for me. It was
clear that she loved Junie more, and who's to blame her, yet she
allowed Alice a pride beyond her years. To prick that pride, all I
had to do was follow the family tendency and indulge Junie, and
at the same time follow my natural inclination and ignore Alice. I
was well on my way to isolating her—diminishing her influence
by contradicting her, by fashioning advice to suit Mary's wishes
and adding sweeties of one kind or another as ballast for Junie,
and none better qualified than I to do that—when, canny as a
cornered rat, she called my bluff.

It was Sunday morning. Mary, Junie and I were having
breakfast. Alice, who was going to take communion, did not join

us. Instead, she stationed herself behind Junie's chair, and after a while, not looking at me, she said, "Mama, Junie can't go to church with that cold."

Or anywhere else, she meant, and I could see our little outing going up in smoke.

"If she goes out in this weather," she went on, still looking at the ceiling or wherever, "it'll go to her ears, and she'll miss a week of school again."

She turned to me at this point.

"Junie has trouble with her ears. She's not supposed to go out in the rain, the nurse told us." Educating the stranger in their midst and at the same time quelling her mother's resistance by quoting some ignoramus at the clinic.

"We can take a taxi to the train," I said, knowing how this would appeal to Junie.

"She should be in bed, Mama." Alice was talking right through me. "Or it'll be the pneumonia again."

The diagnosis came tripping off her tongue like a line from the play she was studying. The whole situation was an act, and I could just hear her calling down the curtain next time round with a speech on rheumatic fever or such.

"All this to-do about a couple of sniffles," I said, contenting myself with a smile at Junie. Her hand was lying next to mine on the table, but I deliberately did not touch it. "I'll call Sam when we get to the other end, and he can pick us up in the car."

"Get back in bed, Junie, and I'll bring you a cup of tea," Alice said, making it all too clear that she was not taking a blind bit of notice of me. She sat down and began to eat. Nobody was going to church that day.

Mary, Mary, quite contrary, made no effort to scold Alice. After all my preparation, my outing had been ruined by a meddlesome chit of a girl. I was shaking with anger as I put on my hat, and I slammed the door so hard, Mary told me later, that I shattered the gas mantle. They had to use the oil lamp the rest of the day.

Alice, Alice, full of malice, somebody should have taught you that pride goeth before a destruction and a haughty spirit before a fall. You may have won that particular battle, but there was no way you could win the war.

I did not go back that night. For much the same reason that I kept Mary waiting for our second meeting, I delayed my return until the following morning. By then she was only too anxious to promise, come what may, that the girls would go with me on my little excursion the coming weekend. She even made an effort to please me that night, but I pleaded fatigue. I had lost all interest in her.

Some kind of attention appeared in order at this stage, however, for my show of temper had alarmed Junie. Her smiles were as sweet as ever, but she did not chatter as much. It seemed to me, too, that there was a holding back on her part, a tendency to stay close to Alice, though Alice was so wily it could all have been her doing. Lord knows what she had said about me after I slammed out. Whatever; it was essential I get back into Junie's good graces.

I worked hard and spent fast that final week. I showered them with presents, including a radio—their first—that I bought secondhand from the foreman at work. Mary, of course, was delighted that my affection was taking a form so easy for her to bear, while Junie, with the natural tolerance that is the hallmark of a sunny nature, dropped her remaining reserve and grew ecstatic.

Alice alone remained the fly in the ointment. Alice Blue Gown, I called her, smiling, as though I was unaware of her dark moods. But she would not wear the dress because I had bought it, any more than she would wash with the scented soap, Mary's one concession to vanity, that had become a major outlay in my budget. Mary and Junie would waft of lavender or lilies of the valley or whatever I had just brought in—though I never once caught them at their toilette—but not Alice. Never Alice. In her mother's castoffs and reeking of carbolic, she would watch unmoved as Junie, smelling withal like the Rose of Sharon, would tie new ribbons in her hair. Alice would drop her guard only when, sitting around the kitchen table, I told them bedtime stories. Junie cajoled me nightly, but it was Alice, her book still open in front of her, who really listened to my tales of King Robert the Bruce and the spider, and O'Neill of the Red Hand. She listened so intently, as a matter of fact, that I grew alarmed at what she might be storing in that tidy brain of hers—for to hold Junie's attention, I would put in all the accents and the sound effects that had appealed to Robbie—and I was forced to abandon my entertainment. Is it any wonder that living with Alice was no picnic? She would have made a right rare orphan.

Nothing, however, not even Alice's cold manner, could spoil my good humor those last days there. Having won Junie back, I could smile easily as I helped Mary pack her rubbish—though the smile was strained, I admit, when Mrs. Butler came crawling round, looking for an invitation, children in arms included, to see Mary's new home. Junie's excitement matched my spirits, and she swooped through the rooms, squabbling with her mother about what not to take and rearranging and repacking all the little trinkets I had given her or describing the house to her playmates on the steps outside and taking leave of them several times over. We were celebrities on the block.

Alice did not pretend to pack. She was too busy with her play, she said, but politely, for now that the battle lines were drawn between us, we each treated the other with the formality of long-term enemies. Someone less experienced might have thought from her manner that she had forgotten her victory over me; but I knew better.

She waited until the last minute to lower the boom. Like one big happy family, we were sitting around on Saturday afternoon, waiting for the weather broadcast. Sunday, the radio finally reported, would be fine and clear. Junie cheered.

"Junie," Alice began, and right away I was on the alert. "I'm sorry, Junie. I have a special rehearsal at school tomorrow, a dress rehearsal. We won't be able to go."

There was finality rather than regret in her voice. Junie, bless her, recognized it and began to cry.

I was not to be thwarted this time, however, and this time, too, I did not refrain from patting Junie. Alice gave me a quick, darting look, and I knew that she had known for days about her rehearsal.

"We're not going to disappoint Junie two weeks in a row," I said. "They'll just have to get on with the play without you, Alice. It's a question of principle and your mother agrees, don't you, Mary, we are not going to disappoint Junie again. Fair's fair, Alice."

"I can't go," Alice said after a while. "I have to go to school. Miss Morris gave me a note saying I have to go."

There was another silence.

"Miss Morris says Junie can come and watch." She smiled at me.

I smiled right back at her.

I had been toying all week with the matter of the order. Appetizer and main course; main course and dessert. Even if I changed the names, the order still gave me pause. Somtimes it was better to receive than to give. I would alternate my preferences, savoring this advantage over that. But the overall plan was set.

Now Alice had presented me with a third choice, and a not unpleasing one either, and I made my accommodation with it. I had no wish to make Junie suffer.

"I see no reason why Junie should suffer," I said. "If you must go to school, Alice, then go to school. But I warn you, we shall take the trip without you."

"I didn't get to go last week. When Junie couldn't go," she said in her bully-boy voice to Mary. "Fair's fair both ways. And I don't—" She stopped and stood up, tossing her head the way Junie did, except Alice's hair was too short to fling. For dark hair, it could have been pretty, if she had only let it grow. "Oh, nothing," she said, and left.

The nothing meant something, of that I was sure, and victory or no victory this time, I was glad that, one short day, and I would be clear of her. My turn at the helm was at hand.

It was hot after our hike from the station. Junie was sweating; I could smell her, it was lilies of the valley today.

"The ocean's over there. Behind the hill," I said, pointing.

Beyond High Tor was the sea and the boats and a room of her own. You can pass off anything if you keep your voice firm.

I stooped to help her pick some of the flowers growing wild in the yard.

"Not far now," I said. "It's just around that bend up ahead. We'll get you a drink of water first."

I pushed open the door.

"I keep the house key here. It's my workshop."

I had spent two weekends tidying it up. The bed, no longer in its winter vigil beside the stove, was stored in the back room, and the tools were hanging neat on the wall next to the sink. I had covered the table with an old tarpaulin that reached to the floor. If you take care of the little things, the rest will take care of itself.

I showed her how to use the hand pump, and watched as she refilled the jam jar and stuck the daisies in it.

"See those little knives over there?" I said when she had finished. "When I make a sculpture of you, those are the ones I'll use to carve your face."

I took down a plane and in fatherly fashion showed her its use, though I could see that she was itching to get on to the house.

"But there's something I have to do now, before we go." First things first.

I turned at the door to the back room. If she stayed where she was, the table would form an effective barrier between her and the front entrance.

"Watch your fingers, Junie. Those things aren't toys, you know."

Out of modesty, I closed the door before I began to untie my shoes.

10

It seemed to Celia Lynch as she waited for Jim at the top of
the subway steps that only as an adulteress did she feel free of
deceit. The irony of her reaction, that duplicity was the well-
spring of her probity and that in her duplicity she had forfeited
the power to mask herself from him, made her smile. She saw herself, a girl again, chaste before the chaste nuns, and deceitful, too,
wondering with lowered eyes if they felt the heat of periods, the
weight of breasts. She had these kinds of thoughts whenever Jim
kept her standing in the cold. It was a way of deflecting anger.

He could not meet her at the house, of course. Since the
night he had first made love to her, they had rarely been seen in
public together. When Con stayed away on the odd weekend, five
times in twelve months, they had celebrated with a Saturday-
night movie or dinner; always in Manhattan. She had gone with
him several times to the Schnitzers', but she had felt too keenly
her position and her inability to return their generosity, and after
Etta became pregnant, he had stopped insisting. He talked of

Con not finding out, as though the secrecy was all on her behalf, but she knew it was because he did not want the world to have anything on him. Yet, over the year, it had been impossible not to tell, and people knew. Bobby, of course, and the Schnitzers. Her sisters, Liz and Nora. She was not sure when he had told McCoy, sweet croppie boy. The thought of gentle McCoy as homespun rebel made her smile again.

She had found safety in the isolation at first. "Nothing lasts," she said to Liz—it was in telling her sisters about him that she had talked herself into loving him—and together they had mourned the inevitable future as they had when Ceil, bitter and bleeding, had tried to will away the contractions of the second, inescapable miscarriage. She had expected her excitement to fade, the feeling that she was always slightly drunk and that the dreary weekends with Con were shadows from which she drifted, swaying, into the glow of her evenings uptown with Jim; and loved him as redeemer when it did not.

She watched the car turn the corner and held her breath, letting it out in short, triumphant puffs as he drew alongside. (She had been with him—a safe place, Manhattan's Inwood section—when he bought the car, a black, anonymous Plymouth, from a cousin several times removed. "You would've got it for less if I hadn't been with you," she had said, and he had nodded. "He's just jealous," he said, flushed with pride of his possessions. "You're worth the extra ducats.")

"I can't feel my feet," she complained, climbing in.

"You wanna stop for a drink?" he asked without precedent, and frightened her with his sudden carelessness about being seen with her. He is no longer thinking of me, she told herself, as someone who can compromise him.

"You've already had several," she said calmly.

"It's not a bad idea, though. Jesus, I'm tired," he said, and her stomach flopped with panic. Pan who held orgies in the olive groves. Not Pan; Dionysus, Bacchus, Iacchus. Three in one. Unholy trinity.

"Not of you," he said, reading her silence. He put his hand on her thigh. "Never of you."

"You can't keep changing the rules," she said. "They're your rules."

"I was late, is that it? I'm sorry I was late."

"There you go again," she said.

Without warning he pulled the car to a stop, ignoring the rest of the traffic. "What's wrong? Is it Con?"

"When was it ever Con?" she said. Then: "You don't seem in much of a hurry to get uptown."

"Of course I want to get uptown, what's the matter with you?" He unbuttoned her coat, checking. She had worn the dark green, and even to her critical eyes she had looked good. Which was why she feared something bad was about to happen.

"I love you," she said miserably, the wrong thing at the wrong time. It weakened her, made her despicable perhaps, to say such a thing when he was cold. It was what he liked to hear when she knelt before him and her ministrations made him swell until she nearly gagged. He liked that, too.

He put his arm around her, and with the other tilted her head so that she was facing him.

"You are very beautiful, Ceil," he began, but his eyes were bleak.

Here it comes, she thought. The good-friends speech.

"You make me greedy," he said, and put her hand between his legs. "Here. Feel the greed grow."

"You're not so tired."

"I'm tired of all this hiding, all this running round in secret circles. That's the part you like best," he accused.

She had told him as much in the beginning, when it had been true. The sly beddings and the sensual phone calls excited her, had become vehicles for her ingenuity, and the triumphs of her masquerade lingered in her mind and warmed her in his absence. She had told him some of this, believing he would confess the same to her, giving him absolution to confess; and thought him dishonest when he didn't. Only gradually did she perceive that the clandestine, which was necessary and familiar to him in his role as son, as cop, left him feeling soiled in their context. In sympathy with his reaction, her own impatience grew, yet mitigated by the fear that she would not be able to face Con. Jim knew this, too, and she found it reasonable to assume that her cowardice allowed him to indulge in feelings that would be dangerous if she were free. Because—for all his jeers about secrecy —it was at his insistence they held themselves apart. To Ceil he seemed like one of those men rescued from the desert, able to take only small sips of nourishment at a time. Too much, too soon, and he would spew forth one of his rages, deadly and as indiscriminate as the plague.

"I must be out of my mind," he would say on the phone the next day, and she, patient as Griselda, would submit; to prove she could withstand him.

To her sister, though, she was less sanguine.

"Before me, he never went with anyone longer than four months. Usually four nights," she told Liz after a particularly bad fight that had started, lightly enough, with a joke about his mother. His joke. "How do I know I'll be able to convert him?"

"Ceil, Ceil," Liz said, whispering over the phone so that Danny would not hear. "It's been almost a year. You already have."

"Then why don't I feel it? One look that gets a little too appraising, and I'm waiting for him to lapse. To leave," she had clarified; then hung up, cheated by her sister's impenetrable optimism.

He pulled her toward him and kissed her, then reached to restart the car.

"The part I like best is right here," she teased, stroking, and he eased forward in the seat so that she could unbutton his fly.

She had met him at her aunt's wake. He had come with Bobby Brennan, who was doing the flowers.

"I haf been vatching you all evening," said a voice behind her. "Your legs belong in Hollyvood."

"But not the rest of me?" She turned, disdainful, and looked up into his face. A Mick, in spite of the accent.

"Haven't seen enough of the rest of you." He was on the verge of being drunk.

"Ceil," Bobby said quickly. "This is Jim Hackett, an old friend. Jim, Celia Lynch."

"Niece to the deceased. A maiden lady." She had not liked her aunt, but still; it was more than she had meant to say.

"You or the deceased?" He smiled unpleasantly, knowing better. She had seen him look for her ring.

She watched as Con, taking over the dead aunt's gambit, snubbed her mother. She caught Liz's eye, who had seen it, too, before turning back to him.

"Née Blake," she said.

"Such a pretty name. To have given up." Then, clearly hunting to fill the silence: "You related to the Blakes on Fifteenth?"

"We're from the Heights," she said, reluctant to move.

"Out of my league. All that lace."

"I used to know an Eileen Hackett," she said. Con was looking. "A teacher."

"No," he said. "I'm son of the dipso on South Ninth."

She nodded. "That Hackett." And spoke to Bobby, silent and uneasy at her side. "Tell your old friend he's had enough."

"Does she," he said to Bobby, "always talk in clichés?"

"It's the company I keep," she said, looking directly at him, and was disconcerted when he flushed.

Three days later he phoned her.

"I wondered if you'd call," she said.

"Brennan gave me the number. Bobby, I mean," he said quickly, but she had already known. Bobby had told her two days before, at the funeral, and for two days she had sat by the phone.

At her suggestion they met by the bridge, at the subway stop that became their regular rendezvous. It was three months before his promotion to second grade and the car, and they took the subway across to Manhattan.

"How long you and Con been married?" he asked at the gin mill in Greenwich Village where they ended up. The bar was dark and noisy, and through the gloom she counted only two other women; professionals. Yet she did not feel out of place there.

"Four years," she said.

He nodded, not looking at her. "You see that man behind me? The one to the left. That's Buddy Tambor with friends."

"You know them?" The two women were among the friends.

He shrugged. "Cops and crooks, they hang out in the same places sometimes. Two sides of the same coin."

"Sometimes," she said, "they're the same side of the same coin. I read the papers."

There was a short silence.

"You ever play around before?" he asked, and she let his presumption go unchallenged.

"I've given it some thought," she said when he had lit her cigarette.

He nodded, staring at her. "How old are you?"

"I'm as old as my tongue and a little older than my teeth." He should not expect everything to come easy. To soften the rebuke, she tasted her drink and choked. "I'll be thirty in March," she said hoarsely.

"And no children, that right?"

"I may be barren," she heard herself say, and smiled a cold, social smile.

"Watch your ash," he ordered, playing cop, and took the cigarette from her gauche fingers. "May be? Don't you know?"

"It's hard to know." She was still smiling idiotically. "I thought Bobby must have mentioned it to you. I thought that's why you asked. Con tells anyone who'll listen."

"Jesus," he said, and she was to echo him many times in the months ahead. The "Jesus" became a talisman, the magic charm that had bonded her to him at that moment when she was powerful over him and ignorant of her strength; and later, when she loved him and he had the power, she would say the word in a half whisper as he had done, yet audible in all that noise. And hug herself with love.

He took the lead and his pace was slow. He called her twice, often three times a day, and guided her when she was free (and with Con away during the week, she was nearly always free, ruthlessly breaking commitments with family and friends) to run-down bars where she would sit and watch him drink. On the phone his conversation was suggestive, almost schoolboyish, but in person he held back, put off, as they all were, by her coolness. He filled the silences with questions about her family, about Con; but did not give her the same freedom of inquiry.

"He lived on my block," he said. "Con. We brawled once when we were kids."

"I know. It was one of the first things Bobby told me. Naturally."

"Naturally," he agreed. "He put up a fair fight till the end." It was the only nice thing he could find to say about Con.

"It doesn't make sense," he would go on. "You must have led him into believing he rated you. He's stupid as the day is long, he'd never've thought of it for himself. It must have been your sin."

For a godless man, she thought, he chose some odd words, and she watched him struggle not to let his scorn of Con spill onto her. Then with a patience she did not feel—it was like trying to explain the impulses of someone she had not known very well; the shame alone was intimate—Ceil held herself up for judgment.

She was the middle of three sisters, and as if to compensate for her median position, she grew into the tallest, the smartest, the prettiest. A swan above ducklings, she dominated the family photographs. She usurped her sisters in real life, too, charming the boyfriends of the oldest, cowing those of the favored youngest. Yet apart from a brief period of civil war in their teens—fewer than four years separated the firstborn from the baby—they had always been each other's closest friends. In her troubled womanhood, Ceil was forgiven her arrogant adolescence; and their advice to one another, though not always realistic, at least lacked the distortions of pity.

Their father had been a lawyer, and they lived in a large corner house detached from the rest of the block. All three girls went to college, and Ceil taught English and Latin in a parochial high school until her marriage. She had married later than her sisters, who were both on their second child when she met Con. Her mother had begun to give up hope for Ceil's chances. "It's all very well being educated, Ceil, but not when you use it to keep nature at bay," her mother would say resentfully. By nature she meant the men who, attracted by Ceil's looks, came calling—in droves, her mother exaggerated—only to retreat before Ceil's satiric tongue.

It was not until her father died, in the bed of his mistress of fifteen years, that Ceil saw the trap she was in. (Ceil had gone for the priest at one in the morning. "What goings-on," Father Blake, no relative, had said; then remembering Ceil's bereavement, had hurried with her to the other woman's house. At the funeral her mother, with a dignity that made Ceil sob out loud, had crossed the aisle to kiss her rival on the cheek.) A few weeks into widowhood and her mother, Ceil noticed, had stopped talking about nature and spoke instead of redoing Ceil's room: They were to be companions in loneliness. Con, tall enough and slow-moving, had come along at this point and, mistaking his insensitivity for strength—Ceil glanced sideways here to see how Jim was taking all this—she had married him. "You have to remember, I'd driven all the others away by then," she said defensively.

"So why not go looking for somebody new? You might have met me," he said, and she was up half the night over that one.

"I'd run out of time. I wanted to get the whole thing over with, get on with my life, start a family. I never thought about having a baby until then. I just assumed it was something coming to me, like old age. It didn't seem to matter much who the father would be. Besides, it wasn't so bad at the beginning." No wonder people lie, she thought, and wondered why she hadn't. The truth is so unmalleable.

"It still doesn't make sense," he said, defeated; and of course he was right.

Three weeks passed. He drank and questioned and listened, but except for a good-night kiss, he did not touch her. Just as she was despairing—she had neither eaten nor slept properly since his first phone call; her mother, attributing Ceil's pallor to grief for the dead aunt, rejoiced to foresee the sorrow her own passing would bring and stayed to overhear but not to listen to the convoluted phone calls. Ceil, knowing all this, yet oblivious—just as she was despairing, he met her one night in a borrowed car. In dense silence he drove her uptown to his apartment.

"I've been here five months, but I can't seem to get around to finishing it," he said at the door.

Ceil took care not to sit down, awkward and inaccessible in one place. She ambled through the two rooms—three; a New York landlord would call the tiny, windowed kitchen a room—as though she were touring Versailles, what she had read of Versailles. The living room looked unused. A sofa, two small chairs, a table between the windows, which were covered in tan draperies. Curtains. The wooden floor was polished and bare. Only in the bedroom, with his books and his photographs—a wedding group of the Brennans, Jim a best-man blur to the side; a fat, indolent baby, his godson Jimmy McCoy—was there softness, and she saw in his paraphernalia something of herself, of her own bedroom filled with sterile claims to familial embrace. She returned to the living room and came to a halt in front of the print over the fireplace.

"Braque. One of those clever Frenchmen. It doesn't make sense, but it's easy on the eye," he explained, and turned her around to face him.

In her attempts to seduce him she had worn as little as possible, had met him each time freezing half to death. She was dressed in a low-cut black blouse—she was still in mourning—and two large, easily manipulated buttons were all that separated him from her skin. With one quick look to check the curtains (he had planned this in advance, he had left them closed that morning; she hoped he was feeling some of the nausea that was making her tremble), he undid the buttons, and his hands were on her breasts.

"No," he said as she reached for him. "I won't last long as it is."

In spite of his words, she must have been expecting him to enter her slowly, a guest's gentle slipping, for she was startled by the swiftness, brutal and selfish, with which he took her.

"You were good and ready," he said afterward, still in her.

Wondering if it was an apology of sorts and deciding it wasn't, she said, "I've been ready for weeks."

He smiled and kissed her slowly, relaxed enough to be tender, and began again.

"Wait awhile," she murmured, but he ignored her and, her throat arched on the pillow, Ceil looked up at him, at his face frowning slightly, and he seemed to her like a monk lost in agitated prayer. He opened his eyes and saw her watching; and came a second time.

"You always look?"

"No," she said truthfully.

"I think I like it," he said, her rhythmic jack-in-the-box, full of surprises.

The next night she was on time at the subway stop, and he was not waiting. He won't show up, she thought at the end of ten minutes. Ten minutes; and the day spent reliving the evening before, devouring every minute in place of the food her stomach couldn't hold, trying on and rejecting half her wardrobe, was blanked out in her misery. He got what he wanted, and that's the last of him.

He came running up the stairs, sweating. Under the hat his eyes looked black, beady with fatigue.

"I got stuck at the morgue," he said. "A rotten day. And on top of it all, I couldn't get a car. Do you think you can bear the subway?" (She learned to love the subway. She could stand with him in public, and when it was crowded he would take her arm to let the creeps know and she would press against him and watch his mouth quirk.)

"I gotta take a shower," he said when they were uptown, and as though she were not there, he stripped. "You wanna come in?"

She had spent the day in curlers, getting ready for the night.

"I've just washed my hair," she said, not yet trusting him to see her with it straight.

She had a drink waiting for him when he came out. Balancing the glass in one hand, he turned down the blanket with the other and stretched out on the sheet.

"Supine," he said, ready to concentrate on her.

"With possibilities Cicero never dreamed of," she punned, approaching the bed.

"Don't you believe it, teacher. You've been reading the wrong stuff."

She held his eyes, smiling, and his legs parted unresisting as she slid down him. Careful of her teeth, for he was larger than Con, she began to play with him.

"Whoa," he said, not meaning it, and she ignored him. He propped himself up on his elbows, moving with her, and with one hand she brushed her hair aside, to let him watch. Then, as violently as he had entered her, she slipped a finger into his rectum; and choked on his responding climax.

"Oh, yes," he said after a while, and pulled her up and across him. She was still clothed. Then: "You always swallow?"

"No," she whispered, fearing his drift.

"You swallow Con?"

He was undoing her dress and invoking her husband.

"Who do you think you are, the Inquisition? The department said, Hackett, go get yourself a fallen woman and come back and tell us the dirty bits, is that it?" She was off the bed and at the door before he reached her.

"Not fallen," he said, holding her close. "Full of grace."

"Blessed among women," she said softly, and he kissed her to shut her up. He was trembling, from the cold probably.

"It's the Stephens case again," he said. Ceil was making scrambled eggs, and he was standing in the kitchen doorway.

That was what his mood had been about, she thought, and was disgusted with her self-absorption.

"What's happened?" she said, a refrain from when the case started.

"Poor little bitch," he said as though he hadn't heard her. "Junie Stephens. She flits in and out like a ghost, unreal somehow. To me, at any rate. Not to them. Mary Stephens and Ali." He paused. "She reminds me of you. Ali. There's something about the way she stares at me."

"Perhaps we see you the same way," Ceil said soberly, putting the plates on the table.

"And how's that?" He was eating the eggs, his jaws hardly moving, and she wondered at his many parts.

"A lion among the Christians," she said. "A vegetarian lion."

"Sounds good. What's it mean?"

"I'm not sure. Because sometimes you're a Christian among the lions, and that's what makes her stare. But a tough Christian."

"Not so tough today. I spent too much time worrying about the mother going off her head and Ali having to handle it all."

" '*Mihi filia rapta est.*' Ceres mourning Proserpina."

"Golden-haired Ceres," he said, and she saw he meant it literally.

"What happened?" she asked again.

They were lying on the bed in the dark. He was holding her casually, one arm around her, like a husband; and like a husband, without urgency, he was telling her about his day. It was at moments like this that Ceil would have bartered the excitement of their lovemaking, or some of it, at least, for the possible tedium of marriage to him—arguing about his drinking, cooking his meals at odd hours, but remembering to cut off the fat first—and the right to show him off to her family and lie next to him as he talked and to know that never again would she have to get up in the middle of the night to return to her own cold house.

11

While Ceil had still been getting her beauty sleep, Hackett's day had begun, as most of his days began, with Hackett sitting on the toilet, reading the paper as he waited for the water to run hot. The old lady in the next apartment, whom he suspected unreasonably of drink because she sang as she climbed the stairs, would leave a *Mirror* outside his door every morning. He was up by six-thirty when he was working the day shift, and the paper was always there.

When he was a child, Jim Hackett had read only the sports pages and the funnies. Now that he was a man, he had put away childish things, postponed them in any case, and these days he read the news section first. Except for Sunday, he had forsaken the funnies.

Hackett banged on the pipe again and turned the page. Juxtaposed with an article on further corruption in the Vice Squad—continued on page ten, but he didn't bother, it had turned into a reprise on Polly Adler—was a story on Maria Rasputin. The daughter of the mad monk was on her way to join a big-cat act in a Peruvian circus, and Hackett was deep into a catalogue of the lady's eccentricities when he realized the room was full of steam. He showered and shaved quickly because, ironically, it took him much longer to get to work from West Seventy-sixth Street than it had from Brooklyn; even longer now that he drove.

It was hard to run a car on an annual salary of $3,200, minus the compulsory cut all city employees took, due to the bad times. Hackett had heard of cops, perhaps the ones the *Mirror* had in mind, who banked that and more in a month. Corruption, moreover, was not confined to the Vice Squad, though it was more visible there. Rank throughout the department could be bought or finagled, and location—whether a cop worked the lucrative fleshpots of Manhattan or languished in the Siberian wastes of Queens—depended more on pull than on performance. Or it had.

Valentine, the new commissioner, was supposed to change all that. The first cop to have achieved the position, Valentine had been an early bulwark of Costigan's Confidential Squad, the shoo-fly boyos whose job it had been to flush out crooked cops. The appointment, part of the reform movement that swept the city with La Guardia's election, had been a popular one. No sooner installed, however, and Valentine was up to his old tricks. After a bare twelve months in office, he had already transferred every plainclothesman in the department; had reactivated the hated DD4, the form on which a detective was required to list his daily activities; and for good measure, had put the entire Detective Division on probation. Rumors of further predations had been rampant all summer, and indeed, in October, Valentine had reorganized the eighty-five precinct detective squads into sixteen district squads, promoting and reducing officers with what the department considered fearful and erratic abandon.

Long had been one of those who had fallen by the wayside during this period of upheaval. He had failed to gain promotion mainly, it was said, because he drank too much. For on top of everything else, Valentine, a protégé of La Guardia and the Wets, had turned out to be a professional Dry, and stories of a drunk drawer in which he kept the names of the more flagrant departmental boozers flew from precinct house to precinct house, garnering strength as they went.

And all the while from Downtown came the antiphonal, pious rumblings: Valentine, like an ambitious precinct detective, shooting his mouth off to the press.

Hackett, courtesy of the Missing Persons Bureau, was outside most of the trouble; for the bureau, while not exactly Siberia, was a backwater in department prestige. It was considered a safe and monotonous place to work, with little opportunity for either graft or showy police work. Promotions came slowly and, because the work was considered specialized, transfers came hardly at all. Only when the bureau functioned as a disaster squad did it come in for public—that is, press—attention. "Remarkable teamwork. Invaluable," the papers would banner when it was announced that the bureau had identified all victims. "What we could use is a few more floods and fires," Cahill and the old-timers would mutter then, and would recall the Wall Street explosion as the watershed of the bureau's early struggle for approbation. You could not even rejoice when a case turned into a homicide, for, likely as not, the precinct concerned hogged most of the headlines.

Yet in spite of its lack of status, the bureau was the most effective unit in the department. Since its founding, after a lot of political pussyfooting, in 1917, it had annually registered a success rate in the high ninety percent range, though this statistic did not include the people—mostly men—who skipped: who went missing on purpose. After the Crash, the numbers had skyrocketed of men who had taken off to look for work or who had run away when their dreams vanished with their savings, and the figures were shot to hell. Looking at the grim, hopeless women, Hackett could not tell if their husbands had left from economic desperation or if running off had become a convenient form of divorce. Either way, he went through the motions and filed the reports and found his time hard to account for when he filled out his DD4. The activity sheet was the only one of Valentine's far-reaching reforms that affected his daily life, and like everyone else, Hackett was running out of lies.

With the *Mirror* tucked under his arm, Hackett drove down-town to Headquarters. It was part of his ritual to swap his paper for McCoy's, and he was curious to read what the *Times* had to say about the latest Vice Squad scandal. It was his guess that the *Times* would understate the story on the front page, then sneak into its second section an article deploring corruption as a wide-spread disease. Like Lewis Valentine, the *Times* could never leave well enough alone; was always looking to generalize a city phe-nomenon into a national trend. Or so ran a constant squabble with McCoy, at any rate, and the time they spent arguing they put down as Case Review on their DD4s.

Hackett went in the side way at Centre Street, to avoid the tarpaulins. They were painting the place again, a makeshift mod-ernization, and the smell brought back the stress of his move to Manhattan and gave him a headache. Any day now, the painters would get to the bureau's quarters, and it was too cold out to open the windows, even if access to them was not blocked by the extra row of filing cabinets.

Jack McCoy was making tea when he entered. McCoy had been born in the Bronx, but he spoke Irish with his parents, had married late like a true son of Erin, and after a few drinks on St. Patrick's Day could be counted on to cry when Dunne, the bu-reau's sweet-toned tenor, began to sing. What could you expect from a man who read the obituaries before the rest of the paper? He was so guileless Hackett wondered how McCoy could have landed in the department in the first place, and why no one took advantage of him. He was like some kind of holy innocent; one of those men who marked the passing of time on a calendar of happy events. In spite of all this, Hackett liked him.

"Nothing happen over the weekend?" Hackett asked, swap-ping newspapers. Meg McCoy was expecting her third child in as many years. Hackett had not seen her stomach flat since her wed-ding.

"She says she's not ready," McCoy said, "though why she thinks I should take her word for it, I don't know." His wife went in for one-hour labors—unwitting gratitude on her part, Hackett told her, for having been rescued from spinsterhood at thirty-two; smug, she had twisted his ear—and their second son had been born in a rush of fluid in the hospital elevator. "She's looking for a girl this time. God willing," McCoy added, maneuvering himself into a chair. Six desks were crammed into a space designed to fit three, and McCoy had put on a lot of weight since his marriage. He and Hackett listed the same height, six feet, on their dossiers, but bulk made McCoy look bigger. The department had twice warned him about it.

Mike Lewis, the sandy-haired man at the intake desk, looked up from the funnies.

"The Tenth just called," he said to Hackett. "Long's looking for you."

"He say what about?" Hackett asked, not turning. He and Lewis had once found an old man in a cellar. Rats had eaten away the man's nose, and Hackett, new then, had puked. A few days later, Lewis, by way of a joke, had put a dead mouse in Hackett's desk, in the drawer where he kept his cigarettes. When no one was looking, Hackett had thrown everything out.

"He did not," Lewis said, still with the funnies.

The connection was bad, and with anybody but Long it would have been difficult to hear.

"It's about the Jameses," Long howled, "the Stephenses, whatever the fuck they're calling themselves these days. Somebody sent the mother a doll, a real doozie. Yeah, a doll. A toy. You gotta see it. Mailed yesterday afternoon, with a Grand Central postmark. The mother's half out of her mind. Says it's from him, of course. Shit, I wish I knew what to think. And bring the letter with you, huh?" He hung up as usual without warning, and Hackett was left hoping that Mary Stephens was not within earshot.

Everything was out of order because of the paint job, and it took Hackett fifteen minutes to hunt down the file; another fifteen to reread his report. The letter, his one tangible link to James, was discoloring fast. He left it where it was and took instead a photographic copy.

It was nine-fifteen when Hackett got to West Twentieth. Long met him upstairs in the squad room.

"You took your sweet time getting here," Long said, glowering. He was rattled, Hackett decided. That's why he's yelling so much.

"They're in Rossi's office," Long said into Hackett's silence. "I brought the things in here."

He had been keeping himself busy. A bundle of white tissue paper—inside which, presumably, lay the doll—was clumsily shrouded in cellophane. The outer wrapping paper was smoothed between more of the cellophane, and through it gleamed the name and address of Mary Stephens, written out in full, society-matron style. Mary James, rather.

"Well?" Long said.

The nights Hackett had spent staring at the letter, the minute he saw the script he knew he had a match; the way a lover recognizes the handwriting on a delayed billet-doux.

"She's right," he said. "It's him."

"How can you be so sure," Long said irritably, "in this shitting light?" He did not like the switch in their roles.

"I'll have it checked," Hackett said. "But I'm sure. Let's see the doll."

Wordlessly Long removed the cellophane, and with one finger unrolled the tissue paper.

"Jesus," Hackett said. He had never met Junie Stephens, but he guessed it was her hair; knew, from the report, that it was her dress. He was surprised by the doll's small size.

"The mother says the hair is the girl's. Says the dress is the girl's," Long said, in charge again.

Hackett nodded, staring at the fringe of hair and the obscene baldness behind it. His gaze moved unblinking to the scarlet mouth. Breaking the spell of its smile, he lifted the tiny dress as carefully as he would have lifted Junie's. Underneath, the torso was a utilitarian rectangle too long for the limbs pegged to it. The unpainted eyes were empty. Like those of a corpse, he thought.

"Of course," Long said, "our doll maker could've read about the dress in the papers. By the time the mother got through talking about it, there wasn't an undesirable in the city didn't know where she got it and for how much. The dress by itself don't mean shit. It comes to that, everybody knew she was blond, too.

And at best the hair's a could-be, am I right?" He was doing nothing to control the volume of his voice, and the whole room was openly eavesdropping.

"You saying"—Hackett turned to him in wonder—"our doll maker's some guy who found an old newspaper and got inspired? Is that what you're saying? He's the murderer, Bill, and he's pullin' the puddin' over a child six months dead." Until he said the words, he had been unaware of the thought, but their man— Hackett would put money on it—must have been reliving the murder for months, had butchered Junie Stephens many times over as he created her in effigy. Even before the doll, Hackett had been sure of the butchery. "Now he's looking for a little credit, a little appreciation," he added, "for being so goddamn smart. Let's hope we're the ones to rescue him from anonymity."

"Say it's James." Long's tone conceded without capitulating. "Why send anything at all? He was home free. Unless he's one of those types that wanna get caught?"

"No," Hackett said sharply. He raised his voice to include the listeners. "Not after all this time. The doll's about being clever, not about getting caught."

Like a mute Greek chorus, the listeners nodded. Long shook his head, full of doubt and independence.

"There was this guy I read about," Hackett said, lowering his voice. "He killed seven women, mutilated them, but he didn't rape them. He'd go looking for sex afterwards. So he said."

There was a short silence.

"You saying," said Long, persistent, "our man could've killed the girl and then, maybe months later, he sat down and carved this thing? Just to get it up?" Shaking his head again, he answered himself. "No. If he was that dippy, he'd have introduced himself by now. We'd be dealing with a whole string of cases by now."

"Could be he's just warming up," Hackett said, and there was another short silence.

Hackett turned back to the doll.

"Why did he take such care with the face, but not with the sex organs?" he fretted. "He's crazy, he should've enjoyed that, right?"

"What were you hoping for, Jim?" Long winked at the others. "She was ten. No, nine. Nothing but currants on a pastry board. You were looking for a red slit maybe? Something to titillate our inky-fingered brethren?" Projecting his own tactics, he was mimicking Hackett besides. The room laughed, and Long, encouraged, turned on Hackett.

"Jesus Christ, Jim, you saying he murdered her but you ain't sure he raped her? Am I reading you right? Fucking wishful thinking is what that is. We bring him in, he'll say he didn't, of course, and he'll be lying. He'll stand there and talk his head off about the kiiing part, but he'll grow shy when it comes to the sex. They all do, and that's a fact. However far gone they are."

Far gone, Hackett thought. Not far away in California, but far gone into the shadows of an interior landscape. It was unnerving the way they—Long, the others, himself, too—could be so knowing of a stranger's madness. The consistency, when madness should be inconsistent.

Sad-faced Moylan spoke for the first time. "You find her, there won't be enough left to know." After all these months, he meant. "He's true to type, he just flung her away afterward. You'll have to sweat it out of him. The rape."

"Yeah," Hackett said, publicly conceding. True to type, he thought; not false to type. "God only knows what he did to her."

"And He's not telling." Long tapped the brown paper. "This came wrapped around an Altman's box, if you please. I sent it over to the store, care of Ryan and a dozen of New York's finest. Fucking wild-goose chase, if you ask me."

A uniformed cop put his head round the door. "We got two sambos downstairs for the Klein job," he said to Long. "You wanna be there?"

"I've got work to do," Long said, standing up, and Hackett, trying not to feel like a dismissed schoolboy, found his own way to Rossi's office. His eyes were watering in the cruel light, and he blinked them rapidly before he opened the door.

Mary Stephens was sitting in the chair next to Rossi's desk. Ali stood behind her, her arm resting along the back of the chair, and the first thing Hackett noticed about her was her height. Ali must have grown two inches since he had last seen her. Her nose looked less prominent because her hair was longer; or perhaps because her face had filled out. A beat passed before he realized that the rest of her had filled out, too; all in five short months. She's grown too old for James, he thought, allaying an early fear.

"Detective Hackett." Mary Stephens rose to greet him. The cop at the door tensed; waiting for her to do what? Hackett wondered. "It's him. Surely as I gave life to her." Her voice was steady, but she stumbled as Hackett helped her back to the chair. All her movements were in slow motion, and he waited until both hands came to heavy rest in her lap before he spoke.

"Yes," he said, risking the truth, though with Ali there he had no option. "It's him." He nodded but did not smile at Ali.

"I've known all along that she was dead," Mary Stephens said, talking through him. "The first time you spoke to me, after that I knew she was gone. I didn't need no doll to tell me that." She began to rock back and forth in the chair, her shoulders hunched like an old woman's. "She was born in a cellar and she never had the chance to get the sun she needed. He made sure of that. He was sitting and smiling and talking in my kitchen, and all the time he was planning to take her away and do—and do—"

"Mrs. Stephens," Hackett said. "What time did the package arrive?" Long would have already asked that.

"About eight," Ali said after a pause. "We came right over."

"It was Mary dear this and Mary dear that. He was a real sweet-talker, that Ananias. We almost lost her to the measles when she was five, did you know that? That was the year her father died. Junie was so weak, and I was run ragged, and to this day I don't know if I let Frankie die to save Junie. Seems to me now that I did. That I sacrificed the both of them. I saved her just to hand her over to that man, and not all the Hail Marys in the world can change a day of it."

"The carving, the doll, is covered in a fabric that you have identified?" Hackett was hiding, shamefully, behind officialese. Long slipped in through the door.

"It's the skirt," Ali said, "of the dress she was wearing. You can see where the tucks were." It was painful, Hackett found, to watch Ali's face: the way it had not moved a muscle as her mother spoke.

"I'm losing her," Mary Stephens said. "The other day I tried to remember when it was I trained her. I couldn't even remember how long it took, except it was a long time, what with the roaches and no light in the toilet. That was one of her first words. Roach. She was frightened of them." She began to weep softly. "I would've taken more notice if I'd known." She looked up at Hackett. "I can't bear to bring up her name, did you know that? It's like she's the one did something bad." It was hard, Hackett was finding, to look at either of them.

"The hair," Long prompted from the door.

"It takes so long to comb, her hair. She's always late for school. She always gets up with it so tangled."

"Mama," Ali said.

"He crouched over her and he pawed her and he killed her, and then he stole her hair. Oh God," Mary Stephens said without blasphemy. "I can't sleep with my eyes open." She began to keen.

Hackett watched her out of the corner of his eye as she thrashed in the chair. She had forgotten they were there, and it crossed his mind that she was trying perhaps to forget everything. Ali, red-faced now with pity or embarrassment, he couldn't tell, made a small movement as he approached and touched her mother tentatively on the arm. Mary Stephens shrugged him off, brusque as his own mother, but the movement brought her back to them and the wildness left her.

"I pray for her," she said, smiling sadly at him. "But it's hard, not having a grave."

"Let's get you a cup of coffee," he said, too gently, and she almost lost control again. It was Long's harsh tones that saved her.

"She'll be better off with the tea," he honked. "The coffee's liable to poison her. Come on, then. We'll go get you some."

Ali watched expressionless as Long shepherded her mother through the door. She turned to Hackett. "I'd like to talk to you. In private," she said reluctantly.

Hackett had to nod twice before the cop noticed. He went out, yawning, closing the door ostentatiously behind him.

"Yes?" Hackett said finally.

"I don't like him. Long," Ali said. "He calls Junie the girl all the time. I'm the sister. I don't think he knows our names."

"You mustn't mind him. It's just that he's standoffish with people," Hackett said, and wondered which of them he was describing.

"I tried to hide the package," Ali said. "I knew it was from him."

"You guessed?" He was trying not to look at her breasts through the thin sweater.

"I know his handwriting. Me and Junie read his letters," she said. "I thought it would be a lot worse, the package." She dug into a skirt pocket and produced an envelope. "This is Junie's. Mama keeps it with the christening gown. I only remembered it when I saw the doll."

One corner of the envelope was water-stained, but the lock of hair curling inside, white-blond and unbelievably fine, was undamaged.

"Mama doesn't know I took it, so you better give it back to me when you're finished."

She was learning too soon that the ends justify the means, sometimes.

"If you find Junie," she went on, out of the blue, "you can't ask Mama to look at her. It'll have to be Sol. Or Mrs. Butler."

She had stayed behind, then, not merely to give him the hair.

"Even Jesus got crucified only once," he said deliberately, and watched her face turn young with grief.

"I brought that newspaper into the house," she said.

"And you once took Junie's last cookie or you wouldn't help her with her homework. It's not your fault, Ali. Not Junie's, not your mother's. He's the only guilty one. If you take the blame on yourself, you're lightening his load. Try hating him, why don't you. It's a purer path to sorrow than the road you're on."

She was crying but making no sound.

"Look at us," he went on bitterly, gesturing at the empty room. "We're the experts, right? He's fooled us, too, don't forget."

Still silent, she stepped forward and touched his cheek, then turning quickly, she left the room. It was as shattering a gesture as Hackett had known, and he sat there awhile before looking up Long.

"That's some way to begin the day, huh?" Long greeted him in the squad room.

Hackett was saved from answering by the arrival of Ryan, back from Altman's with the box. A round-shouldered man at his side dumped a large carton on Long's desk.

"Jeez." Ryan addressed only Long. "The way they leave stuff lying around over there, you could walk off with half the store. Hanrahan here's got most of his Christmas shopping in his pockets."

Ryan put down the box, which was encased, like the doll, in cellophane. The lid had been sealed separately, and Hackett wondered idly if the neatness was in honor of the public viewing the box would have received at Altman's.

But they had come back with something more than Hanrahan's haul, Ryan was explaining. The Merchandising Manager had identified the box. It was the new design, introduced in January. That was when the store had changed its logo—its signature, Hanrahan interjected—from the old "& Company" to the new "& Co." of the police specimen. Of the doll's coffin, Hackett thought.

"We got their personnel files, too," Hanrahan said, opening the carton. "Had to threaten the bastard with obstruction before he'd hand them over."

"All the files?" Hackett, the former assistant buyer, intruded. "Shipping, Maintenance, Display?" Departments that might have use for a man good with his hands.

"That's what we were told." Ryan was speaking directly to him for the first time. He plucked a card at random from the carton. "Yeah. This one's a warehouseman. In Queens, it says here."

"We'll send someone over," Long said quickly. "We'll do the cards, too. It'll be faster."

"Would a warehouse use someone as little as James?" Hackett said spitefully. Mary Stephens, guessing James's weight at 140, his height at five seven, had used Long as her measure. "I'll drop these off at the lab," he added, folding the doll and the wrapping paper into the box before Long could counter. "It'll be faster."

It was in and out, back and forth, the rest of the day.

Downtown, Hackett buttonholed Cahill on the threshold and gave him a précis of the morning's events. "Long's back in, trying to hog everything, as usual," he finished. "Unless someone takes over part of my load, there's no way I can keep up with him."

"Can't do nothing yet, you ain't got enough," Cahill said. "But do what you can on your own, with my blessing." Pass the load unofficially, he was saying.

"Another thing," Hackett bulldozed.

"Christ, Jim, I hope your timing's better, other areas. I'm due upstairs."

"Not one word's to get to the papers yet, and I'd like your say-so on that. There's three versions doing the rounds already at the Tenth. I don't need a pack of busybodies telling me I ain't doing enough with the little I got, especially when the little I got is being filtered through Long's greedy fingers."

Cahill looked sideways at Lewis, listening at the desk. "Long already called," Cahill said. "He don't want you to jump the gun on him either. Nobody's to speak to the press yet." He edged past Hackett.

"While you been running around making your DD4 look good," Lewis began, "your mother called. We had quite a chat." He smiled.

Hackett said nothing. The first time he had heard Lewis bantering with her, he had thought it was to some dame who didn't know any better.

"And the Gigli thing came up," Lewis said. "Pyzelli took it."

"Just as well," Hackett said, still at the door. "He speaks the lingo."

"Let's see Long's toy," Lewis said, nodding at the box under Hackett's arm. Showing he knew all about it.

Hackett hesitated, frowning, then spun on his heel and went back along the corridor. Keeping his head low to avoid greeting anyone, he crossed Broome Street and entered the Annex. The place, opened with City Hall fanfare in the summer of '34, still looked new on the outside. Inside, though, the ceilings were beginning to peel and nobody seemed to clean the fire buckets that were choked with cigarette butts. It was fast taking on, in Hackett's jaundiced view, the impersonal, slightly sinister dinginess that was the hallmark of police structures.

The elevators were not working, and he took the stairs to the lab. Handwriting was out, drinking his lunch, but Fingerprints, in the shape of fat Burroughs, was wandering about the room.

"It's urgent," Hackett said, snapping for emphasis.

"Everything's urgent," Burroughs said happily, but he took proper care as he opened the cellophane. "Maybe," he said, twinkling up at Hackett, "maybe your friend doesn't know the cute tricks I get up to with silver nitrate." Using tweezers, he unrolled the tissue paper and beamed at the doll; which had as much effect on him, Hackett noted, as if it had been a bunch of old firewood. Burroughs saw everything, wood, cloth, paper, as nothing more than surfaces on which to perform his reverse sleight of hand: First you don't see it, then you do.

"Whose can I expect to find?" Burroughs asked.

"On the wrapping, God only knows. On the box, the mother's, Long's maybe. And our friend's." Ali had not touched the box. "On the doll, if we're lucky, just our friend's." Mollified by Burroughs' interest, Hackett was speaking slowly, keeping pace with Burroughs' scrawl.

"I'll begin with the doll then. And you want to know yesterday."

Hackett handed Burroughs the photostat of James's letter. "Cunningham'll need this. And the wrapping, when you're through."

"Of course." Burroughs bobbed his head toward Handwriting's empty chair as he read the letter. He turned to the doll with increased interest. "I remember him now. We didn't make him, right?"

"Right," Hackett agreed, and fingered the lock of hair in his pocket. He was trying, without success, to picture Mary Stephens as a bride.

He was barely back at his desk when Cunningham called.

"Course they match," he said. "You go to trial, we'll need an outside graphologist maybe. But you can take it from me, the same hand wrote the both of them. And, oh yes, Burroughs says to tell you it don't look good. So far, only smudges on the box. He's still working on it, but I think you've ruined his day."

"He ain't helped mine none," Hackett said, and dialed Long.

"Half the personnel is female," Long said disparagingly. "Of the rest, maybe a dozen possibles, and that's stretching it."

"The women may have husbands, fathers," Hackett said, thinking back to Martha Butler. A man about the house.

"Tomorrow," Long said. And Hackett could tell from the tone that Long's enthusiasm for this particular chase was once again waning.

At least, Hackett told himself, at least this time I hung up first. He turned to Lewis. "One word of that outside this room, and I'll have your guts."

Pyzelli, who had come in halfway through the phone call, waved. "Time for a quick one, Jim?"

"You and Old Nick," Lewis said, low; Hackett ignored him.

"You shouldn't ride him," Pyzelli said outside to Hackett. "He's stupid, but he don't mean no harm."

The bar, a block from Headquarters, was full of cops. Cahill was sitting in the corner talking to two men Hackett did not recognize. Pyzelli, after one drink, was swaying slightly.

"It ain't booze, Jim. It's battle fatique."

They had been talking about Gigli, Hackett remembered.

"You know this is his third time?" he said, trying to concentrate. "After this, he stays lost."

"He's senile, Jim. He don't know how he got there, how long

he was gone, nothing. Anyway, there was a lot of kissing and crying when we walked in, and everybody promises to keep a closer eye on him. They brought out the homemade grappa, and while we was toasting Mussolini, the sly old bastard tries to take off again."

Hackett shook his head. "All that sipping. No wonder you're worn out. And thanks."

"My pleasure. I owed you anyway."

"Not by the end of the week, you won't. I got a couple of things I may pass along, you got the time."

"My pleasure," Pyzelli said. "Long as Cahill knows."

"Cahill will know," Hackett said, and ordered another round.

And what with one drink and another, he had been late meeting Ceil.

It was after midnight when he drove her home. He stopped the car at the end of her block.

"I ever tell you," he said, leaning across her to open the car door, "that I like your voice? It's so soft. And low."

"Like my pubic hair," she said primly, climbing out, and Hackett saw that she was very pleased.

Which was why, when he got back uptown—creeping up the stairs like a burglar, the bastards shouldn't know his comings and goings, pouring himself a nightcap—and the phone rang, he expected it to be Ceil.

"Where've you been? I've been calling all night." It was his mother.

"Hither, thither and yon," he said lightly, shaking open McCoy's paper. She had no sense of time.

"The house is so empty," she said.

"Yeah?" It was going to be one drunken Hackett to another; those family ties will get you in the end.

"Walter got took sick last night. He's in the hospital."

McCoy had circled the article. A source high up in the Police Department, the *Times* said, had confirmed that Commissioner Valentine was investigating the latest charges of corruption in the plainclothes squad. Mayor La Guardia was investigating, too. Quotes from Boston and Chicago claimed scandal for their cities as well. It seemed, the *Times* said, to be a nationwide disease.

Not Valentine, Hackett noted, but a source high up. It must be serious to make the commissioner so coy.

"It was a heart attack. Walter," his mother was saying. "The house seems so empty."

Hackett sneezed into the phone. "There's always the birds," he said.

"I found him on the stairs in the middle of the night. All dressed up. His wig fell off, and now I can't find it. It was his heart."

"I got time," he said, all graciousness, "I'll stop by tomorrow." One-handed, he folded the newspaper.

He was undoing his tie, part of Ceil's birthday present, when the thought struck him. Ali must have assumed at first that the package was for her. The doll had arrived on her birthday.

That night Hackett dreamed, among other dreams, that he had found a set of dentures, chipped and stained, in a birdcage; Mary Stephens, her shoulders spattered with droppings, had held him as he wept.

12

Teeth and hair and the washed-out eyes of old saints were on Hackett's mind when he woke the next morning. To erase the images, he switched on all the lights, just like they did in the movies, and stared down the street at the park. The tops of the trees were splayed ugly against the sky, and either the bums were sleeping somewhere warmer or they had already moved on. The benches were empty. A sheet of newspaper, the discarded blanket of somebody's former son perhaps, drifted up, then down and out of sight. They're in the subway, he remembered. They had been evicted from the Hooverville near the fountain, he had seen them on the newsreel; they had smiled for the camera, no ill will, the police had bribed them first with booze and real blankets.

So once must an Indian have looked at the land around him, Hackett thought, still staring; looked up one dawn into the face of a smiling Dutchman. He closed the curtains, foiling the eyes that would pry in the dark. The room was ready for Ceil.

In the bathroom, a smiling Dutchwoman and more teeth:

Mrs. Roosevelt at a performance of *First Lady* accepting flowers from a couple of kids who would never lose their look of underfed scrawn. Nobody loved the rich like the poor, he reasoned, rustling the newspaper so that the kids' mouths sneered lewdly. That's why they loved Roosevelt, trusted him for his wellborn ignorance of the facts they lived by and wished they didn't. They had nothing to fear but fear itself. Except the fear of fear kills: It shrivels the weightless old women in their beds, smothers the big-boned men in the mine shafts.

Hackett turned the page. Another woman, this one not smiling: Mrs. Bruno Hauptmann, wife of the convicted kidnapper in the Baby Lindbergh case, seen here in Chicago petitioning for a second stay of sentence. She was wearing black; she must know it was a lost cause. One of these Tuesdays, her husband would fry in Trenton, and that would be that. Baby Lindbergh, Hackett mocked his reflection as he shaved. The almost anonymous victim in an unhappy fairy tale. He could not himself recall the child's first name, but the law that bore his last name would avenge the remains of Junie Stephens, poor little Match Girl; would send her killer to the chair, God willing, like Hauptmann. Like Hauptmann, he repeated, patting his face dry. Since the arrival of the doll yesterday, he had endowed John James with Hauptmann's obstinate face. Carpenters both.

Lucky Lindbergh Junior, it came to him on the stairs. The baby had been named for its father. Charles Adolphus, Augustus. Swedish.

Some of the trusting poor were removing the last of the trolley tracks from Central Park West, and the detour down Columbus found Hackett stuck behind a limping bus. He was late for work, and his sense of efficiency was further threatened by the sight of the lab reports waiting on his desk.

He was skimming through them when Long called. "Well?"

"Yes on the handwriting. No on the prints." Hackett was nettled by the spurious firmness of his response. He could not handle Long this early in the morning.

"What we figured." Long the born leader had no memory for past discord.

"About the cards," Hackett began. "You might check if Altman's ever hired carpenters, maybe for—"

"Yeah, yeah, we already done all that. We checked everybody who was a John or a James, too, anybody with any kind of 'J' in their name. Jesus himself couldn't get past us. Nothing. Besides, I been talking to Rossi, and I ain't so sure James even made the doll. He could've got it anywhere. He could've just stuck on the hair and stuff himself, you know? A peddler, a pushcart, he could've got it anywhere."

"No." Hackett spoke carefully, as to a child. "James made the doll. Slow and easy. The only thing he did fast and careless was send the Altman box. And it's not anything he dug out of the garbage, that box. It looks new." He shuffled aside the box and reached for the doll. It too was sealed in a lab envelope. Not sealed, he saw, as he took it out; Lewis had picked over that as well. "What we gotta hope right now is that sometime in the last few months he had some kind of connection with Altman's. And that we make that connection." The tiny knife marks around each of the doll's eyes looked identical. James had a passion for symmetry as well as for little girls.

"What we gotta hope, more likely, is he makes another stupid move. A grab for the sister, maybe. Or another gift through the mail." Long's voice perked up. "Make life a lot easier, he did something like that, huh?"

Hackett closed his eyes. "You got a man on the house?" he said finally. "You alert the Post Office?"

"You ain't got all the smarts down there, you know that, Hackett?" Long bristled through the wire. "Sure we got a man on the house. Round the clock, at least for the time being. And the Post Office is cooperating. Though that don't mean shit this time of year. Not their fault, Christmas, but there it is. Listen. Rossi says if Personnel don't work, we should get a customer list out of Altman's. I ain't got an almighty lot of faith in that place, it don't have the right feel for this sort of thing. But it's worth a try, what d'you think?"

"He's no customer," Hackett said flatly. He could see all too clearly his image of James limping his way into the *Gazette* offices; Altman's, the other end of Thirty-fourth Street, was a world away. "He's no more an Altman-type customer than I am."

After he had hung up, Hackett sat digesting Long's closing line. "You don't never put yourself on his level, Jim," Long had said. "No way at all, you don't never do that." He had been very serious.

The phone rang. Long with another bon mot. But it was McCoy, who had not shown up for work.

"What's the best news?" McCoy sang.

Hackett smiled. "You tell me."

"Would you believe? Another boy. But we made it in time for a change. Eight pounds seven tell Pyzelli."

"A boy for McCoy," Hackett told the room.

"A girl next time," Pyzelli of the harem called into the phone.

"Would you believe? That's just what she said."

"So when's it gonna be your turn to middle-aisle it, Jim?" Lewis asked afterward.

Hackett, the sole bachelor holdout in the room, had been expecting something of the kind, had watched the thought struggle up from the brain in Lewis' ass, how else would he know when to shit, to the one in his head. Like a dumb dinosaur, Lewis needed two. One brain by itself, and he'd still be wallowing in his own dirt.

"When you make sergeant," Hackett said, but Lewis had turned away and was talking to Pyzelli about hunting, about Christmas. About hunting again.

"Save an evening Christmas week, my boyos," Lewis said, smiling at Hackett to show he hadn't heard. "Mrs. Lewis' son Michael's gonna bring back meat for the table this year." For two seasons he and Pyzelli had been promising venison.

"What you doing for Christmas, Jim?" Pyzelli asked through the jeers.

"The usual," Hackett said, and to escape the phone, to escape them all, he grabbed the doll and got out of there.

Rain was falling when Hackett left Headquarters; not Portia's gentle drops either, but lancing sleet that nearly blinded him

as he ran for the car. He drove slowly north, then west, then
north again. The streets were washed of color, and the people
marooned in doorways looked a long way off, blurred. They were
talking, some of them, gesticulating at the rain. Conversation was
not casual in New York, where people acted as though the sound
of their own voices was too defined an intimacy to share with
strangers. It took a catastrophe or a celebration, or a sudden
downpour, before they would entrust themselves to one another.
The rain drumming on the car roof drowned out the engine, and
the absence of its noise left Hackett feeling isolated. I will never
be at home in New York he told himself, and melancholy again
seeped through him.

Like flares at sea, traffic lights bleared out of the rain. He
stopped short. The doll fell to the floor, the soft clicking of its
jointed limbs riveting him in mid-motion. The car stalled, and a
drenched, skinny Santa Claus swam into focus and waved in
derision.

"For Chrissake," Hackett said aloud, and pulled over to the
curb. He locked the door, leaving the doll, innocuous in its envelope, where it had fallen. Then watched by the thousand eyes of
the Empire State Building, weeping opposite like those of some
inconsolate giant, he entered B. Altman & Co. Or maybe it was
back to being B. Altman & Company. Depending on what they
were doing with the logo this year.

The saleswoman on the ground floor assessed and found
wanting the cut of Hackett's coat.

"Perhaps something French?" she said doubtfully, smoothing
ugly, shingled hair.

Dirty pictures, six months old, floated through his mind.

"Perhaps," he agreed, and favored her with the smile Ceil
hated. He watched as the saleswoman folded the scarf into a box,
then wrapped the box in Christmas paper.

He handled money like a peasant, her thank-you suggested,
but it was because he was trying to hide his bitten nails.

Upstairs and lost among the plump-fronted matrons, he
bought a pink garment for Schnitzer's daughter. The baby had no
name that he knew of, and he addressed the package to Etta.

"Oh, yes. We always seal the boxes that are to be mailed," said the saleslady—this one was a lady; she had succumbed at once to his show of avuncular ignorance—in answer to his question. "Or delivered." For the rest, policy seemed to vary from department to department. The scarf for Ceil, under his arm, had not been taped. Chances were, then, that the doll's box had been walked out of the store. Not by James as customer, though; Hackett couldn't swallow that. Maybe as custodian? But he had not shown up in the Personnel file.

Christmas was around the corner, but both transactions had taken no time at all in the uncrowded store. 'Twas not the season to be jolly, in a city full of empty pockets. With an hour to kill, Hackett debated the merits of a visit to the man Ryan had seen in Personnel—Davis Taylor, Taylor Davis, someone with two last names, Mayflower-style—and rejected the idea as premature: Tomorrow would be soon enough to tread on Long's corns. Instead, made respectable by the package under his arm, he wandered through the men's department, reassured by prices scarcely higher than Macy's; the same, really, if you counted in the fancy wrapping paper and the cost of the loudspeaker system that was piping in carols. He stopped and tried on two overcoats, appraising them with the critical eye of the shingled saleswoman downstairs. Neither coat passed muster, and when the salesman tried to intimidate him, Hackett turned Brooklyn and bullied his way out. He marched through the street door to the tune of "O Little Town of Bethlehem," played too fast for his taste, and was waiting, thirsty and hungry, when Schnitzer emerged from Bellevue for their lunch at one.

Schnitzer, who was conscientious and stuck to the regulation thirty minutes, led him to a nearby deli, the kind of place that looked as though it would smell bad, but didn't. It was clean, Schnitzer promised, and he was fussy about such things. ("When a Jew stops being kosher," Schnitzer had instructed on one of those nights when he did most of the talking and Hackett most of the drinking, "he spends the rest of his life waiting to be struck by food poisoning. One twinge in my gut, it's ptomaine.")

"So what's it gonna be?" Hackett said when they were settled at the counter. Himself, he could've used a drink.

"Marsha Sandra," Schnitzer said, misunderstanding. "That way we keep both sides of the family talking to each other. At the moment she looks like a cross between Herbert Hoover and Etta's dad, but she's improving by the day. Come see for yourself, Friday. The grandparents'll be there, all four of them, dividing her up, claiming eyes, nose—everything but her hair. Which is indisputably mine. Come and get drunk, they'll expect you to."

Friday was usually a Ceil night, but Con was coming in early for some meeting.

"Marsha Sandra Schnitzer," Hackett said slowly. "A bit sibilant. But classy, definitely classy."

"You wipe that smile off your face, or I'll tell Etta. It was her idea. Besides, what's it matter? She's gonna marry David the Doctor, who'll have a nice name like Miller, changed to avoid the coming of the Cossacks, he'll tell you, but really it's so he'll look like a goy in the New York *Times* when he marries my daughter. Marsha Miller, that's not bad, huh?"

"Bologna on white," Hackett interrupted him; he had eaten no breakfast. "And he"—tilting his head—"will have pastrami on rye. Lean." He waited until the counterman had retreated into the small back area before he opened up the envelope. "Speaking of little girls . . ."

Schnitzer looked at the doll with distaste.

"You got no feelings, Jim, you know that?" He rubbed a lock of the hair between his thumb and finger, and shook his head. "Your man is seriously insane."

"Speaking of hair." Hackett took from his pocket Ali's stained envelope and handed it to Schnitzer. "Tell me more, but not so loud." Though there was no one close.

Schnitzer did his bit with the finger and thumb again.

"Both came from a prepubescent child, Caucasian of course. More than that, though, not even God himself can tell you at this stage. You find her, the hair's good circumstantial. But it's never definite. Not like teeth." He paused. "Christ, but he has to be stark goofy."

"Not too crazy. Not too crazy to fry, I catch up with the bastard."

The orders arrived. Schnitzer, adding more mustard to a

sandwich soggy with it, stopped to look at Hackett. "How come," he said, taking a large bite and smearing his chin, as Hackett had known he would, "how come it's always the Christians who want blood? Whatever happened to all that turn-the-other-cheek business?"

Hackett sighed. It was an old theme. Schnitzer was the only cop alive who had qualms about the death penalty; the other had died in a gun battle on the East Side, his weapon drawn but not fired.

"Any nature," Hackett said, watching Schnitzer dab at and miss the mustard, "will permit the harming of one of its parts in order to save the whole. Aquinas."

"That anti-Semite." Another old theme.

"Better to cut off a leg than let the cancer creep into the rest of the body. Any doctor will tell you."

"What happens when the bastards cut off the wrong leg, then let you die rather than admit it?" Schnitzer took another bite, and a second smear joined the first. The part of his chin facing Hackett was beginning to resemble a yellow map. "Sacco and Vanzetti, that's what happens. Your homicidal saint tell you how nature handles that one?"

Hackett faked weariness. "There you go again. Throwing out the baby with the bath water, and no thought of clogging up the drain. I never said every murderer should die, did I ever say that? All I'm saying, not every murderer shouldn't die. And James is one of those that should." He leaned forward and signaled with his cup for more coffee. "To me, it doesn't matter a fuck if James is crazy or not, and it won't to a jury either. Because it's beside the point. Because he's a violator. Not just of Junie Stephens, I mean. He's a violator of trust, and that's cancer, that's dangerous. And that's why he'll die. It's got something to do with common sense, Larry, and that's not something you know a helluva lot about."

The counterman edged toward them, this time squinting openly at the doll. With his free hand, Hackett slid it back into the envelope.

"What you're hearing is the death throes of a Catholic education," Schnitzer said pleasantly to the man, who spilled coffee into their cups and fled. "Correct me if I'm wrong"—Schnitzer swiveled and continued in the same tone of solicitude—"but it seems to me that with all your ignorant medical talk, you've failed to diagnose the real disease. You don't, for instance, see any parallel between private murder and the public variety we choose to call justice?" He nudged Hackett with his elbow.

Schnitzer had fallen into their late-night debating style—such as it was—and Hackett followed suit.

"The wheel wasn't invented by anybody living on a hill," he said, unperturbed. "And the present terrain ain't suitable for putting up that particular house of cards. Maybe it never will be. You introduce an idea before its time, and either you'll watch it die a natural death or you'll find it's upset some balance you didn't know anything about." Hackett drained his cup and stood. "You know," he added innocently, "like that Egyptian, that pharaoh who got himself trepanned because he'd dreamed up the one-God thing. Before the Jews did. Who were the ones supposed to be doing it, right?" He counted out the money; it was his turn to pay. "Justice, the man says," he said. "Justice has got nothing to do with the death penalty. That's God-over-Satan business and always has been."

"Now it's the unbeliever who knows so much about God," Schnitzer said, and stood up, too. He moistened his napkin with his tongue, and with an unselfconsciousness that left Hackett jealous began to clean his chin. "Besides," he went on, turning next to the crumbs that were stuck like confetti to his coat, "it's not before its time. The English are doing a lot of talking about it these days. The ultimate punishment, they call it." He swept like royalty through the door Hackett was holding.

"The English! What do they know about justice? Or God, for that matter. The closest an Englishman gets to Heaven is when his boot's on an Irishman's ass."

The rain had stopped, but a sharp wind was blowing up the avenue. Schnitzer, his coat billowing, was trying to cross against the light, and Hackett waited until he was partway over. Then: "Hey, Larry," he said, too loud on purpose. "What happened to all that eye-for-an-eye business? They'll be getting you to sign the Hauptmann petition next."

Schnitzer turned and made a rude gesture. "Friday," he called, clutching unsuccessfully at his coat.

"Friday," Hackett repeated, smiling. His spirits had lifted.

He locked the doll in the trunk and walked the block to a bar on Third. He drank standing up, holding his coat open so that the gun showed; it always helped on the check. He carried his second drink to the back of the bar, sipping and studying the posters on either side of the pay phone as he dialed.

"Hi," he said.

"Hi," Ceil said, soft and low. "I was just thinking about you."

"What were you thinking about?"

"Things."

He listened to the silence, seeing her face. "You're very beautiful," he said as if she were in front of him.

"You always sound surprised when you say that." Accepting the compliment as her right. "As if it's something that hits you fresh each time."

"Like Cleopatra. 'Age cannot wither nor custom stale—'"

"Stop talking about me as if I'm embalmed." She was laughing at him. "When you're the one pickled."

"I almost called you last night," he told her.

"You should have."

"If I'd called, what would you have said?" He turned his back to the bar. "You still there?"

"I'm here."

"Well, go on."

"I know what you're up to," she said, and he could see her face smiling.

"Go on," he urged gently.

As if frightened of being overheard, though he knew she was alone, she spoke faster when someone was there, she murmured, "I was just thinking. I was just thinking, some men have nuts. You know, small and hard." Con she was talking about, he thought, jolted as he always was by the contrast between her quiet voice and her casual crudeness. "And then there's you. With maybe the most beautiful balls in the world. That must be why there are so many different names for them, do you think?"

In no way misled by the deliberate innocence of her tone, he
didn't answer. He grinned instead at the poster of Joe Louis to
his left.

"Where are you calling from, Jim?"

Are you alone with a hard-on, he translated. In the beginning, on night duty at the bureau, he would call her and grow
stiff at the sound of her voice. One night he had been close to
masturbating at his desk, and it was the night after that, though
still unsure whether she was more lonely than interested, he
hadn't learned the language yet, that he had risked making a fool
of himself and invited her uptown to bed. When he had told her
about it later, she had laughed. "You just didn't want to defile
your files," she said, turning confession to pun.

"I'm lonely in a bar," he said. "I may love you, you know
that?"

"In your way," she said after a while.

"Let me count the ways."

"There's a law against this sort of thing, copper. Why did
you almost call? Last night, I mean."

"I was having a bad dream." He hesitated, reluctant to break
the mood. "About Ali. One of those things where she got lost and
I couldn't find her and somebody else did but it wasn't her—"

"It was you," she said. "You see yourself in her. You were
the one lost."

"Damned, anyway," he said lightly, but she didn't laugh, and
her voice when she said goodbye was drained of its earlier buoy-
ancy.

Hackett got himself another whiskey before phoning downtown. There was a message from Brennan, Lewis reported, but no
word from Long: He was playing possum. Hackett, still bardic,
cut short the rest of the news on the Rialto and phoned Brennan.

"A double funeral," Brennan said happily, "and the fucking
roses wilting all over the place. The Lombardi brothers, you
remember them?" Not a guinea fell in Brooklyn who wasn't
buried under Brennan's wreaths. At twenty, he had knocked up
old man Walsh's only daughter, and in return for marrying her
had entered the family flower business. Over the objections of his

brothers-in-law, he had prospered, parlaying one store into three, all in the borough. Fertile in every way, Brennan.

"Lunch tomorrow?" Brennan said.

"Tomorrow's good," Hackett said, hoping it would be.

"The usual, at one, I don't die of shame first. Fucking roses."

Hackett stopped at the bar on his way out, coat wide open in case the man had forgotten.

"Not a betting fight, Louis and Uzcudun," the bartender said.

"It's Baer and Braddock all over again," Hackett agreed.

"That's all right," the bartender said, waving away payment. He nodded. "Baer and Braddock. All over again."

The poster of Joe Louis showed him posing confidently for his first bout at the Garden: Friday the thirteenth, against the unlucky Basque. The poster to the right of the phone, just outside the can, incongruous, had been of Shirley Temple in a sailor suit. Someone had drawn large breasts on both posters, and driving crosstown, Hackett considered the way in which Louis came off looking better; on him the breasts were just so much extra flesh he would have no trouble protecting.

At exactly half past three, Hackett drew up outside the Stephens' house on West Seventeenth. Dallying and delaying, it was where he had been heading all day. By way of lunch with Schnitzer yet.

13

"Take this mantle, take this sheet,
Go Thou slow and steady.
'Ere the dawn this day we greet,
Thou shalt be full ready."

Ali was singing in a strong contralto to the tune of "Good King Wenceslas." She took off her coat at the appropriate time and wrapped it around an unresisting plump child standing in the center of the stage. There was a brief silence, then, responding to a poke from Ali, the fat girl trilled something that could only be guessed at. A thin wail was all that reached Hackett at the back of the hall.

The nun halfway down the room tapped a small baton against a chair.

"Constance," she called, and her impatience was as clear as her voice. "Our Lady is supposed to be tired, not at death's door. I can't hear a word."

"Thank God," Hackett muttered, pious, and though the nun could not have heard what he said, she swung slowly round and saw him.

The role of the Innkeeper had been transubstantiated by the all-girl cast into Mine Host's compassionate wife; with Ali doing the honors. Hackett watched her as she retreated with poise to the side of the stage and joined the tall girl who had howled her way through Herod in the preceding scene, and who still wore the same unhappy frown. His gaze shifted back to the fat Virgin, piping reedily as she staggered, then sank to a sudden heap on the floor. Mary full of gracelessness.

There was a confused hubbub at this point until the sestet of little girls at the back of the stage ranged themselves forward. Raggedly the strains of "Hark! the Herald Angels" floated back to Hackett; none too melodiously, it was true, but with the traditional words intact. Ali was sucking in her cheeks. Herod, her scowl gone, was shaking with laughter.

Out of the corner of his eye, Hackett saw the nun drift toward him, approaching with the seeming lack of motion he remembered from his youth. The air shuddered, moving for her. She was older than the clear voice and erect carriage first suggested; her face had hardened permanently into the expression worn by those who deal constantly with children and have learned that obedience is next to godliness—and saves time, too.

"I'm Sister Cecilia," she said, halting directly in front of him.

"Detective Hackett, Sister," he said, beginning to regret the whiskey. "Missing Persons."

"You'll be wanting Ali," she said, and her voice softened in lieu of her face. "A terrible thing. We all miss Junie so much, especially at this happy season. She was always one of our angels, and now, we can but pray, she is with them. She sang like—like a lark."

Clearing his throat, Hackett said, "Ali doesn't do too badly."

The nun bowed her head, and they both turned to the stage, where Ali was again singing—with the same unfortunate clarity—of fear and near, troth and broth, in a minor-key chant he did not recognize.

"We're doing it as an opera this year," Sister Cecilia explained. "With recitative," she added, giving each syllable equal emphasis. Double spondees.

"Yes," he said, interrupting further explanation. "You wrote the words?"

"I did." And her smile was so quick and feminine that he nearly forgave her the awful masculine rhymes.

But Ali, still in strong voice, released him from his amnesty. "Kine, divine," she sang, trembling inexplicably on the meter. "Thine, mine."

The play's a hit but her rhymes are shit. Sister Cecilia ain't Cordelia, Hackett told himself as the nun glided toward the stage, calling for Ali.

Word of his presence put a stop to the chaos, at least. As though his intrusion were part of the plot, the girls turned as one to stare at him. Reluctantly he paced forward, and the tableau onstage fractured. Ali made a swift lunge for her coat, a quick leap down; Sister Cecilia took command again, and confusion returned.

Ali's face, her new full face with the new height to go with it, was as grave as usual as she came toward him. There was no embarrassment left lingering from their closeness of the day before, no sign of her recent hilarity. Kids are like that, he reasoned, refusing to take personally the change in her manner. Time after time he could remember cleaning up after his mother, willing her to choke on the vomit, and ten minutes later he would be laughing it up with Brennan. Or the other way round. Kids grew sideways, feinting, then withdrawing in guerrilla confusion that had nothing to do with the disciplined line of advance that adults pretended. That men pretended, perhaps. Who was it, he wondered then, said women were children of a larger growth? Next time Ceil got prickly, he would hit her with that one. He smiled at the scene in his mind, and Ali smiled back.

"How did you know where I was?" she said as he helped her on with her coat. She buttoned it with the concentration a younger child would give to such a task, and he read into the tight, precise movements a resistance to her own burgeoning womanhood. Like a father returned from the war, he picked out the features—the almond-shaped eyes, the jutting nose—that revived the child he had earlier known. Then as now, he had observed her, unobserved. He ran a hand across his forehead. All it is, she's outgrown the coat. Less protective, he stepped back from her.

"Mrs. Butler said you might be here," he said.

Martha Butler, hanging out the window, letting him know she knew why a cop had been standing across the street since yesterday. "She dropped off her books first, so she should be at the CYO. For the Christmas pageant," she had called down, her voice raised over the noise of the truck pulling out of the warehouse opposite. "Otherwise, she'll be at Sol's, with Mary. Ali doesn't like to stay down there alone these days. They don't light the stove till they get back from Sol's, for one thing. If she's got nothing better to do, she comes up here." Ali's guardian angel, with a halo of hair curlers. He had smiled, then remembered the doll's halo.

"Sister is right," Ali was saying. "You can't hear a word Connie says."

"That wouldn't be the one and only Connie Costello? Boston's pride and joy?" He chanced the reference, satisfied he was sober. "The one who took your part? Puck, was it?" To show that he remembered.

Ali nodded, her attention fixed on the stage. "I was supposed to be Mary this year, but I signed up too late, so she got it."

"They should make you Mary anyway. You've got a much better voice."

"Not with these lines," she said, pleased. "Sister Cecilia is not"—she hesitated, glancing up at him—"is not Shakespeare."

Hackett stared at her.

"Fat Puck," she said, turning to lead him out. "She should put a girdle round herself."

Sol's was crowded, and they did not stay.

Hackett waited by the door as Mary Stephens, her eyes averted after the one quick nod, made up a sandwich for Ali. Sol, drowning in worry, came over.

"What's he up to, doing something like that? What's it mean?"

Implicit in Sol's words was the suggestion that they were helpless against James. He was included, Hackett saw; that was why no one had yet asked him when he was going to collar the bastard. He looked past Sol at Ali, standing on the counter rail and whispering to her mother. Mary Stephens nodded. Giving permission to light the stove early, Hackett guessed, and with growing fear sneered at his omniscience in things trivial while a murderer avoided him as easily as Mary Stephens lowered her eyes.

"It means," Hackett spoke without inflection, "that the craziness has overwhelmed the cunning." For the moment, he almost added, but checked himself against the superfluity. Instead, turning to stare through the naked windows, he said, "I'm driving Ali home. I'll stay till her mother gets back."

"I'll walk Mary home," Sol said after a while. "I'll close early, if you like. Say six?"

"Yes," said Hackett, still in neutral, and they waited in more silence until Ali was ready.

"Unclean, unclean," she said, ringing an invisible bell at Sol. She flicked her eyes, to include Hackett, and said, "He doesn't like ham."

"It upsets my stomach." Sol paused. "Lots of things upset my stomach."

"He's delicate as one of those Dionne quints," Hackett confided as he propelled Ali quickly through the door. Before Sol could come up for air.

They crossed to the car parked outside the Catholic Youth Organization. "I was in one of those plays once," Hackett said, nodding his head at the marble-faced building that looked like a failed bank. "Herod. Hissing through my teeth." And trying not to collapse as Brennan, tipsy on sacramental wine, pawed the Mary on loan from Holy Face.

"You must've made a good Herod," Ali said unexpectedly, and smiled to ease any sting. "You're so tall." She was casing the car and trying not to be too obvious about it; noting every move as he started it up.

"How's the new school?" he asked, keeping on with the patter. He was driving slowly, as though she were an invalid.

"It's nice. Hard but nice. Nobody at Washington Irving knows about me. About Junie, I mean. Nobody whispers behind my back, you know?"

"Oh, I know," he said, and he did.

At the house, he parked carefully, and again she made a homework assignment out of watching him. "It's a long way, the school," he said. Then, jesuitical: "Maybe you could move closer."

"That's Sol's line, too," she parried matter-of-factly. "I'm not blind, you know. I know why there's a cop across the street. Why you're here."

Tongue-tied as a Saxon, Hackett followed her down the stone steps.

"You think he's gonna come back and murder us in our sleep, don't you? You and Sol both," she said, unlocking the door. Inside, she went straight to the gas lamp and lighted it, and with the same match started the stove. It seemed to Hackett, still at the door, that the petty economy had about it the stamp of ritual. He closed the door, and with a feeling of déjà vu sat down in the same chair; in the same place, anyway. They both kept their coats on.

Ali struck a second match. "He could've killed us anytime he felt like it, when he was here," she told the stove. "And he didn't. That's what Mama says, and she's right." She adjusted the flue and, without pausing, unwrapped her sandwich and began to eat.

She doesn't have gloves, Hackett thought irrelevantly, noticing her cold-reddened hands.

"You know why he sent that doll?" she said suddenly. "To torment us, that's why. Just in case we're getting over Junie. It was a little reminder. Letting us know he can torture us anytime he feels like it." She sat down abruptly, and Hackett could tell by the look on her face that she was hearing echoes. "And he'll feel like it again," she said, her voice rising. "I know him. I know he looked in the papers this morning for something about the doll, and he'll be furious there's nothing there, and he'll send something else. Only next time it will be—worse." She faltered and stopped.

She had said it yesterday, about the package: I expected it to be worse.

Ali shifted her chair, and the scraping sound went through his teeth; like a nail over a blackboard.

"Tea?" she said formally, and without waiting for an answer she went to the sink. She kept her back to him.

What had she feared to find in the package? An ear, a finger? She might have expected something closer to the size of the box, the way a Christmas present was supposed to fit, giving you a chance to guess. A hand, then, or a foot. Under Hackett's eye a nerve began to throb, and he wondered if it showed.

He watched her go about the business of making tea. For six months she had been going about her other business, changing schools, running errands. Waiting for the bogeyman to surface: She had been certain that they were not rid of him. Though Hackett should have known better, he had not foreseen the relentlessness of the nightmare.

Don't worry, it won't happen, he thought as she carried the teapot to the table. But he did not say it. She would see comfort as condescension, or as a lie. And it would be a lie. James, diseased animal, might well be hiding in the bushes.

She poured the tea, then placed a felt cover over the pot. The heat from the stove had not yet reached the table. He helped himself to sugar, was stirring before he felt the tension of her stillness. She was measuring him.

"Next time it will be worse," she said quietly. "Unless you stop him."

He gave a quick nod, relieved that she had found him worth challenging. "I intend to."

"Listen," she said. The rapt expression was back. "There's someone on the inside stairs."

Not echoes after all. Her open schoolbag was slung over a chair, and Hackett sneaked a look at the spine of the book on top. A First Year of Latin Poetry; its bark worse than its bite.

"It's somebody going to the coal bins," Ali said. Then: "He always used the inside stairs, did I tell you that? The outside steps hurt his foot. He never said that, but they did. That way, too, he didn't have to pass the window. My only warning he was back was to listen for him on the stairs. Or to watch for Junie's smile. Because she listened for him, too." She looked down at her teacup, and Hackett waited for the tears. He was surprised when instead her voice hardened. "I try not to think about her. Whenever I think about her, I end up thinking about him. It's like I'm not allowed to think about her unless I think about him as well. Whole days go by when she's not on my mind at all, then somebody'll come down the inside stairs, I can tell by the way they come down that they're not going out, they're coming down to the bins. Or the garbage. And I'll start thinking about it all over again."

And it doesn't help much when a cop comes calling, full of false promises, he thought. I didn't promise, he corrected himself. Nothing that bold, Hackett. Good intentions are your limit on the road to Hell.

Ali went to the stove and added water to the teapot; watching her, Hackett felt restless. He patted himself, located the cigarettes. She brought back a saucer for the ash.

"You're going to ask me more questions," she said.

"Something like that," he agreed. "Nothing too hard, I hope."

"Questions are only hard if you don't know the answers."

There was no end to her surprises.

The sounds from the back basement were in retreat; heavy breathing, heaving footsteps ascending the stairs. They were both listening, Hackett saw.

The silence went on so long that she looked up. Questioning.

"You think he made the doll?" he said then.

"Of course he did," she said, taken aback. She went on more slowly, "He worked with his hands, you could tell that right off, just by looking at them. He was no storekeeper. Sol has storekeeper hands. Besides, when the bottom step broke off outside, he fixed it real good. Said he could've fixed the others, too, except we were going to be moving, and anyway, he wasn't gonna fix something for nothing. For the landlord, he meant." Her mouth curved, suddenly ugly. "He was always bringing up about how we were going to be moving."

Hackett studied his hands. I've been working on the railroad, he thought, but that had been his father. If he were not smoking, his hands would still be hidden in his pockets.

A heavy shrouded look was on her now, and Hackett searched for a way to get her talking again.

"Besides," she said, as if his silence was contradicting her, "he could sew, too. He mended the cozy." She touched as if it were hot the teapot cover, an orange object Hackett remembered from his summer visits; its color then had seemed to add to the heat of the room.

He examined the cozy, wondering if, like fingerprints, the small neat stitches could be matched with those of the doll's dress. They certainly looked the same.

"Mama threw it out, it was so torn, and he brought it back in. He liked the way it went with the pot, he said."

Hackett stared at the teapot. It was apple green, like the cup that cast a bilious glow around Ali's mouth whenever she sipped her tea. Around his own, too, he supposed. The cups and pot must be the remains of a service. The saucers were white.

"Orange over green. A welcome sight at peep of day, he used to say. He always made the tea in the morning." She shrugged, disassociating herself from the words. "That's the way he talked."

Orange over green: a jarring combination; but James, it was known, had tainted tastes. A warring combination, too, Hackett realized then, and broke into a sweat in the freezing room. Under cover of his hands he looked at her, but she was gazing sightlessly into her cup. She knows not what she says, he thought, and made himself turn away from the cozy. In case she read his mind.

"Of course he made the doll," she was saying quietly. "He was telling us a story one night, and he made two little men from the wax around a cheese, and they looked just like the doll. The same shape and all." She smiled thinly. "He squashed them when he saw me looking at them. He knew I thought they were good. That's when I was sure he didn't like me. That he hated me."

"And you him."

"I don't know." Considering, not objecting. "I knew I didn't like him. But I can't remember anymore when it was I began to hate him. It's all muddled up. I don't remember if it was before, or if I only started hating him afterward. When I knew what he had done." -

"It doesn't matter," he assured her. "What you thought about him afterward is just as important as what you thought at the time. To me, I mean. Because," he added, smiling to let his affection show, "the brain has its own sense of order, its own way of connecting things. Haven't you ever taken an exam and not known the answer to the first question, and then halfway through, you remember it?"

She nodded slowly, measuring him again.

"Those stories he told you," he began slowly. She had mentioned them before, Long had shut her up in the middle of a gory one about a king who'd cut off his own hand. "You remember what story he was telling you—"

"The night he made the wax men? Yes. Because it was the last one he told us. Junie got a nightmare from it, and after that he didn't tell us any more stories." She frowned, concentrating. "It was a ghost story. About two men who hid in graveyards and sneaked out in the middle of the night and dug up bodies, dead bodies. He put in whispers and mists, he was pretty good at that sort of thing, but he frightened Junie." She suppressed a sigh. "He liked to frighten her, I think."

He liked to frighten both of you. Hackett could see her eyes.

"He give these characters names? The dolls, I mean."

"Yes. He always did that. You know, to make them more real."

More scary, she meant.

Ali bit her lip, and Hackett could see it coming. "I don't remember the names." She was flushed with distress. "One of them began with a 'k'—I think. Ordinary names, that's all I can remember."

"You got a piece of paper?" he said, steering her away, and before she knew what he was doing, he had taken the sheet sticking from her schoolbag.

Surprised, she dug out a pen, too; a fountain pen.

"A present from Sol," she said; whose gifts she accepted.

"You remember how long he'd been here when he told you that story?"

"Two weeks," she said promptly, trying to atone for the lapse about the names. "It was the Friday before the church fair, and we got there late because Junie had overslept. Because of the nightmare." The shrouded look was back, and Hackett busied himself jotting down the date on the back of the paper. The nightmare would have come halfway through James's stay with the Stephenses, he reckoned; though they would not have known that at the time, of course.

"I bought a mug, a cup, at the fair," she said after a while. "It was cracked down one side, but it was pretty. It had this motto on it, like a scroll. It was in French, he told me. 'Evil be to him who evil thinks,' he told me, and then he dropped the mug. He smashed it on purpose. And I let him know I knew. If I hadn't done that, he might not have taken Junie so soon. I rushed him, you see."

"No." Hackett, writing, spoke without heat. A part of him was still justifying the filching of the paper. "May 21: Junie sent to bed with cold. May 28: Junie goes on outing." He pivoted the paper so that she could read it. "See? You gave her an extra week of life. Think about that instead." School was hard but nice, he thought. Nothing like a little Latin to keep your mind off things. Grief, he recalled from somewhere, was a sense of sin turned inward.

"And Mama, too," she said.

As if on cue, footsteps were descending outside, and for a moment they sat there listening. Then Hackett stood up, twirling his hat and not looking at her.

"Maybe I'll drop by the school tomorrow. The names in the story, maybe they'll come to you by then."

"Burke." She faced him, radiant. "One of them was called Burke."

"With a 'k' in the middle," he said. "You see what I mean? About the brain connecting?" And as though the entire purpose of their talk had been to prove that point, his returning smile was as delighted as hers.

Then Mary Stephens entered on the arm of Sol; Sol strutting like a bantam cock. Hackett fled.

Inside the car, under the eyes of the cop on guard, Hackett

opened up Ali's sheet of paper. It was a poem, as he had known,
and feeling like a shit, he read it.

> I have a gift
> I can see into the sun
> And see all of the fire
> And see all of the warmth
> Without opening my eyes
>
> I have a talent
> I know what's around the corner
> And inside all the cracks
> I know all the hidden things
> Without wondering what they are
>
> I have a promise
> For myself and only me
> To keep part of myself
> Off limits do not touch
> So I have my gift and my talent
> Without showing who I am

Across the top, in red ink, some cunt of a teacher had written: "Watch your punctuation, Ali."

Ten minutes later, Hackett was in the Forty-second Street library. Too proud to ask for help, he wandered through the reference room, his heels clicking on the polished floor. He disturbed a
turbaned lady, in there for the warmth, and she frowned at him
before resting her head back on the table. More quietly, he saun-
tered to the index cabinets. The clicking had reminded him of
the doll, still locked in the trunk of the car, thank God. Ali might
have guessed the envelope's contents.

False starts. He checked a likely-sounding title that turned
out to be a character assassination of the wrong Burke. He read
too much of a treatise on Jack the Ripper, knowing it was useless
but fascinated anyway. He hit pay dirt on his third try. Mort
cages, see illustration, page eighteen. Dutifully he flipped to a
photograph of a cemetery, its graves banded by iron hoops: necessary precautions, he learned, in certain areas during the nine-
teenth century, to protect the newly buried from the depredations
of grave robbers ("resurrectionists," they were called; gallows

humor) who sold the bodies to medical researchers. Insert above, he read: "An artist's impression of Burke and Hare at their murder trial in 1829." The pair—the most infamous of the resurrectionists—had tired of loitering in the chill graveyard mists and had taken instead to suffocating the unwary. The bodies were fresher that way, worth more. Ali hadn't told him that part. Probably she had not known. James might have found it too close for comfort.

In contrast to the elusiveness of Burke and Hare, however, the rest of what Ali had told him was easy pickings, and after another fifteen minutes, Hackett was ready to go.

He took stock in the car.

Early on, Hackett had discarded as purposeful fictions most of the titbits James had let drop about himself. The very real fact of Junie's abduction, together with the weight of the circumstantial evidence—and not only the false name and background; ominous in hindsight, to Hackett at least, was the obvious pleasure James had taken in deceiving Mary Stephens, relishing the subsequent pain it would cause her—had seemed at the time to warrant an attitude that Hackett now saw as mistaken. He had always assumed, of course, that some truth was sprinkled among the lies: James had indeed liked Junie, though he had hidden from all but Ali the unwholesomeness of his feelings. Equally indisputable, James had disliked, probably hated Ali, in whose cool eyes he must have feared appraisal of his forbidden daydreams.

What Hackett now had to come to terms with was that he, like James, had underestimated Ali. The cop in him had sought—and she had tried to give—tangible facts: the faint accent, the intermittent limp. Yet it was her personal recollections, observations plucked at random from seemingly thin air, that were proving most concrete. James, long-winded in his lies, had been more eloquent than he knew.

Hackett read the poem again. The second verse he read twice and considered the possibility that Ali, quick-witted but unaware, might have filed away as dubious reference a truth she did not know she had. It's like a jigsaw puzzle, he warned himself then: Ali may have some of the pieces, but they'll turn out to be fillers, bits of the sky. No, he amended, the library fresh in his mind. They are signs from Heaven, albeit indirect signs. He smiled at himself in the car mirror. "You're a good-looking son of a bitch," he said aloud. For the first time, he felt, he was in the driver's seat.

He was waiting at the subway stop when Ceil arrived. He was not often the first one there these days, and she made a point of trying not to make too much of it. He was smiling before she got into the car, and there was a tension in his movements as he leaned over and kissed her, it took the form of not seeing her, that made her sit farther from him than she usually did. The excitement had nothing to do with her.

"I got something for you, teacher," he said, and shoved a piece of paper at her. He started up the car. "A poem."

She read it slowly, angling the paper to catch the bridge lights.

"Well? What d'you think?"

"Sad." She was watching his profile. " 'Off limits do not touch.' Like signs in a museum." She was not sure what else she was supposed to read into it.

" 'I know all the hidden things without wondering what they are,' " he quoted jubilantly. "And so she may. Ali, I'm talking about. Inside that little girl may be everything I need to know about the bastard. Getting it out of her, though, knowing what to ask to get it out of her, how do I do that?"

If he is thinking of Ali as a child, Ceil thought, then he doesn't know much about thirteen-year-old girls. Or is he saying that for my sake?

He turned to her, waiting for an answer. The question had not been rhetorical, then: He did not understand thirteen-year-olds. Fourteen-year-olds.

"Talk to her, I suppose. Get her to trust you, I suppose."

"She does trust me," he said at once. "As much as it's possible for her to. Considering the circumstances."

"She does well then," Ceil said softly. "Considering the circumstances." She stared out the window; Herald Square and Christmas lights. "Get her talking," she repeated, tapping the paper.

"It takes so long. And time ain't something I've got a lot of."

Nor I, she thought. You're shortening my life, she thought. Only the hours she spent with him seemed real to her. She saw herself losing him, perhaps for days on end, to Ali.

"Listen," she said. She kept it light to counteract the weight of truth. Truth always seemed to put her at a disadvantage. "Ali's a young girl, not a little girl. You're probably the first tall, dark and handsome man in her life, and if you end up making her trust you, too . . . well, it's a responsibility." It makes me sound jealous of a child, she thought, if that's how he's still seeing her; but she went on anyway: "You may be a real hero to her, you with a gun on your hip. I know how I would have seen you at that age."

The car shot across Columbus Circle. He seemed to be driving faster than usual, and Ceil braced herself to take most of the jolt in her arms.

"Tall, dark and handsome, is that how you would have seen me?" he said, smiling. "But you may be right. I've been picking up something off her." He patted her knee. "You jealous?"

Ceil could now consider this out in the open. "No," she said finally. "Not of her. Maybe of what she's feeling."

"We'll soon take care of that," he said. They had arrived at the brownstone. "Shit, it's starting to rain again."

"That's all right," she said, deliberately slow about climbing the steps. "I'm a wee bit moist already."

"You're always so clean," he told her later. "Beggars can't be choosers, I know, but some women . . ." He was pausing, to avoid coming too soon, as he had last night. She had never known him so considerate.

"And you're so—tasty," she said later still. Protocol did not give her the right to evoke other men, to tell him, for instance, that he tasted different from Con. Though that was an observation left over from earlier days. Con had not touched her since the Fourth of July picnic, when, timid rapist made bold by the solidarity of a family picnic, he had blundered past her protestations. Shame of the memory dismayed her, and Jim—feeling and misinterpreting the sudden warmth of her face—pulled her up and kissed her.

"I went to the library today," he told her afterward. He was watching her make his hamburger, checking to see that she burned it suitably. "I'd forgotten how nice they smell, all those books."

"Because of something Ali said? Something in the poem?" The tension that had nothing to do with her was back, and she concentrated on the hamburger. There was still some blood showing. Not mine, though, she prayed, and her stomach lurched: seepage. She ran to the bathroom. God was good; it was only semen.

"James is Irish, ain't that something?" he said when she came back out. "From Ireland."

"How do you know?" It had taken a moment for his words to register on her, but he appeared not to notice.

"Things," he said, preening, and though the grooves in his cheeks deepened when he smiled, he looked ten years younger. "It hurt my pride," he added, "the way the bastard kept coming up with things I didn't know anything about. So I checked. A French motto that turns out to be English. And stories of kings and criminals, all Irish. Schoolboy stuff."

"Does Ali know?"

"No. And I won't tell her. It wouldn't be—useful." He looked up, 'pausing between bites, and his face went into the sleepy, preoccupied trance she knew from his lovemaking. "We hook the bastard, he's gonna find he's got no monopoly on the torture trade."

"This will help? Knowing he's Irish, I mean."

"Everything will help," he said softly, still seduced by his own thoughts. "Though it's hard to know what's big or little at this stage." After a while, he said, "It's a pity all this didn't come out in June. But better late than never. It's the doll, of course. It's making her dig up stuff she'd buried."

"What stuff?" she remembered to ask, but he was already talking again.

"Shit," he was saying. "I forgot all about it. I was supposed to be seeing my mother tonight."

"It's too late to phone?"

"I'll go tomorrow." He had already dismissed the problem. "She won't know the difference."

"I'll be late tomorrow. My aunt is sick." She was giving him time with his mother, with Ali. She was made generous by love, he would think, but love was, in fact, making her nervous. If she listened to her mother, love could be dangerous right now. And if her mother should be listened to, Ceil worried, then why had she put it from her mind for three hours?

"This the old one that's always dying?"

"None other." Ceil's aunt, rumored to be rich, bought tickets to concerts, plays, ballets—the Dance, Ceil would mock, using her aunt's genteel voice—to everything in sight. A day or so before culture was due to claim her, she would fall sick and blackmail her nieces into buying her tickets.

"Who gets to see what this time?" He knew she took only the weekend events; to escape Con.

"Nora. *Winterset*, tonight."

Ceil normally lingered over the dishes, part of her leave-taking ritual. Tonight she rinsed them rapidly, then shrugged into her coat. She was going home earlier than her usual time, but he appeared not to notice that either.

Driving her home, he entertained her with his account of the Christmas pageant. More soberly, he described his talk with Ali.

"So he's Irish. But not Catholic," Ceil said.

"That's right," he agreed, and turned to her in high good humor. "Who else but a heretic quotes the Bible?"

At her corner, she got out carefully, though it wasn't safe to loiter. When it snows, she anticipated, he'll have to drive me to the door. She could not risk slipping.

"You should feel happy more often," she said, smiling. "It leaves me feeling good, too. And sore."

She was halfway down the empty block when he called softly to her, "Hey, lady. Why you walking so funny?"

Different schoolboy stuff, she thought, and in between her trips to the bathroom that night, she hatched cheerful plots in which she killed off Con in varied and untraceable ways. The faster Con died, the more painless the death she allotted him.

14

Hunger and the call of nature woke me.

You would have thought, after all I had been through, that I would have been unable to sleep; but when it was over, I collapsed on the bed in the back room and slept the sleep of the just. I have always had the true sea-dog trick of putting down my head any old place and snoozing. When you have stood storm watch, as I have, through a Bay of Biscay gale, four hours on, four hours off, you soon learn to catnap at a moment's notice.

It was the middle of the night, I wasn't sure of the time. I relieved myself hurriedly in the privy—hurriedly, for I was still in my birthday suit and a glow like an eye opening was coming up behind High Tor; winking, more like, as the clouds passed in front of the mountain.

The trip to the privy got rid of one of the problems. The other had to wait. Though I was starving by this time, I did not dare stop to eat. I had to get a lot done before Monday dawned full of Nosey Parker schoolgirls. Besides, I hope I have made it clear by now that I am not a man who fancies eating with a messy sink facing him.

I had left her in the sink. Afterwards, I realized I could not get at the pump; she was in the way, and I had to wipe off the worst of it as best I could on the grass out back. I did none too good a job as it turned out, for the mattress got stained, though I didn't notice that until later in the day.

The little part—the legs and the edge of the body—was the first thing into the hollow behind the bushes. The middle section was surprisingly heavy, and even over so short a distance I found myself sweating as I maneuvered it next to the legs. Last but not least went the head. During the night, unfortunately, the head had fallen at an angle in the sink—I take full blame for that, for not thinking ahead and propping it up better—and the blood had matted her hair so that it stuck out, stiff and black, disfiguring her. The few locks lying on the table, a memento I'd had the wit to snip off earlier, were the only proof of her former fairness. She was too young to have the telltale other hair.

I had hoped to place the head in the proper position so that she would lie as one piece, but the hollow was deeper than it was long, and the head would not fit. In the end I had to put it at the bottom of the ditch with the legs straddled across it—they had set in that position and, short of breaking them, which I was not prepared to do, there was no way to force them together—and the large middle chunk on top, covering the rest. The geography of the place had to be accommodated, I know—the topography, I mean—but it bothered me to mix her up like that, all out of order.

I was by now beginning to worry seriously about the light. As quickly as I could, I rolled the boulders back over the hollow, then scattered earth all around. I stood off a bit to survey the possible danger, but there was very little sign of disturbance even then. A few rainfalls, and nobody would ever know that the boulders had been moved in the first place, let alone the effort it had cost me to put them back. I'm not as young as I used to be, and I was glad I'd had the few hours' sleep. All this done, too, as you can imagine, to the rumblings of an empty stomach.

I need not have worried about the light. I'd had a good wash all over—the sink now being clear—and had finished my sandwich a full hour before the first bus passed my door; it must have been nearly two hours before the convent girls began showing up for school. By rough calculation, it meant that I had got up sometime between four and five in the morning; later than I had intended, I admit, though it all seemed to have worked out for the best. It was nerves, my windiness, which was natural enough under the circumstances.

I had smothered her—burked her, they call it where I come from—on the kitchen table. I held a corner of the tarpaulin across her face and pressed my knee into her chest, to get the job done that much faster. Through the canvas I could feel her mouth sucking against my hand, trying to draw in some air. Clean and quick; it was over in no time. Child's play.

There was a bruise on her middle part where my knee had dug in, and a couple more on the back—from the same pressure, I presume—but the rest of her was unmarked. She could have been sleeping, except for her neck, which was arched at an unlikely but delicate tilt to the left—possibly as a result of her struggle to suck in air.

Taking care not to disturb the artistic angle of the neck, I undressed her where she lay. First the coat, a $4 luxury from Gimbels basement and good as the day I bought it. Next the dress, an earlier present, $1.99 from Cohn's on Eighth Avenue and no bargain, judging from the shoddy side seams. And then the rest. She was as fair of form as of face.

The pleasure was over. It was time—three o'clock of a sunny afternoon would be my guess—to get down to the work. I took the scissors and cut off some hair from the right side, the side facing up. I would have taken more at this point, and looked longer, too, had I known then how my carelessness with the head would mar her. I wrapped the canvas around her while I set out the tools on the shelf next to the sink, first taking care to move her flowers without spilling anything. She had overfilled the jar, of course, as children tend to. Then and only then did I uncover her completely and carry her to the sink. The bucket was already in place.

I positioned her head over the bucket, and though that made

the work harder—the bucket kept teetering as I shifted position— it also made the whole business a lot less mucky. I could have done it all with the big knife—nobody's ever said I don't know the tools of my trade and I could tell just by handling it that the knife would do, it was heavy as a cleaver—but since the saw was there, I used it. She was an exceptionally fine-boned child.

The kitchen had one of those high-up country windows, and if anyone had been passing by, on a quiet Sunday stroll, say, what a sight would have met their eyes: a man as God made him, moving in mysterious ways at the kitchen sink. No one did pass, of course, and anyway, I was not born yesterday. They would have had to be giants to get a glimpse of the wonders I was performing. Just to be on the safe side, though, I waited until sunset before I emptied the contents of the bucket down the privy. It was the last thing I remember doing before I fell asleep.

All told, things had gone pretty much the way I had planned them. It was a good omen, I felt—her destiny, if you will—that she had not tried to run away. She stood rooted to the spot as she watched me emerge in that state. Only as I reached her did she try to pull back.

"I'll tell Ali," she said then, and then she began to cry, and then my hand was over her mouth, cutting short a scream. After that, as I've said, it was a matter of minutes.

I am a stickler for detail—there's no other way to stay afloat in this world, the merchant marine taught me that, if nothing else—and the next morning it took me longer than I had anticipated to rinse off the tools, to stow away her clothing and to get the mattress as clean as I like a bed to be. On top of that, it had taken my fancy to strew around the boulders those last flowers we had picked. I was not insensitive, you see, to the joy a little girl takes in daisies, as in gifts. I had thought to put the whole jarful where she lay, but when I tried that, the effect was too funereal for comfort, and I had to content myself with scattering my largesse broadside.

Anyway, on account of all this activity, it was late on Monday afternoon when I arrived back in New York, just in time to read the first version in the evening editions. I was not displeased with the coverage, though it held forth with certain inaccuracies, and I cut out all the pictures, good, bad and indifferent. I still have them somewhere.

Much wants more, and that first week in the city I bought every newspaper on the stands. On Tuesday, I ousted H. G. Wells's war prophecies from the front page. Wednesday, Cincinnati's decision to play nighttime baseball, the first ever, was shoved aside in favor of police speculation on the case—speculation, I might add, of the highest imaginative order. By Thursday, however, rumors of a darker nature began appearing, libeling me outright, by name, and in Friday's editions I was given inferior billing between a report on mass sterilization in far-off Germany and the latest story on the derring-do of the man-woman pilot, Earhart.

I knew who had been doing the slandering, all right. I knew at whose door I should lay both the distortions and the demotion. Console myself as I would, though, the upshot was that by Friday night I was so distressed I had to retreat to Rockland County for a breathing spell. I had planned to stay for just the weekend, but once there, the Celt in me became so overwhelmed by renewed passion that I could not tear myself away from her.

Now, I am a man of tenacity, a particularity that has sustained me through stress that would have buckled a weaker sort. It has enabled me to absorb as lessons my abandonment by a mother, my betrayal by a wife, and my castration in the daily press—attempted castration, rather—by a daughter. Stepdaughter, rather. From three generations of women in the school of life have I learned these ABCs, and none so diligent a pupil as I. In other words, I did not go to the county to hide. With all that I have been through, it would take more than the ravings of a demented child, aided and abetted by a pea-brained police force, to worry yours truly and make me change my plans. I stayed there to suit my own purposes, but I went there for the reason given, neither more nor less. When I got there, though, I found both more and less than I had bargained on.

Once upon a time there was a baby girl who was fat and pink and who hardly ever cried. She had the kind of beauty that is said to excite the fairies, but the fairies in this instance were not given the chance to yearn for her, because the mother—more by good luck than good judgment, for of the latter she had none and of the former, precious little—because she did not once lift the netting that protected the babe not only from the fairies' jealous gaze but also from the flies.

But the fairies might have won her in the end. They might be playing with her right now at the bottom of my garden, for that is where she sleeps. Certainly the flies played with her, as I discovered when I returned that first weekend.

I am a man of the world, but let me tell you, it took courage for me to stay around after I had rolled back the top boulder. It was not the smell, I had expected that. It was the flies; their progeny, that is. Maggots were seething everywhere, the fat white kind that fishermen drool over. Her head was in pieces from them, and thousands more poured from the neck cavity when I poked it with a stick—not the proverbial ten-foot pole, alas, but a short twig that had me leaning too close to the destruction before me. There's no other word for it, that's what it was: destruction. After one short week, there was more left of the daisies than there was of her. It was not at all what I had anticipated.

As I looked down at what remained of my sweet, pink fairy, my first thought was that I had been a fool to worry about the order in which I had placed her in the hollow. Only second did the plan come back to me that I should make a model of her. Given the action of the vermin—it must have been the warm weather that caused them to be so fruitful and multiply that fast—she would be nothing but bones in a week or two, and it seemed shameful, with my talents, not to keep her alive in some way. A carving would make more of the less that was left, so to speak.

I was not moved right then and there to begin work on the idea, but I did take steps to keep secure the locks of hair I had put by as a memento. I retrieved them from their hiding place inside her underwear, and from then until I used them for their true purpose, I wore them about my person. She had always brought out the sentimental in me.

One of the very good reasons I could not immediately sit down and carve her was my natural desire to keep body and soul together. Playing the part of the rich and foolish bridegroom had drained me by this time of most of my resources, and I was badly in need of a job. Without a job, I could not stay in Rockland County, and in the county I had decided to remain. For just as passion had first compelled me to linger near her, so now a growing prudence made me realize I should stay with her—at least for the time being, which is the only measure of time I care to deal with. Passion followed by prudence, it is the story of lovers the world over—the caution brought on in my case by the increasingly ugly stories in the newspapers. After all those smears, I had no wish to run the risk of meeting a stray neighbor in the city. Only a simpleton would press his luck too far.

I badly needed a job, then; but work in my area of the county was confined either to coddling the crazies at Rockland State Hospital or to traprock quarrying around High Tor. As we all know, I could no longer count on a welcome at the nut house, and my first attempts at the quarry were not exactly productive. I was turned away twice. But try, try again, like Robert the Bruce, and my third visit resulted in a day's labor. After that, I managed to put in enough hours to stay alive, and then some. The foreman knew a worker when he saw one and, once in, I was not averse to blowing my own trumpet. Modesty is a fool's game; like taking risks.

If my work by day was a tiresome necessity, my work by night brought me a pleasure I have rarely known. Unaware of the passing of time, I would sit up till all hours, my eyes streaming from the kerosene fumes, and the next morning my back would be stiff from sitting so long in the one position. It was not all smooth sailing in the carving line, either. Like my attempts to find work, my first two efforts at rendering her were a waste of good wood. But once again it was third time lucky; almost from the first nick of the knife, I knew it would be a gem: not unlike her, yet not so like as to be unimaginative.

Her body held no challenge for me, for I always knew she would be clothed. Carving the head, however, and in particular the face, produced in me a feeling of such intensity that it became vital to maintain that state for as long as possible. My holding back reached the point where I would deliberately ration the hours I would spend in one session with her, allowing myself to complete only one part at a time—her left arm on one night, her right on the next, and so on. Like a child at supper, I left my favorite portion till the end, then made it last the longest. I had never done anything on so small a scale before—her delicacy had demanded that of me—and I almost came to grief over the mouth. A little glue, though, a little paint, and no flaw showed.

All in all, what with the sanding and the hair, it took me much longer to make her than to break her. I stretched a twenty-hour job into one that took well over thirty, and that does not include the time spent sewing the dress. I can knit, too.

During this period, I had followed my lifelong habit of setting aside part of each of my pay packets. As my savings accumulated and as coverage in the press dwindled—daily newspapers from the station were the one extravagance I allowed myself—it became clear to me that I would soon feel the need to move on. Two days after the doll was finished, I realized that the time had indeed come. During those two evenings of enforced inactivity, my mind would not stop working, and I was in a ferment from all the ideas and longings. I could foresee a rosier prospect than the sunrise over High Tor.

I gave formal notice at the quarry. I could not afford to pull a vanishing trick there and queer my pitch with Benton, the foreman. Unlike the lilies of the field, who toil not, neither do they spin, I might need to come back to the job the next time I retreated to the county. Besides, I had given him my real name. I was an honest and rehabilitated man; in case anyone brought up the schoolgirl incident.

I invented an emergency. A sick daughter in the city, I told Benton—observe the ethics of my little white lie. An illness of uncertain duration, I said, and set off for New York with his blessing.

At the beginning of July, then, it was back to Amsterdam Avenue with money in my pocket and a mission in my heart. It was, as it happened, a month of heat waves, of white glares and black tempers, and the city's climate—Roosevelt's pep talks on national recovery notwithstanding—was in no way improved by the inclement outlook on the job front. I did well to snap up some menial night work that gave no credit and little recompense, but where at least it was cool, and where I was left alone with my memories. Lying on a shrouded sofa, I would recall at will her first smile, her hair shining in the sun; then her presence —something like the smell of Evening in Paris, her favorite soap and the most expensive—would fill the warehouse, would come floating past the stacked chairs, would peek through the rolled-up carpets, and she would smile, letting me know that her orphan soul soared free.

For of course you cannot lock up a soul to rot in the ground with only vermin for company. Just before I left, I saw a solitary rat there, though there was little enough to attract him that I could see. Where once her North Sea eyes had shone, blank sockets now stared at me. Kneeling there, I was moved to pity for the loneliness of her estate. O Lamb of God, which taketh away the sins of the world, have mercy on her. O Lord, hear my prayer. And let her cry come unto Thee.

Her mouth may be gone, but her teeth can still talk, can still tell some prying dentist who she is, and where; though never why. The next time I go back, I must wrest with that problem. I am a man of tenacity, and I know that in spite of what He may do for the lilies of the field, the Lord helps those that help themselves.

15

The telephone rang six times before McCoy picked it up. "For Chrissake, Jim, I'm a new father. You any idea how little sleep I've had in the last twenty-four hours?"

"I waited to call," Hackett lied. It was not yet eight in the morning. "I knew you wouldn't be up at peep of day."

"Yeah, well, they're doing fine, the both of them. Hell, Meg's in better shape than I am. She ain't got anybody waking her up at the crack of dawn." McCoy stopped. "What did you just say?"

"I said I knew you weren't one of the peep o' day boys."

McCoy was interested. "You know who they were, the Peep o' Day Boys?"

"They're part of a riddle," Hackett said, and ignored McCoy's groan. "I have me an Irishman who's not Catholic, who says that orange over green is part of the natural order of things, who—"

"An Orangeman," McCoy interrupted, and Hackett relaxed,

as pleased as a car owner who had diagnosed the fouled plugs ahead of the mechanic.

"An Orangeman," Hackett repeated, and wondered in passing why Ceil had failed to come up with it as well. "But he's shy about his origins," he added.

"Not so shy if he's bringing up orange and green and the Peep o' Day Boys," McCoy said.

The Peep o' Day Boys. Night riders putting the fear of their Protestant God into the local Catholics. They got so good at terror, those boys, they had grown into men. Orangemen. In honor of William of Orange, King of England . . . Hackett remembered it all, from Brother Gregory's rantings. Cromwell, too, though not the dates.

"He's an arrogant bastard of an Orangeman," Hackett said.

"That sort." McCoy yawned. "You should really be talking to my dad about this stuff." Irish stuff. " 'Poor croppies, you know that your sentence has come, When you hear the dread sound of the Protestant drum. In memory of William we hoisted this flag, And soon the bright orange put down the green rag.' "

"How long's this been going on over there?" Hackett said when McCoy was quite through.

McCoy hesitated. "Hundreds of years. But nothing ever changes over there. They're still using that drum, my dad says."

Hackett digested this. "Tell me," he said finally. "Those potato eaters. They know yet the world ain't flat?" He meant the lot of them, McCoy's old man included.

By nine o'clock Hackett, who had followed the Third Avenue el north, had crossed into the foreign territory of the Bronx. He stopped at a gas station that was offering gas for fourteen cents—and was dispensing free the urine that flowed under the wall phone. Standing to the side of the stream, Hackett yelled at an angle into the fixed instrument.

"That's right, Michael, you've guessed it. I am not, as you correctly divined, downtown. I am alone, uptown." He looked around at the circle of listening men; bums and winos, whose can he had usurped. "If Long calls, tell him I'll see him after lunch. . . . Right, Michael. After lunch means this afternoon."

Pyzelli was right: If you could overlook the stupidity, Lewis was harmless.

Perhaps because he was rehearsing the call to Washington—"A Protestant from the North of Ireland, sir, though that's only an educated guess. A little girl told me, but out of the mouths of babes . . . Sir, I don't know his name and his age is approximate. I don't know when he entered the country, nor even if he's legal. He is, however, male. That part's definite. Sir."—perhaps because of that, Hackett made the wrong turn off Westchester Avenue. He was well on the way to Throggs Neck before he caught his mistake, and by the time he had backtracked through the wilds of Pelham Bay it had taken him twice as long as it had in June to get to City Island.

He liked the place better now than he had then. In summer it had been crowded with people and boats and pushcarts selling fresh crab sandwiches. Today it resembled Mary Stephens' shattered dreams. The cobbled streets were empty; the little boats naked, without sails or sailors. The sullen gray sky had swallowed or been swallowed by the sullen gray sea, he could not tell where one began and the other ended. John James had seen it in summer, Hackett decided, and shivering in the freezing wind, he set off along the curved waterfront. The hand carrying the doll was already chilled.

An hour later—two carpenters and a chandler later, to be precise—he was back in the car, neither surprised nor deterred that none of the three had recognized the doll, its workmanship or the revised description of John James, Irishman. Hackett had never believed in City Island in the first place and could not now remember why he had come. Somebody had to, he reminded himself. Because John James must have been there at least once, if only to gather descriptives. And because of the doll. Hackett locked it in the trunk.

Maybe I'll buy a boat, he thought then, knowing he never would, and without a backward glance began the long drive back to the real world.

Brooklyn had shrunk to a few stunted trees, bridge lamps; a place to slip through in the dark, meeting and delivering Ceil.

Waiting in the bar in Flatbush, Hackett worked out that it had
been months since he had seen Brooklyn by day. It seemed to
him, too, when Brennan finally did show up, that he hadn't seen
Brennan by day in months either, though it had in fact been only
a couple of weeks. The Brennan who was now approaching
looked thinner on top and thicker around the middle than the
nighttime version, yet he walked with the same energy, smiled the
old smile, and was indifferent as ever to the clock. Twenty minutes late, and even then he clowned at the bar and stopped to
talk at every booth before sliding into the seat opposite Hackett.
He did not spill a drop, of course.

"To the Lombardis," he said, raising his glass. "Both the
quick and the dead. *Slainté.*"

"You'll be late for your own funeral," Hackett said, and
drank. But the toast was appropriate, he had to concede. Although Brennan did weddings and christenings, too, it was at the
funerals he came into his own. His candid eyes would moisten
spontaneously in the presence of the dead, endearing him to the
bereaved, especially the widows. The older widows he would call
Mother, and he used his own time to round up friends and free
booze for a wake for the dear departed; who might otherwise have
gone neglected. His comfort of the younger widows—if rumor
was to be believed, and Hackett believed; in rumors as in tabloids
—ran to physical rather than to floral tributes and seemed only to
increase his popularity; perhaps because Brennan in manner
wooed everyone. Hackett had seen him at it for effortless years.

"Poor Eddie," Brennan said. "Though I could see it coming
with Joey. There's a certain type dago not destined to make it
past thirty, and Joey was always one of those."

"Course he was," Hackett said, who remembered Joey as a
punk. "Girls, gambling, all the booze he could drink. Nothing
worth living for was his problem."

Brennan shook his head in sorrow. "Knocking each other off
like flies these days. And those two lovely girls. All alone in the
world. Especially Eddie's."

"Not all alone," Hackett said, wondering when Brennan was
going to get to the point. "There's a spider in the pretty flowers."

"What you got to remember"—Brennan, circling in toward

target, looked at him with bland blue eyes—"what you got to
remember, Jim, is women are just like men. A little bit different,
is all."

"You expect me to swallow these pearls of wisdom, you gotta
buy me another drink."

Brennan gave an entirely businesslike nod, and the waiting
bartender came running.

"The food, too," Brennan said to the man, who returned on
the double with their plates.

"Steak?" Hackett said, poking suspiciously at the meat.

"A double funeral, of course steak." Brennan stood up and
removed his coat, three hundred dollars' worth of black cashmere,
he used the same tailor as Jimmy Walker. "You're drinking too
much, Jim," he said as he sat down.

"Ceil," Hackett said at once.

Brennan ignored him.

"Ceil is worried about me. Because I'm drinking too much.
Last month I wasn't eating enough, I'm surprised she didn't call
you about that, too. Jesus, Bobby, all it means is Ceil's getting
her fucking period—one of those little differences you haven't
finished telling me about. The first sight of blood, and she carries
on like some guinea peasant, like it's the world coming to an
end." That's why she'd been so quiet in bed last night; why she
hadn't picked up on the Irish-Orangeman connection. Selfish
bitch, she might show a little interest. But then, nothing was ever
her fault. It was always her biology doing the dirty on her. On all
of them. "You don't know, the only time that woman feels safe is
when we're in bed." Yet the moment he said it, Hackett saw his
quandary. In betraying Ceil, he had confirmed the intimacy her
complaints laid claim to.

"That can't be all bad," Brennan said, and stared at Hackett
speculatively. "Listen," he said then. "I don't need to tell you
this. I know people."

"Tell me anyway." Hackett put down his fork, but it wasn't
much of a loss. His steak seemed to be tougher than Brennan's.

"I can fix things. If you want it, that is. Ceil would have
to stay where she is, Brooklyn's the best place in the world when

it comes to annulments, but you'd have to make yourself scarce; be careful at least. You'd have to get Con to go, but that's no problem, what I heard. If you want it, I mean."

Hackett said quietly, "You tell Ceil any of this?"

"You think I don't have all my buttons or what?" Brennan changed sides immediately. "You know I know better. Would I tell a dame a thing like that?" Shaking his head and putting Ceil in her place at one and the same time.

"Words, words, words," Hackett said sententiously, and finished his steak with something of an appetite after all.

In much the way that Headquarters dominated the tenement landscape downtown, the outside of the Tenth Precinct rescued West Twentieth Street from the demoralizing shabbiness of the surrounding area. Inside, though, the peeling green paint reduced it to the level of just another station house; but that could be the people, not the paint. Hackett was considering this point as he studied Ryan's closed, unsmiling face.

"It's something political," Ryan said. Something more important, he was saying. "Long's Downtown now. Some Commie who murdered the comrade who was fucking his wife."

"Don't sound almighty political to me," Hackett murmured. "Where's Himself keeping the Altman files?"

"We got a photo of them at the May Day shindig. Best friends until the comrade got corrupted by the capitalistic way of life. Spanish, all three of them, you know what they're like."

Hackett, who didn't, persisted. "The Altman files."

"Locked away." Ryan, smug alchemist guarding fool's gold, smiled and picked up a blurred snapshot. "The bearded one's our man. No wonder she wandered, right?"

Disarmed, Hackett looked over his shoulder. Courtesy of Commissioner Valentine, he thought. Valentine, La Guardia's man, had issued the license for the May Day parade, over a chorus of protests. In the interests of democracy, he had declared with his usual pomp. And then had ordered the department to photograph the paraders; in his own interests. Bleeding Heart Valentine, a wily cop bastard and nobody's man. He, too, had quit school at sixteen, so they said.

"Pity she didn't wander farther," Hackett said, and Ryan laughed, showing large, very white teeth.

"Rossi's office free?" Hackett asked then. One of the boys.

"Sure," Ryan said, expansive. "He's never here anyway."

The Tenth's operator was a lot more stupid than Lewis, and it took ten minutes of repetition, cooling his heels and admiring the truant Rossi's taste in whiskey, bottom drawer left but unfortunately sealed, before Hackett was connected to what he hoped was the right person at Immigration and Naturalization in Washington.

You could say this much for the call: It was less embarrassing—Hackett assessed it later—than he had anticipated.

A little girl kidnapped and murdered, Hackett began (he got that bit in right away, making it sound as if it had happened yesterday) and heard the laconic voice at the other end soften and expand. By the time he had finished his précis, the voice was matching Hackett's own in patient courtesy.

Yet for all their mutual politeness, the outcome was a rash of conditionals, no less frustrating for all that it was expected. If John James or whatever his real name might be was a naturalized citizen or a legal alien, or if John James or whatever was a former illegal who had filed for respectability under the amnesty of '29, along with some eighteen thousand other illegal brethren, then . . . (Ironic that the land of opportunity had become a haven of Depression in one and the same year: Hackett's thoughts were drifting at this point, waiting for the calm voice to continue. If Washington didn't get a move on, the call could end up costing more than Rossi's bottle.)

If, on the other hand, John James was none of the above, "then, I'm afraid, he won't be traceable . . ." The voice slowed, then recovered with a spurt of energy. "But you give me a couple of days now, and I'll send you a list. You never know, we might just come up with something."

Fat fucking chance, Hackett thought, but his goodbye was cordiality itself.

Did dirty old men see themselves as dirty old men? That was the question. Did they begin by doing what he was doing now, sitting outside Washington Irving High and watching several hundred schoolgirls spill from the building? And did the dirty old men then go off with their minds full of clean faces and obscene images to pull the puddin' in some doorway? Or did they start off at a keyhole, like Brennan and himself watching Mary Margaret Farrell get undressed? Probably. But they stayed at the keyholes and with the envelopes of smutty pictures, and they made a vocation of knowing the alleys little girls would walk along, the movies they would sit through in the dark. The men with the candy and the wandering hands knew all this without thinking about it. No, Hackett debated. They thought about it all the time, and enjoyed the thinking. They knew, in other words, that they were dirty old men.

And how come I know so much about them? Hackett catechized, looking around for dirty old men and seeing Ali emerge from the doorway. Because we are all sinners; all in thought, some in word, only a few, thank God, in deed. Because we were all once fifteen, and that's the outside respectable age for a dirty old man. Though—he suddenly hedged, serenely bridging the gulf of two decades—it was all right to like the look of the tall blonde standing behind Ali even when, say, you were thirty-five. That came under the heading of objective appreciation and had nothing to do with the one-track mind that sought out and damaged, sometimes destroyed, others in its perversity. Schnitzer, who had been to night school, said it was because the men were arrested developmentally. Not arrested often enough, Hackett had replied. Schnitzer said, as if it was supposed to count, that the men had themselves been damaged. Who had not been? Hackett had wanted to know. It was not a defense that could be expected to solace the Junies of the world; nor their sisters.

The swarming schoolgirls, their eyes as speculative as Brennan's, stared as Ali got into the car. The stupid bitches couldn't tell the difference, that's why they were always getting themselves into trouble. He caught the smile of the blond girl he had noticed before, and flushed. Falling back on cop procedure, he straightened his shoulders and glowered at the whole mindless bunch of them.

"What I usually do," Ali said, apparently not minding the stares, "is go to rehearsal now. Only there's no rehearsal today."

"Well." Hackett was anxious to get away, but disinclined to spend another session in the freezing kitchen. He looked at the bulky schoolbag lying between them on the seat. "We can drop off your bag, and I'll take you for ice cream."

"Ice cream in December?" She laughed, playing carefree to the spectators outside the windows.

"Whatever," he said, close to exasperation, then remembered her gloveless hands.

Kitchen scenes, restaurant scenes; food. Hackett felt as if he was eating his way through a play, feeding off Ali's memories. He commandeered a table, stage left, and distributed hats and coats on the other chairs, preventing intrusion. Ali was shrugging in front of Hot Food—he could tell what she was going to choose; her shoulders would lift just before she slipped in the nickels—when she turned and caught him watching. She hesitated, then walked to the end of the row and back before deciding on anything more. Telling him not to look.

The Automat itself had been Ali's idea, and Hackett, for somewhere else to look, tried to visualize the place through her eyes: the high ceiling, the tiled floor, the veined marble pillars. It probably looked quite grand to her. Except for the noise and the smells, sour rags and pea soup, it could almost be the Aquarium, he decided, appraising the windowed tanks that lined two walls. Shark sandwich, hermit crab Jell-O . . .

He had run out of fish lore by the time Ali dumped the loaded tray on the table: beef pie, a piece of seven-layer cake, a glass of milk. To the side, separate, was a cup of coffee and a purple mess that looked as though it was breeding ptomaine. Piranha pie.

"The coffee and the blueberry pie's for you," Ali said, confirming his fears. She handed him the leftover nickels.

"I'm not hungry," he protested, and without missing a beat she moved the pie to her side of the tray.

"It's nice here," she said, and looked around with satisfaction.

"Nice and warm," he said, glad that he hadn't offended her about the pie. He took a careful sip of the coffee.

Halfway through the beef pie, she paused. "You married?"

"No, not yet. Not so far, I mean."

She smiled ruefully. "I had it all worked out. I figured your wife must be tall and blond, too. From the way you looked at Barbara Auslander. Mr. Butler only looks at girls who look like Mrs. Butler. She's very dumb and boy-crazy, Barbara. And she peroxides her hair. Everyone knows about it."

Miss Auslander must be as careless about her roots as she is about her smiles. His own smile shifted, and Ali gave him the fisheye.

"So does Jean Harlow," he told her. "Dye her hair."

"No!"

"But you were close," he consoled her. "There is a lady, and she is tall and blond. But not dumb or boy-crazy."

"What's her name?" She did not look consoled.

"Celia," he said after a while.

"Cecilia? Like Sister Cecilia?"

"I suppose," he said, taken by surprise. He was not sure, any more than he was about the boy-crazy part. He stirred. There had been more than enough talk of Ceil for the day.

Ali must have picked that up, too, and in the silence they both listened to her jaws chomping as she put away the blueberry pie. She was saving the seven-layer for last.

Alarmed that she would have wolfed everything down before he had said his piece, Hackett told her, "I went to City Island this morning."

"Oh?" Her eyes darkened. "Which part, the old or the new?"

"The new," he said finally.

"The new part is where the store was. Where the customers lived, the rich people and the foreigners." She caught herself. "Where he said the store was."

Hackett looked at her with interest but without surprise. This child who was eating like there was no tomorrow had early rejected John James's lies. Yet here she sat, believing in City Island as though she had been there. As, in her mind, she had. She had retained the image from a time when, in spite of her protests now, she had believed in the rosy future James had painted. Hackett could remember one of his uncles, a great-uncle, red-faced and featureless, who had told him tales of the old country. It wasn't until after the funeral that Hackett discovered the silly codger had arrived in America when he was two. Senile fancies, then, but the windowless cabin had stayed with Hackett, coloring his dreams; it was still with him. Adults were always lying to children—from habit, perhaps, from a need to seem wise—and most of the time, he supposed, it did not matter. James, though, by virtue of his authority over Ali, the authority of a father as well as of an adult, had subverted for more lethal reasons a child's willingness to believe; had played on a truth that was, like poverty, relative. The cabin's sod floor had existed, after all, even if Hackett's great-uncle had not been the one to trample it.

"There's no store. And no new part either, Ali. He was describing someplace else."

"Yes," she said. She was toying with the cake, her appetite gone. "He called it City Island, but it was someplace else."

"How did it come up, City Island, do you remember that?"

As though his voice had alarmed her, she was suddenly wary; childish. "The first time, you mean?"

"Yes." Hackett was having trouble with her age swings.

"Junie," she said, and frowned. "He was telling us about the store and the house and how one of his neighbors, one of the customers, was so rich he was building another house even though he'd already got a big one. Junie asked him where, and he wasn't sure what she meant, I guess, because he said it was by the side of the road. I said where was the road, and he said it was in New City Island. After that, he told us about the boats in the old part." She paused; she had talked her way back to being fourteen again. "That's how it was."

"Did you think he was lying?" Hackett rummaged for the phrase. "Did his eyes go funny?"

"That was only his second visit," she said in apology. "I didn't know what he was like then. You know, what he was putting on and what was really him."

As if she had ever really known him, Hackett thought. He

nodded anyway, but Ali had turned to examine the fair-haired girl who had arrived at the stand-up table, packages by S. Klein on the Square between her feet—all this out of the corner of his eye: Hackett was not about to let Ali catch him looking.

"Why couldn't she have screamed or something?" Ali said abruptly. "Why couldn't she have run away or something?"

"We don't know that she didn't," he said gently. She had not, of course. Surprise and terror had pinned Junie helpless, a mouse before the marauding cat, he would have pawed her at will. She might at the last minute have screamed, but nobody would have heard, no rich people or foreigners. He would have thought of that, he had thought of everything else.

"She liked him, you see," Ali said bitterly. "She was dumb and she liked him. I told her she was dumb, and she was."

It was ten to seven by the clock on the bank—the green-domed Williamsburgh Bank, the "h" in memory of the Dutch who had settled the area, it had been clean those days—when he turned slowly onto South Ninth. The colored had taken over one side of the block; half of the other side was abandoned. The house in which Paddy Boyd had barricaded himself the night the Day Street boys came after him had long since burned down. She would have to move one of these days; be moved.

He let himself in and startled her. Her hand slid automatically over the cup.

"I thought you were coming tomorrow," his mother said. She meant yesterday. Her dress at least was clean, her hair pinned higher than usual.

"It is tomorrow." He breathed in cautiously. Gin and birds and a lingering smell of cabbage, her scent never varied; it was his personal time machine. There was nowhere to sit, the chairs were piled with junk, so he stood, lounging against the door. The birds calmed down.

"You're all dressed up," he pointed out.

"I went to see Walter." She shuddered, peering at him. "They're places to die in, hospitals. Tea?"

"No. Yes." His stomach was still jumpy from Ali. He had driven her safely home, and she had sat unseeing in the corner,

stone in her slitted eyes. Doing penance for her outburst against
Junie. He moved a stack of junk from one of the chairs and sat
down. The birds started up again.

"How's Walter?" he said.

"I found his wig. I must've brought it in here and not
remembered."

"I see it." It was hard to miss: a curly cap on top of the big
cage.

She went over to the sink and filled the kettle. He took the
cup she gave him and wiped the rim carefully with his handkerchief.

"I went to see Walter today," she said, watching him. "I
didn't tell him about the wig, so he doesn't know I lost it."

"Just as well," he said heartily. "Since you found it again.
He's got others anyway."

"Much comfort they would be. This is the only blond one."

The first thing Hackett had known about a boarder was coming in the door after a two-month hiatus, and there in the middle
of the stairs was a tallish figure in black evening frock and long
black hair. Only when the figure turned and bolted up the stairs
had Hackett seen the hard, hairy legs.

"Godallfuckingmighty," he had said then.

"He does no harm," his mother had answered. "It's nice to
have a man around again, and he does no harm. It's a small sin,
Father says, as long as he stays in the house."

"He fancies himself a blonde these days," she said now, sipping at the cup.

Hackett smiled. "What was he wearing when he went to the
hospital?"

"A lovely red velvet. From Mrs. Malone." Mrs. Malone ran
the old-clothes store two blocks down, and Walter was her constant customer. "The men from the ambulance were very nice
about it. The dress."

"He ought to be put away," he said, not meaning it. He was
grateful to Walter.

"He's close on seventy, who'd have believed it?"

Walter as ageless cherub, with hard, unholy legs. "How's he
doing?" Hackett said again.

"It's his heart." She put milk and sugar in his cup without consulting him, and poured the tea. "But he says they'll let him out by Christmas. Which reminds me. Willie phoned today. Yesterday."

Hackett nodded. It would be the usual. Christmas morning he would pick up his mother and take her to her brother's home above the funeral parlor. He would stay for a drink or two, listening to the ramblings of his uncle ("But you should only know the things your sister says about you, nights, Uncle Willie") and watching Aunt Helen as she counted the glasses his mother put away. At exactly one o'clock he would phone Ceil's mother's house, and Ceil would pick up and wish him a Merry Christmas, Maureen. Cousin Joseph, with his father's moon face and his mother's sly eyes, would try to listen, as he had last year. Hackett had worked briefly with cousin Joseph at Uncle Willie's funeral home, one of the jobs before he became a cop. Briefly, because on his third day there—a bare half hour before he was due to pick up his first customer, client, never corpse—Hackett (fear had robbed him of imagination, he excused himself in retrospect) had locked the sneering Joseph in the prize coffin, a mahogany affair with silver-plate handles and trim. "Hooligans and drunks, the people I've married into," Aunt Helen had moaned as her husband pried Hackett off the airtight box, denting the trim. Until Uncle Willie's stroke, communication between the two families had come to an end. Since then, though, Hackett's mother, Auntie Ann, had gone back to spending Christmas with her brother, but it was understood that cousin Jim would stay only for the odd drink or two. Hackett whiled away the obligatory hour flirting with Joseph's wife, a large, watery-eyed girl with bad teeth and, given encouragement, a tendency to mock her husband. Aunt Helen's lip would curl, and what with keeping one eye on the clock and the other on her sister-in-law, her face was as busy as Long's forehead. At her signal, Uncle Willie, half bagged and reluctant, he had forgiven Hackett the damage to the trim, would grunt his way out of the chair and see Jim to the door. Hackett would spend the rest of the day at Brennan's, leaving cousin Joseph to take Auntie Ann home. Hackett tried not to think about how Joseph got her in and out of the car.

"You won't be late, Christmas," his mother said, and switched on the radio.

"I'll be here at noon."

Amos 'n' Andy. He watched her as she slumped over the set, laughing. Her face was beginning to flush.

"I missed most of it," she said as soon as it ended, and turned the radio off with a snap. Blaming him. They sat in silence, even the birds were still, until twenty to eight, when the phone rang. They both jumped. Hackett had installed the phone when he moved out; the only phone on the block. This was the first time he had heard it ring.

"Walter. He must've died," his mother said as she moved to answer it, but after listening for a moment, she handed it to him.

"She's really sick this time," Ceil said hurriedly. "My aunt. I can't get there till eight-thirty, is that all right?"

"Fine." He kept his voice businesslike. "You okay? You sound tired."

"No." She hesitated, and it occurred to him that she might be lying. *Honi soit.* "It's just that I've never seen her really sick before."

"She'll outlive us all," he said, turning to smile at his mother. "That kind always does."

"Celia Lynch she called herself," his mother said as soon as he had hung up. "She any relation to Con Lynch?"

He went back to the chair. "Yep," he said, nodding lazily.

"She the one you're running around with? The one you moved out for?"

"I moved out for myself," he said, then, forced to look up by her sudden immobility, he met her eyes and saw that she knew all about it.

"She's the one can't have kids, right? Walter told me. He got it from Con." She took down the gin bottle from the shelf and poured a generous one. "She doesn't know when she's well off, tell her."

Con tells anyone who'll listen.

"Can't you shut them up?" he said irritably. Unsettled by her movements, the birds had begun a new racket.

"Con know you're running around with his wife?"

Hackett stood up. "You know what's wrong with this world? Too many crazies running around the streets, that's what's wrong with it. And too many bird-brained women listening to them." Walter the pipeline should only drop dead.

Not listening, she said, "Con's running around himself, is it?" The overhead's shadows smudged her face as she nodded. "That'll be it. That's always the way."

Fearful of what she would say next, he left her sitting there, unheeded Cassandra. He did not bother to say goodbye. Once in the car, however, his mind flicked over the obvious—if she knew, the whole block knew, Con knew—and began poking at her assumption until it rolled over and showed itself as fact: Con as philanderer. Hackett could not now understand why the idea had never occurred to him. And where, he wondered, suddenly breathless with anger, had Ceil been that she had not warned him? She had told Brennan. Con will have to go, but that's no problem, what I heard, Brennan had said at lunch, and then the councilman had joined them and there had been no chance to ask.

Hackett calmed himself with words. Nothing's new. Con's still a callous coward: Head rhymes. It's fear not fact that's sending you off half cocked. He smiled grimly. Not any cock at all would he give her. For the first time he saw her and Con as a couple, joined in their desire to drive him from cover, turn him from stalker to blind prey.

His hands sweating on the wheel, Hackett circled from Tenth Avenue onto Seventeenth Street, halting a little way in from the corner. He smoked two cigarettes and watched the dark bulk of the cop standing in the warehouse doorway. From time to time the cop stamped his feet; freezing his ass off or making known his presence to whoever was sitting in the car. There was a glimmer from the second floor of Ali's house: The Butlers, listening to a radio tuned low, the kids were asleep. Certainly not fucking with the light on; it took a classy type like Ceil to be so shameless. Whatever she claimed, she was probably still sleeping with Con. Not that it mattered. He wondered if Con had held on to the blubber he'd brought to the wake, then sucked in his own gut, softer than it should have been. The light went out in the

Butlers' place, and there was a flash of white as the head of the watching cop bobbed up, seeing it, too. Reassured, Hackett wheeled the car and headed back to Brooklyn. Out of concern for his belly, he did not stop for a drink: Getting ready to take on Con.

Hackett was on time at the subway stop, and Ceil was so late he began to wonder whether the aunt had died. The delay in meeting her, the break in their routine, reminded him of the early days when they had not had a routine, and against his will he could feel his anger softening, dissolving. When she finally turned the corner, his heart jumped. But her head, neat in a cloche, was bent against the wind, and piqued by what he construed as a lack of anticipation in her approach—she was half an hour late, she should have been hurrying—he turned on the brights. He saw her face desolate, stunned in the glare.

"Sorry I'm late," she said, tight-mouthed, and he was suddenly tired of women and their problems. The odor of her misery was filling the car: Her period had come.

"She dead yet?"

"No," she said, tensing. Something must have leaked from his voice. "She's not dead yet. She's better than she was, but my mother is staying the night anyway."

"Did you have to tell her your real name?" Adding in a rush of spite, "Why didn't you tell her you were Maureen O'Day?"

"There was nothing I could do." She didn't look at him, she was going into her stonewall act. "My mother was standing right there." My mother and your mother; problems both, she was saying. It was not, he noticed, in any way an apology.

"You knew what you were doing," he said, and when she still didn't react, he pulled her face roughly around. "Con knows, am I right? He knows it's me, doesn't he?"

She roused herself. "That is not a question I have felt free to ask. Obviously." But she felt free enough to push away his hand. "No," she added, reflecting. "I don't think he knows about you. I don't think he knows anything."

"Then he's the only one in Brooklyn who doesn't." He

lunged and pulled her face toward him again. "Let's change the fucking verb, Ceil, if it'll make you any happier. Let's try guessing what you think he guesses."

Responding to the threat in his voice, in the hand squeezing her chin, she whispered, "You're terrifying me," and he dropped his hand. She looked terrified.

"Does it matter if he knows, guesses?" She was still whispering. "There's nothing he would do about it, either way."

Hackett lighted a cigarette. "Why is that, Ceil? Is it because he's getting a little on the side himself? That you forgot to tell me about?"

"Does it matter if he is?"

"Stop asking me if it matters," he said, his voice raised. "It matters if I think it matters. It matters"—he brought the volume down but the words spilled, out of control—"if I think you've been playing me for a fool to get back at that stinking lump of lard. Is that what's been going on here?"

"You know that isn't true. Though I knew that's what you'd say if I told you." Contention strengthened her voice in turn. "And that what you'd be thinking was I might decide I had grounds and get rid of him, and then you'd be trapped with me. And that's exactly what you are thinking."

"Con's the one with grounds," he said viciously. He knew the rules: She was bleeding, barren. Almost too late he remembered the other rules. He was standing above a chasm deeper than he had realized. "Is it legal grounds we're talking about here?" he said.

The word rang miserly. "Yes." It rang weak, too. While her mother was alive, Ceil would not leave the Church for a divorce; any more than she would stand up and admit sterility for a Church annulment.

Calmer, he asked, "Is it one poor sinner Con's stringing along, or does he have a series?" His own day, he felt, was a series he would cheerfully hand over to Con.

"One."

He waited, knowing she would look at him, and when she did, he spoke directly at her. "Who would be so fucking stupid as to stick herself with Con?"

"One woman," she said right back. "Two children."

"Two children? Two?" It was unbelievable and he wanted to laugh, but he knew his laughter would give her permission to cry, she would see that as some kind of balance. "Con?"

"It's been going on since before we were married. He was about to marry her when he met me. He told me about it, all about it, the first time I refused him." She turned to face him again. "So now you know."

She had spoken evenly, but in the low light from the streetlamp it seemed to Hackett that her eyes were set and hurt. If nothing else, it must have jolted her pride the night Con told her. Especially the part about the kids. It was pride that was now making her face him.

"Well?" she said, and he saw fear, not pain, in her eyes. Her forehead was beaded with sweat, and for the second time within the hour he took out his handkerchief, and she sat obedient as a child while he mopped her face and took off her hat, smoothing down the wisps of hair that floated up with the movement.

"Why did you tell Bobby and not me?" he said, jealous.

"I didn't tell Bobby. He told me. He wouldn't say who told him."

"Close-mouthed bastard," he said mildly, and leaned over and kissed her. He would get it out of Brennan, who was playing both ends like a crook.

"It's too late to go uptown, I guess," he said after a while, watching her sideways, watching her body relax as she leaned back in the seat, smiling up at the car roof as he drove to the dark spot on the other side of the bridge; where she went down on him in the front seat.

He buttoned himself with his left hand, and with the right he stroked her hair in silence. ("It's okay to like it," she had told him in the beginning. "You don't have to make jokes." "You're the one with a talent for one-liners," he had protested, glad of the dark. "And a taste for fellatio?" she had teased, to prove his point. "A talent there, too," he had said, and the awkwardness had passed.)

"I'm starving," he said, patting her head.

"That's because you haven't eaten anything lately." Her voice was muffled, she was scrambling on the floor for her hat.

"Don't be crude, and I'll try not to be crass. Fuck Con. We'll get a bite down here."

But the only place open in the entire area, it turned out, was the diner two blocks from Headquarters, and that's where they ended up. Feeling safe behind the steamed-over windows, Hackett ate two hamburgers in a row—properly charred but half the size of Ceil's version—while she, confessing to cramps, ordered the soup of the day; then stared at it when it came as if she hadn't.

Curiosity returned as his appetite was appeased. Appetites.

"How could you have kept it to yourself? About Con."

"There's no mystery," she said simply. "I don't care, so I don't think about it."

She was single-minded or cold-blooded, he couldn't decide which. Edgy again, he said, "You cared enough not to tell me."

"Don't," she said. "Don't let's talk about this tonight, okay?" She put down the spoon and lifted her chin high above any pretense of eating. "Did you see Ali today?"

"Yes," he said. "I saw Ali today. I spoke to a man in Washington today, too, but I did not get to see Long today, nor did I get to make any more sense out of that whole mess than I can make out of you. So what waltz shall we dance to now?"

"I was late," she said, averting her head.

"I know you were late. An entire fucking half hour late. Did I complain?"

"I mean I was three days late. Seventy-two hours. I thought I was pregnant."

"Seventy-two hours," he repeated in disbelief while she sat there crying, where any minute a cop he knew might walk in. Had she actually added up the hours? You counted in hours when a child went missing, an hour could make the difference between life and death; that was significant. You counted in hours before a date, in the beginning anyway, before it had settled into something so close to marriage he was stifling under its weight.

"You thought you were pregnant. Small with child," he said,

and his voice silky with venom startled her out of the tears. "Three days, and you had me all tied up, ready for delivery, too."

"It's only because I can't that you stay with me, you think I don't know that?" She rose, in tears again, and fled. He paid hurriedly, not looking at the man. He's never on at lunch, Hackett consoled himself, and caught up with Ceil at the car.

"Get in."

She ignored him and continued walking.

"Get in before I throw you in," he ordered, blocking her way, and she got in.

At her corner, she said, "I won't call again."

"Yes you will," he said scornfully. Cocksucker.

Uptown, steeling himself against her tears, Hackett waited for her to call, and when she did not, he was furious that she had once again fooled him. This was the same Ceil who had told him one time that the more honest she was with him, the less he trusted her. There was a moral there, she had said.

He poured himself a stiff one, his hands shaking. The room was freezing. Tomorrow he would take over the files and then he would take on the landlord; a busy day. But fatigue was draining him of anger, the whiskey was not working, not even warming him. His mouth dry, his head splitting, Hackett climbed into bed. He did not bother to finish the drink.

Another time, Ceil had told him: "Everyone's got it backwards, a family's not for women. It's for men. Just look at what men do when they don't have one. They go around inventing one. Look at you. Bobby and Larry are brothers. Lewis is your cousin Joseph." "And who are you?" Hackett had asked, and she had smiled.

Another time, still instructing, Ceil . . . Hackett punched the pillow. He was, he saw, taking leave of her, mourning her even. Well, she wasn't the only fish in the sea. Sighing, he turned in the bed, and under him the springs groaned, protesting.

Sea; and the Automat came floating in, Ali's face swimming toward him. She was his last image before he fell asleep.

At four o'clock, Hackett was wide awake. A sharp needle of

pain was piercing his right temple, a straight steel bore ending just above his eye. It must have been what woke him.

Nothing's new, he thought. Con's still a callous coward, and nothing's new except New City Island which came before the old. He was up and out of the house in five minutes, and by half past four, unshaven and unbathed—it was his season for breaking routine—he was standing in front of the sectioned wall map in Cahill's office. In his hand was the list, grabbed in haste from the James file, of the mountain ranges within a one-day train ride of New York City: the Appalachians, the Poconos, the Taconics, Wachungs. He had spent days compiling it in June, breaking it down to the local names, marking in red the individual mountains that were near water, any kind of water; had spent a fortune in phone calls, though his voice, he knew, had lacked conviction. ("On the word of a kid," Long had exploded at the cost. "I suppose we should be grateful she didn't mention icebergs or you'd've been calling—Alaska maybe." By dying there that summer, Will Rogers had brought Alaska alive, even to the likes of Long.)

Hackett went through the list alphabetically, confined by the map's limits to a fifty-mile radius of the city. Beyond that were the bears and the Indians; he'd have to call in the cavalry to traverse there. If only, Hackett thought. If only he had known in June what he knew now; what he thought he guessed now.

It was a slow night, and the cop on intake wandered in. Doran, his name was, a new man still sullen at finding himself buried in the bureau; a Knights of Columbus pin.

"What's up?" Doran said as if he owned the place.

"The game's up," Hackett said, making like a movie cop. He could not stop smiling.

"You okay?" Doran was nervous, wondering if Hackett was drinking right under the old man's nose. Our Father which art upstairs, Valentine. He was drunk, in a way.

"I've found the fucker," Hackett said then, turning back to the wall. "Or at least I've found where he took her." New City and High Tor vanished beneath his finger. On the map they were less than a pinky-length apart.

16

By eight o'clock, West Seventeenth Street was blocked with trucks, illegal spillovers from the Port Authority garage on West Sixteenth, and Hackett had to park near the corner. He had been waiting half an hour, was just beginning to wonder if he should ask the cop if he had missed her, when Ali appeared at the top of the steps. She did not see him until he called.

"I'll give you a lift," he said, opening the door with a flourish that made her smile. Sleep had washed away the strain of the evening before, and she looked calm and very young.

She struggled in sideways, made clumsy by the weight of her schoolbag. "I thought I was going to be late," she said, pleased, "and now I'll be on time."

"I thought I was the one who was late. I was beginning to think I was going to have to roust you out of school," he said, and saw by the wistful look she gave him that she wouldn't have minded that at all.

Still the chauffeur, he closed the door ceremoniously and saluted the watching cop.

"He's just arrived," she volunteered as Hackett slid behind the wheel. "He's not the one who's been here all night."

Otherwise he would have been too cold to return the greeting, Hackett thought, remembering his own vigil in the dark. It must be Martha Butler, he decided, from her vantage point on the second floor, who was keeping them posted. At this very minute she was probably reporting his presence to Mary Stephens.

Last night's chill wind was still blowing, had ruffled Ali's hair, and Hackett smoothed it from her brow before starting up the car.

"Why were you going to get me out of school?" Ali asked as soon as he pulled away.

"Well. Things are happening." But the face she turned to him was so eager that he hesitated, suddenly aware of how much he was building on how little. It was the same old story, with Ali as the fragile cornerstone. No, he told himself, it'll all work out in the end, and the memory of Cahill's wall map rose to comfort him. But he corrected himself anyway; rehearsing for Long. "Things may be happening."

"And that's why you're taking me to school." She spoke as if by rote, as if she were finishing a line he had left unsaid, and he realized it was not eagerness after all. He had alarmed her. She thought he was there to protect her.

"No," he said gently, trying to atone for his stupidity. "I'm here because I think I know where he took her." He halted at Seventh Avenue to let a crowd of kids cross, and stole a glance at her. She had not reacted to the reference to Junie; not that he could see, which was probably not saying much. "Where he may have taken her," he said, cautious again. "If I'm putting things together right, that is."

This time she picked up on the cue. "What things?"

"Things in his stories, stuff like that." He looked at her. "You've told me a lot, you know."

"How could I tell you a lot?" she said wonderingly. "I don't know anything."

"Yes, you do," he said too quickly, and she stared at him, her head to one side.

"People let drop more than they know," he explained, and she blushed. "Criminals, I mean," he went on hurriedly. "They talk too much. Because they're stupid or vain or something. They get careless. Like him. He talked too much, and that was too bad for him. Because you were listening." Usually it was a stoolie who was listening, he thought, but he didn't say so. Most of the time, as a matter of fact, it was a stoolie who would sell his own mother for a fin; and did. The police brought out the worst in everybody, and much good it did them. Only five percent of crimes were solved by what the public liked to call detection; maybe ten percent, if you wanted to get generous about the plain luck that could sometimes happen along. But he did not say any of that either. "It helps, of course," he added instead, lightening his tone on purpose to hide his dependence on her, he knew all about loads that crippled, "that I'm a good listener, too. In case it's slipped your attention."

She smiled briefly, her mind on other things.

"But he didn't say that much," she said after a while. She didn't look burdened, she looked disappointed. "Not about real things, at any rate. Mostly he went on and on to Mama about the new house. Or he made up stories for Junie." She gave one of her sighs and stretched against the seat.

Hackett shot across Fifth Avenue just ahead of another mob of schoolkids, the streets were alive with them, before he spoke. "Go over the one about New City Island," he urged her then. "How it came up and all."

"It's not City Island, remember?" she objected at once. "You said so yesterday. You said it couldn't be the right place, remember?"

"First you tell me. Then I'll tell you," he said firmly, and again she tilted her head like a question mark; trying to decide if it was an offer or an order. Hackett was not sure himself.

"I was asking him where the rich man's new house was," she said finally. "Junie was, I mean, and then I did, and that's when he said it was in New City Island." She cleared her throat. "That's all."

"That's not all. What about the boat part?"

"You mean about Old City Island?" stressing the Old.

"Yep," he said drily. "About Old City Island."

"You didn't say that before," she pointed out, unmoved, and retreated into another interior monologue. "After he told us about the houses," she said, frowning, "he told us about the rich people keeping their boats in the old part. In Old City Island."

"You're sure it was after?"

"I'm sure it was after." Her voice rang confident, and he could see her already on the witness stand. Never saying anything ass upwards.

"Well?" she said. She was waiting for him to live up to his half of the bargain.

Hackett slowed to a snail's pace. They were at the corner of Irving Place.

"Ali," he began, conscious that he hardly ever addressed her by name. "We have here a man who didn't like questions, who didn't talk much except to tell you stories. Yet this same man, of his own accord, sometimes tells you more than you ask. Not often, but more than once. Now, I find that interesting."

She was nodding before he finished.

"That's why you wanted to know if his eyes went funny," she said in quiet triumph. "Like when he changed the mountain into a molehill, right?" They were nodding in unison now, like a couple of marionettes. "What do you call it," she asked suddenly, "when a magician does a trick with one hand so you won't see what he's doing with the other?" and Hackett would have clapped her on the back if she had been a boy; or a year younger.

"Misdirection," he told her, and she repeated the word slowly.

He brought the car to a stop in front of the school, but she made no move to get out. Somewhere inside the school a bell sounded, and she ignored that, too.

"And now you'll get him, won't you? You didn't think you would, I could tell. And now you will."

"I haven't got him yet," he cautioned. He leaned across her and opened the door; she still didn't get out, though another wind, or the same one following her, began lifting her hair.

"And Junie will have a proper grave, and it will all be over with," she said in the exact voice of her mother. "Will you come to the funeral?"

"I will." A promise.

A second bell rang inside the school. Hackett picked up her bag and nudged her with it. "Go on," he said, smoothing her hair again. "It's getting cold in here." And he watched her as she walked, still listing from the weight of the bag, toward the building.

"I'll try to pick you up after school," he called on impulse; protective after all.

She turned and waved her scarf, acknowledging she had heard. And, he guessed, with a mental nod to Ceil's admonition, for the benefit of the small crowd filing like ants through the doorway; but gawking like schoolgirls.

Hackett looked over the coffee cup at Long's dissatisfied face. They were back in Rossi's office, their home away from home these days, and Long was shuffling restlessly through the Altman cards.

"I'm not saying he definitely took her to Rockland County," Hackett said again, lying again. "I'm not saying that. All I'm saying, New City is worth a try. Unless," he added, "you got something I don't know about."

"That's not all you were saying out there," Long said, nasty. "As I understood it out there, you were telling the entire fucking squad just what he eats for breakfast and the exact spot he's buried her at. You know it all, it sounds like. You and the talking kid." He slammed down the cards. "No. I ain't got nothing you don't know about."

But I've got something you don't know about, Hackett thought viciously. No taste of Orange will I give you, you surly bastard. It had, in fact, been Long's fault that the whole world knew about it. He had rushed in late and ugly and begun yelling as soon as Hackett had opened his mouth. Of course every man in the room had stopped to listen. Long had meant them to.

Hackett started in again slowly. "He's like a forger, a successful forger. Overconfident. Who daydreams at the wrong time and

writes his real name by mistake. So he adds another, to cover."
He shrugged. "It happens."

Long was shaking his head before Hackett was halfway
through. "Then why couldn't he have been talking about the
city? New York City," he asked for the second time. They were
like actors going back over their lines. "That's what I'd like to
know. It makes just as much sense, if you ask me. More."

"You mean a mountain's sprung up on Fifth Avenue since I
last looked?" Hackett said. "The mountain is real—"

"If you believe the kid. Only if you believe the kid, Jim,
remember that." Long dealt out some of the Altman cards in a
fan. "You know, if you spent more time facing facts and less time
playing daddy . . ." He added more cards, and the fan became a
circle. Long was tinkering with the evidence.

"If the train is real," Hackett said, trying to control his
anger, "then the mountain sure as hell is real. The girl, Junie, she
wasn't overloaded in the brains department, but she would've
known the difference between a subway ride and what her old lady
calls a big train. The train was part of the treat. Part of his promise." Unbelieving, Hackett heard the note of supplication that
had crept into his voice. He put the cup down with more force
than was needed; coffee slopped onto some of the cards. "All I'm
saying," he went on with what he hoped was conviction, "for the
first time we've got a couple of things that fit. Okay, that might
fit. Nothing that'll fry him, I know, but they might lead to him.
That maybe we've got him on a train going to a mountain that
changed pretty fast into a sand dune. He took pains to change it,
remember?"

A uniformed cop opened the door, took one look at their
faces and closed the door.

Hackett turned to Long again. "And all you can moan about
is facts I'm not facing. What fucking facts?"

Long went on dabbing at the cards with Rossi's unused blot-
ter. "That we're just not gonna get him, Jim. Not this time
round," he said, and looked up, smiling. He had caught the
whine behind Hackett's words. "And that nobody ever made a
collar that I ever heard of, nobody ever made anything but a jerk

out of himself that I ever heard of, listening to a kid that likes to
hear herself talk. If you think you're gonna drag me or anyone
else for that matter up there to—where is it?—to Rockland
County, to go poking under bushes or whatever on the word of
some kid, then you've got another fucking think coming." He
tapped the nearest Altman card. "And there's nothing here either, why would there be? Would you use an Altman box if you'd
worked there, huh? If you'd done what he'd done? It wouldn't
make sense, now, would it?" He pushed himself back from the
desk and stood up. "And nobody's ever said our man's stupid."

"Nobody's stupid till they get caught," Hackett said. Long
was the one playing daddy, pretending prejudice was fact. It was
all in the tone. Faking his own tone, Hackett went on scornfully,
"There'll be a reason, all right, why he sent the Altman box.
Some obvious sort of reason, like he used a different name, he's
probably got a string of them." He stared at Long. "Or maybe
he's counting on our stupidity. Something as simple as that."

Ignoring him, Long began to shovel the Altman cards into
the carton. He made no effort to put them in order, which perhaps was just as well; several were stuck together with coffee.
"Here," he said when he was through. He pointed the box at
Hackett. "Make yourself useful. Take these back where they belong."

Hackett turned at the door and smiled joylessly. "You know
what I think? I think Rossi's taken early retirement. He just
hasn't gotten around to telling anybody yet. What I think, I
think he's left you the Chivas as a get-well present, Bill. He
knows how you suffer."

"You speak for yourself. Jesus," Long said in a flat voice. His
hand was already itching its way down.

Whatever, if anything, Hackett had anticipated about Altman's Personnel Office, the room itself took him by surprise.
After the hushed air of refined commerce on the floors below, the
place bordered on the homey: Two mismatched armchairs were
stuffed into the small area, and a rug not unlike those found in
the parlors of Irishtown covered most of the floor. A dog, a
puppy, was tied to the desk leg.

Hackett's smile at the homeyness, at the unlikeliness of the dog—in relief that he would not be overawed—made the man behind the desk stare. He was Tyler Davis: Hackett could tell by the center part and the sleeked-back hair that Ryan had satirized. But Ryan had not mentioned the glasses. Too narrow, they turned inward on Mr. Davis' broad face and gave to his stare a disconcerting, walleyed look.

What you do, Hackett told himself as they shook hands, is get out of here and up to Rockland County, by when? The clock as he passed Macy's had said nearly noon. Depending on the traffic, by one, one-thirty? He would need a map. He would call on the local cops, and they would tell him how many people lived in and around New City. And he would check them all. His early-morning euphoria, suspended during the hiatus with Long, was returning; was returning, he noted—with another smile that produced another stare—in direct proportion to the distance he put between himself and the Tenth Precinct. By the time the handshaking was over, Hackett was back to being certain.

"The young man on the phone said you were on your way," Mr. Davis said as he sat down again. He nodded at the carton under Hackett's arm. "With the file."

Anyone who could describe Long's gravel roar as the voice of a young man was a person worth cultivating, and Hackett almost regretted his need to skip.

Mr. Davis nudged the dog with his foot. "He's not house-proud yet," he explained, "so watch your shoes. He's just a puppy."

Dutifully skirting the dog, Hackett dumped the box on the desk. "The file is complete." A bit chaotic, a bit stained, but complete. Free of the carton, he took a step backwards. He was on his way. Only when his hand touched the metal did he realize that he must have opened his coat and sought his gun.

"I thought you wanted to talk to me," Mr. Davis was saying, startled that Hackett was retreating. Or perhaps he'd noticed the gun; it was hard to tell with the turned-in glasses.

"What about?" Hackett stopped in the doorway and looked with curiosity on Tyler Davis, who lacked any sign of the arrogance that, like the hair, Ryan had also scorned.

It will be about the file, Hackett decided. Our Mr. Davis forgot to tell Ryan something, and I'm supposed to stand here and wait while he wonders if the information is worth the embarrassment of admitting imperfection.

Poised for flight one minute, conceding delay the next, Hackett sat down uninvited in the nearer chair, the uglier one. The dog peed into the rug, but Mr. Davis, reflecting, did not stir. Hackett, who should have been in sight of the George Washington Bridge by now, could see himself sitting there until Doomsday.

It did not take that long. Mr. Davis cleared his throat; Hackett leaned forward, urging him on. Mr. Davis, stooping low, patted the dog, and Hackett appreciated now that the man wore the funny glasses not for effect or camouflage, but because he could not see. So much for guns and peeing dogs.

Mr. Davis cleared his throat again. "In the old days," he began, making it sound like Paradise Lost, "we had so much stuff it wouldn't all fit in the warehouse. We had to send the overflow to Greene Street."

If this is the great secret, Hackett thought savagely. Shipping had already explained Greene Street to Ryan.

Cunning showed through Mr. Davis' glasses. "What kind of an, ah, investigation are we discussing? I was never told." Was it worth his while, he meant, to come clean?

"It's confidential. For the moment." Hackett was trying to block the detour. "A felony, though," he added, coming partly clean to encourage the man. As a contrast to tight-lipped Ryan.

"Perhaps it might always remain so? Confidential, I mean. We have the store to think of." Full of melancholy, Mr. Davis stared at the dog.

Your job, too, Hackett thought, not unkindly. In his book fear was a legitimate reason for silence, and other omissions. "We'll do our best," he said. You and I.

"Greene Street," Mr. Davis said slowly as Hackett sat frozen with impatience. "There hasn't been an overflow in years"—one eye squeezed tight in thought—"not since the winter of '30, '31." He sighed. The old days.

"I see." But all Hackett saw in his mind was the street strewn with Altman remnants, artifacts of another time.

"Perhaps," Mr. Davis suggested, once again looking for a hole to hide in, "perhaps you should speak to Shipping? About the flood."

"There was a flood. At the warehouse," Hackett said; not quietly enough to be outright theatrical, but a prompting from the wings, unmistakably.

"There was a rainstorm," Mr. Davis gargled. "The roof buckled and most of the sofas on the top floor were soaked through. Ruined, most of them."

"And what wasn't ruined, that stuff was what you sent to Greene Street?" Hackett, picking his way through the overflow, top hats and linen sheets, saw the promise of a gap in the mess. "When did this happen, sir? The flood?"

"July, of course. That's why we lost so much stuff. We were stocked up for the sales—"

"And the boxes? They get sent to Greene Street, too?" He patted the dog to soften his brusqueness.

Mr. Davis smiled on a world that was kind to animals. "That's the whole point, you see. Shipping says we didn't get back all the merchandise we sent there. It happens all the time, of course. But if we didn't get back—"

"Then they might have stolen some boxes, too." Hackett was already at the door.

Mr. Davis looked sad. "Everybody seems to steal these days."

In the old days, too, Hackett thought. By the time he hit the main floor, he was running like a thief.

In a strictly limited sense, and not that it mattered at all, Long had been right. Hackett, with a good humor verging on the ferocious, was prepared to concede the point: The bastard James had felt free to send an Altman box because he had not in fact worked for the bastards. Something as simple as that.

The crosstown traffic was murder, and Hackett, stuck for a moment near a drugstore, debated calling Long. Caution held him back. Greene Street might be a dead end for all he knew.

Caution and a need not to report to Long every two minutes held him back.

Literally, at least, Greene Street was not a dead end, though it might as well have been. Two trucks were blocking the juncture with Grand Street, and the drivers were hurling primitive insults; like kids in a playground. In case the squabble escalated to war, Hackett parked with care: In case he might need to back out in a hurry. He was a stone's throw from Headquarters.

The loft building was six stories high. Inside, most of the ground floor was covered with what seemed to be half the chairs ever created. Large boxes and corrugated cardboard lined the wall facing the glassed-off cubicle to the left of the door. Next to the cubicle were wooden crates and tiers of carelessly piled cartons, of the size and kind Hackett found interesting—though none in view bore the Altman logo.

A solitary man at the rear was whistling, and the sound echoed in the high space. He was stacking chairs and, watching him, Hackett was surprised at how low they stood: The seats did not come up to the man's knee. It was not anything he'd ever noticed before.

What was obvious, though, was the wide-open door and the tempting junk within. The whole place was an invitation to larceny. Hackett was just thinking how easy it would be to walk off with a pile of boxes, even a couple of chairs if you timed it right, when a man darted out of the cubicle and intercepted him.

"I knew you was a cop," the man said in disgust. "I already spoke to one of you guys, I already told him. I don't know nothing."

Hackett followed him into the cubicle and offered a cigarette.

"You the owner?" he asked.

"I'm the partner. The one that does all the work. Bob York." The man sat down at the table.

Hackett perched himself like a friend on the corner of the table. "The other cop," he tendered. "He didn't know what he was looking for."

"And you do?" York blew smoke at the ceiling. "Jesus." A

thought struck him and, licking a blunt pencil, he scribbled something on the top invoice. "So tell me," he said then.

"I'm looking for a man who was working for you when the Altman stuff came in this summer, this July. A man—"

"I already told the other guy. No."

"A man from the North of Ireland."

"No," York repeated, mouthing figures silently. "It never happened. I never hire Irish. They drink." He looked up. "Except for Paddy back there. He don't drink. And anyway, Ralston hired him."

Ralston would be the playboy partner.

"This one doesn't sound Irish. And he doesn't drink." That I know of. "So you might not have known. That he was Irish," Hackett threw in helpfully.

"I'd have known," York said darkly. "They all drink." He totted up another column, then went on, "Is this the same guy the other guy was looking for? The guy with the limp?"

"Yep."

York put down the pencil and looked at Hackett with heavy scorn. "Would I hire a gimp? Do I look like the kind of guy would hire a gimp? In a warehouse?" Having delivered himself of so much common sense, he picked up the pencil and went back to his numbers. "What's he supposed to have done anyway, this gimp?"

"He's a thief," Hackett said, and wondered how York could run the place at a profit. It would be a duty to steal him blind. He followed York's example and put out his cigarette in the half-empty coffee cup. "You take on casuals?"

"All the time." Said with the air of someone scoring a point.

"You keep records?"

York sighed and took a shoe box from the shelf at his elbow. "Here," he said. They both ignored the minor avalanche brought about by the removal of the box.

Hackett blew dust off the lid. "The other cop didn't get to look at this."

"He didn't ask."

The box reflected in miniature the chaos on the desk: a ball of string, one brown glove and, lying every which way at the bottom, perhaps twenty cards. There was silence as Hackett flipped through them; silence, if he ignored the occasional grunt from York, who was counting surreptitiously on his fingers.

Some of the cards had been used more than once. A fair number included references. None had a Rockland County address.

"This can't be all," Hackett said, dogged.

In answer, York lifted his head. "Paddy," he bawled. "Rooney. Here."

The whistling grew louder, then stopped. The man who now stood at ease in the doorway had red hair and pale eyes and the kind of nose that comes from bout drinking. York, Hackett confirmed, was just the kind of guy who'd hire a gimp and not notice.

"You're Patrick Rooney?" he asked, pen poised.

"Ed Rooney," the man said in a just-off-the-boat brogue. "He calls me Paddy." Neither of them looked at York.

"Paddy knows as much about the place as I do," York said handsomely.

God help us all then, Hackett thought. He said, "I'm looking for a man—"

"Nobody with a limp," Rooney said at once, as if he had been eavesdropping.

"Forget about the limp," Hackett said, staring at Rooney's beacon of a nose. "This man comes from Northern Ireland. And may be hiding the fact. A Protestant."

"An Orangeman?" Rooney said, and spat sideways. "If you can call them Irishmen. Is that who we're talking about here? The Orangeman?"

It took a moment to sink in. Then Hackett, incredulous: "You mean you know him?"

"Sure and I know him. And so do you, Mr. York. He's the old liar Mr. Ralston took on, remember?"

"Who?" Hackett and York spoke together.

"Why, Wallace. The night watchman." A slow smile spread over Rooney's face. "He never said he was at all, but I knew him for an Orangeman. They have this funny way of talking that just seems to stay with them. He used to say 'Good night' with that funny sound to it. 'Good,'" he repeated, hooting like an owl. He was enjoying his role of expert in the face of their blankness. "He's some kind of crook, is it? It fits. An Orangeman, a liar and a thief. I was in Donegal at Partition. When they stole Derry."

Spare me. Hackett was frantic at the file.

"He's not here," he said.

"It'll be Mr. Ralston's," Rooney said, and handed Hackett a tin box from the same shelf.

If nothing else, Ralston was a neat playboy. In the rigorously alphabetical file, it was the last card: Wallace, Robert. No middle name given. With the Haverstraw Traprock Company listed as reference. Haverstraw in Rockland County. Near New City in Rockland County. It was as simple as that.

"Bill," Hackett was whooping at full volume when Long came to the phone. "Call me back at this number." From outside, he meant.

"Will do," Long said without fuss, and hung up. You never knew who would sell you out on a police line.

"Jesus, Joseph and Mary," Rooney said, taken aback. He was reading the card over Hackett's shoulder. "You mean he really was a stonie?"

"What's a stonie?"

"A stonecutter. A carver."

A carver of wood, too, Hackett thought, and picked up the phone on the first ring. "We've got him, we've got him, we've got him," he sang, not caring how he sounded. "His name's Wallace, and he's from Rockland County. I'll pick you up on the way." Generous with victory.

"Hold on," Long said, quietly for him. "Where are you? And Wallace who?"

"I'm in a warehouse on Greene Street." Hackett consulted the card impatiently. "Robert Wallace from the Haverstraw Traprock Company. While you're waiting, call a Mr. Benton there. And call the Bureau of Criminal Identification. See if he's got a record."

"We don't wanna broadcast this yet, Jim. You're only a couple of minutes from BCI, ain't you?"

"I'll stop by there on my way up," Hackett said. He was a hop, a skip and a jump from BCI, and he felt like doing all three.

"He must be a real bad un, this Wallace fellow," Rooney said, studying Hackett's face. When Hackett didn't answer, he shrugged and turned to greet the group of men entering the warehouse. Thieves all, by the look of them. Just returned from selling stolen property on their lunch hour, thank God.

Hackett looked at his watch. Two forty-five. Where had the time gone?

"Glad to be of help," York said. "You can use the phone anytime. Feel free."

Hackett threw a nickel into the mess. "And five and eight don't make thirteen," he lied, to add to the confusion.

And you, he promised Rooney's flaming head. I'll be back with a bottle of the best for you. You sweet broth of a boy, you.

17

At three-fifteen, driven inside by the cold, Ali was standing behind the heavy school door. She was blowing on her fingers as she waited, surprised as she always was that it helped. The door was windowed, and she would see him drive up.

The smell of chalk and ink and paint, especially of paint, was strong in the corridor, and Ali breathed it in, savoring the odor the way a hungry man sniffs before eating. School was nice, she had told him. School was in fact wonderful, the only place where she felt safe and free. Free of Junie. She looked down at her schoolbag, at her foot imprisoned under its weight, and smiled. Free.

Perhaps his watch was slow, and he did not know he was late. She was getting hungry. Perhaps he would take her to the Automat again; she could be late for the rehearsal, she knew her songs.

Flanked by two dark girls, Barbara Auslander drifted past and winked. Ali made an insolent point of staring at Barbara's hair, searching for the black roots: Everybody talks about it, how you dye your hair. But once the trio had swayed through the door, Ali shifted position, lugging her bag as an afterthought. When the next group came along, she was leaning against the wall, looking past them down the corridor as if she were waiting for a friend. Nobody seemed to notice, but she was blushing—and in the same instant fearing that he would ruin school for her. It was the only time she could remember feeling uncomfortable there, if you didn't count the first day, and the way he had looked at Barbara yesterday. It was said that Barbara wore a bra, though Ali could not quite get herself to believe that one. Probably his girlfriend did, too. Ali blushed again, but nobody was looking.

By half past three, the building was to all intents and purposes deserted. Ali had seen most of the teachers leave, sometimes in unexpected alliance: Math arm in arm with American History. Who would have thought Miss Burns and Miss Trameer could laugh like that? It made them look unfamiliar, like younger sisters of themselves.

Ali wrapped the scarf around her mouth; people would notice that if they were looking: The way her lips kept pulling down. When she was quite sure there was no one left to see that she had been stood up, she ran quickly from the school. She had wasted enough time. She still had her morning carfare and, her hand in her pocket, she counted out the exact amount by touch. She put a spurt on as she turned onto Fourteenth Street, and at the last minute caught the crowded crosstown streetcar. At Union Square she stared out past Klein's to the Automat. Perhaps, she thought. Perhaps what? None of the dark blue coats was him.

"You're late," Sol said as soon as she was inside the door.

"I was late leaving school," she said when she had got her breath. She slid onto a stool. "I've got time for a doughnut."

"Maybe you'll come back after and eat good. Like a growing girl," Sol said. "You should phone when that happens. When you're late."

Ali nodded, her eye on the clock over the counter. "I'll leave my bag here. That'll save time."

Her mother brought the doughnut. "That policeman," she said. "He took you to school this morning."

Ali took refuge in the doughnut. Then: "How's your tooth?" She could see her mother's tongue worrying at it.

"It still hurts."

"We'll go to the clinic. Not tomorrow, the play's tomorrow. Saturday. If it's still hurting by then."

Mother and daughter looked at one another. Play, clinic: Junie.

"If only I'd known," Mary Stephens said softly.

If she had only known. She would have taken more notice. Of Junie, she meant. To Ali, suddenly stiff on the stool, it made a lot more sense the other way round. Whenever she went to a movie, she could always tell if it was the kind where the heroine was going to die. One word or one look would do it, and she would know and begin steeling herself against the loss. When the deathbed scene arrived, Junie would sit there weeping buckets while Ali ate candy, stoic. Looking around at all the other people helped, too; to keep the tears at bay.

Not more notice, then. Less.

"What's the matter?" her mother asked.

Ali frowned. "It's another dress rehearsal, and I forgot the costume again. I have to go get it." She dusted her hands and slid off the stool. "He says," she began, and stopped. "Detective Hackett says he's gonna get him. Soon," she ended quickly, and made for the door.

"When's soon?" Sol asked, right behind her.

Ali looked up at him. "Just soon," she said, uncertain. Then with a burst of hope: "He says he'll come and let us know."

18

Behind Hackett, two police cars pulled away at the same time, and for one wild moment he thought Long had ordered a convoy.

"It's close on six now," Long said, giving the car a brief once-over. "And me with tickets to the Garden tonight."

Louis will just have to fight without you, Hackett thought, and watched in the mirror as the police cars turned south at the corner. He headed north.

"It'll be pitch black by the time we get there," Long said. He opened and closed the glove compartment. "The way I see it, it don't make much sense getting there in the middle of the night. Not knowing what we're looking for. Or where to look and all."

It was hard to tell if he was seriously suggesting they should wait another day, or if he was just going through his usual cantankerous routine.

"It would've helped if we'd left at five," Hackett got out finally through teeth as clenched as his stomach. An entire hour

Long had kept him waiting. For all they knew, that hour could have cost them James. Wallace. Wallace could have slipped out of sight in that time, and another six months down the drain. Two cops on patrol recognized them and waved, smiling. Not a care in the world, those boyos, while he was having a heart attack in his gut. He couldn't feel his feet.

He could have met Ali in that hour; he had more or less promised to. He could have been almost up there by now. Wild horses couldn't stop him at this stage, not to mention Long.

"Some of us got work to do," Long said, undaunted. "It don't make much sense, though, you gotta admit it. Us leaving so late, I mean."

Hackett slammed on the brakes at the light. "You can suit yourself. Me, I'm going. I know what I'm looking for. And if you think I'm gonna hand this over to the local bumpkins at this stage of the game, then you're the one with another think coming." He slammed on the brakes at the next light, too, and that took care of the deadness in his feet. They began tingling.

"Let's get there alive, at any rate," Long said. In silent rebuke he produced a flashlight, which he flicked on and off, testing; then a flask, which he stowed in the glove compartment. He had come prepared, he was saying. He had never had any intention of leaving it to the locals either.

"Nice car," Long said after a while; a peace offering. To have taken a police car would have entailed more delay, and even then there was no guarantee it would have come equipped with a radio. Hackett, who had never driven out of the five boroughs, tried not to think about the effect of country roads on his tires, let alone his nerves.

"Maybe," Long said after another silence, "maybe the prelims'll take longer than usual, huh?"

"Well?" Hackett said, accepting the olive branch. Some of the tension drained as he spoke. Talking helps sometimes; he'd told Ali that.

"That guy up there in Haverstraw, Jesus." Long began shaking his head. "That guy up there. Seemed like he was mixing me up with Altman's or somebody. Kept on telling me how hard-working this guy Wallace was, how reliable. Kept on trying to give him a fucking reference, it sounded like."

"Not Altman's. He never worked at Altman's." A reminder to Long that he didn't know it all yet. In spite of himself, Hackett smiled. "You were right about that." A peace offering, too.

Long broke into an answering grin, dropping the last of the cat-and-mouse. "It's James all right. He worked there, must've been right after he'd done the Stephens girl. And before that, he'd been put away for bothering little girls. So it's gotta be James, right?"

Hackett was squinting, trying to visualize Wallace's record. To throw off the hovering desk man at Criminal Id., Hackett had looked up yellow sheets on Walker, Wallace, Wallman, and then had been forced to wade through the whole lot.

"He was in Bellevue for it, this time last year," Hackett said finally. Lewd language, a misdemeanor; the charges dropped. Jesus. "And the shitheads set him loose, can you believe that?" He outmaneuvered a truck for a space in the stream of traffic.

"Stupid don't surprise me none, Jim. I ain't got your faith. They knew all about the little girls in Haverstraw, it was the guy up there told me about it. And they still took him on. He'd paid his debt, the guy actually said that. He's paid his debt." World-weary, Long leaned back. "What else can you expect, huh? They're all sheep and half-wits to begin with, or they wouldn't be up there in the first place, right? And they took him back on, too. He worked there Thanksgiving, a couple of weeks. Then quit again, for the same reason. A sick daughter, he told them."

"You still got a man on Seventeenth Street?" Hackett said without thinking.

"He ain't stupid, Jim. He's out looking for greener pastures. Safer ones, leastwise." Long's forehead wrinkled. "You know someone's still there. What I was told, you was there yourself this morning."

Hackett nodded. "Good," he said, meaning he was glad the cop was on his toes; had reported him.

"It's just that swearing at the schoolgirls and sending the

doll is the same thing," Hackett went on, watching the mirror. Behind them, the outmaneuvered truck was tailgating on purpose. "It's just that he's getting ready to break out again."

"You already said that. Before," Long said, but there was no disparagement in his voice this time. He looked out of the window and sighed. "I used to live around here when I was a kid. In a cave with a door on, we used to call it. Those days, you could take your old mother to Times Square for a walk and an ice cream. Any hour. There was no rough stuff then. Any hour, day or night. But not no more."

Never for me, Hackett was thinking. My mother wouldn't eat ice cream if you paid her, not unless it was pickled in gin.

Long, turning back from his reverie: "Anything else on the sheet?"

Hackett squinted again. "He did eighteen months up the river on a larceny two. A couple of smaller dodges, all on widows. He likes widows."

"The same way he likes little girls," Long said, dry, and they were both silent. Brennan likes widows, too, Hackett was thinking now.

Evading the honking truck, Hackett made a left, then a right onto Riverside Drive. It was a clear run ahead to the George Washington Bridge and the faceless wonders of New Jersey.

Brennan liked widows: big girls. Not the mothers of little girls.

"Holy Mary," Hackett said suddenly. "That's what she wouldn't tell us, remember? The mother, remember? She—"

Long looked around, lost. "The mother? What mother?"

"Those sweet nothings he was whispering in her ear. Mary Stephens, for Chrissake. The stuff she wouldn't tell Moylan, remember? He was swearing."

"Small wonder she wouldn't tell him," Long said softly, and smiled. "Him swearing in her ear. To keep the lad alert. Or to get it up in the first place." Not looking at Hackett, he asked, "What d'you think he was saying to her, huh?"

Hackett shrugged, veering from their shared maleness. He was thinking how little they knew one another, he and Long. How, if the world should come to a sudden end, men might understand the means of their destruction, the nuts and bolts; but never the minds that fashioned it. And would not question their ignorance. Perhaps it was just as well, this acceptance of ignorance: Hackett was veering again. Perhaps it was the price of privacy.

"Trouble ahead," Long said abruptly, staring at the bridge as if it were an approaching enemy.

Another stupid truck, this one stalled in the right lane, had them poised over the Hudson for a full fifteen minutes.

"No way I'm gonna make that fight," Long said, still abrupt.

"Louis is gonna be around a long time," Hackett said, to cheer him up. To end what may have been a separating silence.

"Got your word on that, have I, Hackett?" Long said, dry again, but his body relaxed against the seat. He produced a large, unwieldy map.

It was darker on the New Jersey side. Invisible in the dusk, the Hudson lapped silent to their right. Even in broad daylight, though, the river could not be seen from this angle.

Junie Stephens would not have seen this part of the river either. Hackett was concentrating, picturing his second visit to Cahill's wall map, when he had marked the route as far as the crossroads where the convent would have to be. Marked it mentally, that is, to thwart the omnipresent Lewis. James—Wallace, rather—would have taken Junie across the river, probably on the West Street ferry, the promised boat ride, and from there they would have gone inland on the Erie. The Erie stop was closer to the crossroads, to his house, than the Central's, the walk shorter. And by then James would have been saving his energy for other things . . .

"So tell me about Greene Street," Long was prompting. "How come you went there, I mean. Hanrahan had already checked it."

"Funny thing about Greene Street," Hackett said, glad to talk. "Because the chances are James wasn't the one stealing the stuff. Chances are it was the usual warehouse grab." He saw suddenly how he was fitting into Long's image of him: dwelling on the irony rather than the facts. "Anyway, it's only because somebody at Greene Street walked off with a pile of their stuff that

Altman's remembered about the boxes being there." Sticking strictly to the facts, he brought Long up to date.

"You been holding out on me, Jim," Long said when he was through. "How come you knew he was a whatdoyoucallit, an Orangeman?"

Hackett smiled in the dark. "The same way I know everything else," he said evenly, and gave it time to sink in. "The kid told me."

Even with the credit she had amassed, it was hard to call her Ali in front of Long. Even in her absence, he was shielding her from the possibility of Long's impatience. Shielding himself, too, that went without saying. There was the business of not complying with the rest of Long's image: the father bit.

She would have realized hours ago that he was not going to meet her, and she would have gone on to rehearsal, or to Sol's. Remembering her bare hands, he hoped she had not waited more than a couple of minutes. He should have bought her a pair of gloves and called them a birthday present. He could have done that this morning, while he was at Altman's. No, not at Altman's. Any place but.

Houses, just a couple at first, began sprouting along the road. A ramshackle bus, the first vehicle they had seen in miles, came swaying toward them. Pinpoints of light ahead.

"Nyack," Long said with sudden authority, and Hackett pulled over for gas. They both took a leak; Long first.

He doesn't like the dark, Hackett thought as he watched Long scurry back to the car. The Pride of the Tenth.

"You see the *Journal* today?" Long asked Hackett when he returned. "There's this item about these twelve cops in Trenton, see, who were taking this exam, and one of the questions they was asked was"—he struggled and triumphed—"was who wrote this book. *Ivanhoe*. Not one of the poor bastards knew it, of course. How it got in the paper, only one of the questions'd got anything to do with police work, and they all raised holy hell about it." Unthinking, Long pocketed Hackett's change from the gas. "You heard of that book, Jim? You know who wrote it and all?"

Hackett was amused. "Yeah. I heard of it."

"I knew you'd know. I said to Ryan this morning, I said,

'That's the kind of thing that bastard Hackett would know.' Ask him, Ryan."

I will, first thing.

Yet Hackett was touched when Long did not press him for the author. He trusts me, he thought, and began to wonder then if he should have earlier told Long about the Orangeman theory. Long only likes facts, he reminded himself. Besides, it had helped speed things up a bit, is all. It wasn't important. Uneasy, he found himself trying to justify other conduct, and that alone set him off on another bout of wondering.

"Scott," he said, to break his chain of thought. "The guy who wrote it. But I never read it."

As if in congratulation, Long produced refreshments.

"Rossi's Chivas," Hackett guessed, first sip, and Long chuckled in appreciation.

"Make a right here," he said.

Not right, city boy, Hackett corrected silently. We are turning north. He was remembering the wall map.

The silence grew with the dark. The new road was narrower, and untrimmed branches snapped against the windows, startling Long. He took to the flask each time it happened. There was no sign of life, no dog rushing out to be hit by what could have been the last car left on earth. The lack of traffic was eerie. It was hard to believe they were so close to New York City.

Everything changed when we left the river, Hackett decided. Civilizations always begin along rivers. It's after we left the river that the scattered houses, nestled like encampments within the trees, had vanished entirely. All that gleamed along the road now were large patches of frost; as if, Hackett thought, as if houses had once stood there and had dissolved like salted slugs into the ground.

He sniffed. "I can smell water," he said. "We supposed to be near water?"

"Christ," Long said in alarm and rustled the map. "Christ, no. We ain't supposed to be nowhere near water." He groaned. "No chance I'm gonna make that fight tonight, is there?"

No chance, Hackett was thinking, would Junie Stephens have survived longer than two hours after leaving church. Allow fifteen minutes for the subway ride to West Street; another fifteen on the ferry. An hour at the outside on the train, then the walk from the train to the house—twenty minutes, say, if the house was right opposite the convent as claimed. Less than two hours. No chance James would have let himself get lost.

19

It was always possible, Ali thought, that she had not understood him. She turned her head against the wind off the river. Perhaps he'd meant that he would meet her at the house.

Girlfriends come and girlfriends go, but a wife is forever. Except for Sol's. Sol's wife had died ten months after he married her, and Ali could tell by the way Sol talked about her, as if she was someone in a story, that it must have been a long time ago. Ali wondered what he could really remember about her after all these years.

It was not like that with Junie. Yet sometimes it was. Junie kept slipping around in time. Sometimes it seemed to Ali that Junie had just vanished, sometimes that she was long dead. But not dead like someone who had once used salt instead of sugar, who had done a hundred silly things that became sweet in Sol's telling. Junie was always real; someone who should be doing her homework right now, who would be doing it, if . . .

Ali shied from her thoughts as from the wind.

Mama, she whispered then, struck empty.

But Junie would be buried soon, and after that she would stay still; fixed in time. After that, Ali would never see him again.

Their birthdays were the same week. Give or take a couple of decades, he had told her. When she was twenty, he would be forty. When she was eighteen, he would be only thirty-eight.

There was no sign of the car on Seventeenth Street, and Ali stumbled down the steps with streaming eyes.

She lighted the gas mantle but not the stove. The point was to find the long dress, then get out of the cold kitchen as fast as she could and see if he meant that he would meet her at the CYO, like before. She bundled the long dress in an expert roll, smiling at the memory of his sitting there with his coat on. "Brightly shone the moon that night, Though the frost was cruel"; then stopped humming, seeing the room with his eyes. Everything is so ugly, she thought, and his ties looked the kind that cost five dollars, easy.

Crossing to put out the light, she paused in front of the painting over the old fireplace. It was the only proper picture in the house, with a glass and a frame and all. Junie thought the picture was scary, the way Jesus' eyes seemed to follow her around the room, and Ali had had to explain about the eyeballs being in the middle. Then Junie had got scared about that, about Ali saying Jesus had eyeballs like an ordinary man. It was sacrilegious.

In a way, Ali thought, Jesus' eyes were still watching Junie.

In a way, in a lopsided way—she was smiling now, she was pretty sure he would show up at the rehearsal—Jesus was watching her, too.

One hand would not work, she knew that from past efforts, and she put down the bundle to straighten the picture with both hands. Though by the time she got back from the play, it would have tilted again.

Adjusting it critically, one eye half closed, Ali could see faintly her own reflection in the glass. A shadow passing across Jesus' eyes.

20

They were lost on the wrong side of a skinny lake. They were on a back road heading toward Haverstraw; or possibly toward West Nyack. Once they put their heads together, it was easy to figure out what had happened.

"I see where we are," Long said, sounding surprised. "I see what we did wrong. You made one right too many."

Hackett let it pass.

He was retracing cautiously when, without warning, red eyes glared in the headlights. Almost too late Hackett swerved, barely missing a tree. He had adjusted to the absence of dogs, but he'd forgotten all about nature's fucking bounty.

"Sweet Virgin," Long said, sipping and crossing himself at the same time, which was some feat to witness. "What in hell was that?"

Shaken, Hackett straightened the car. "Four legs and branches all over its head," he said when his breathing was normal. "A deer?"

"Nice," Long said. "To get run in by the locals for slaughtering the livestock."

He meant wildlife.

"Jesus!" he went on. "Ain't this the hunting season? That mean those half-wits up there are prowling around with guns? In the dark? Jesus." He took another swig. "Maybe we should think about this. We're a long way from home, and he's crazy as a bedbug, right?"

"He probably don't carry. He probably smothered her," Hackett said, then realized that was something else he had not told Long. It was the man's own fault. Long could not make a career out of suspicion, then expect people to confide in him. Even the rawest priest knew better.

"We could still call on the local boyos," Hackett added. "It might take some explaining, of course, why we left it so late, but we could still do that. That way," he ended, to shame Long, "you might still make the fight."

Long stared out the window, working out the implications. "No," he said finally. "We couldn't do that. Besides, he probably ain't up there, right? You think he's up there?"

It was a subject close to Hackett's heart.

"We know he was in the city when he sent the doll," he said. "And he could've gone back up there by now, who knows? Sooner or later, he'll go back up, that seems to be his pattern. What I do believe, though, is Junie Stephens is up there. Her we'll find, but maybe not in the dark."

At mention of the dark, Long peered out the window. "I hate the fucking country," he said then, and looked doubtfully from the map in his hand to the blackness outside; for all the world, Hackett thought, like a pirate who's stolen a treasure chart and now fears it is a fake.

Long rustled the map again. "The kid. She told you he smothered her sister?"

"Not exactly. He told them stories—bedtime stories, I mean, not lies."

"He told them those, too," Long said, anxious to get back in the picture. "Lies. Tell me, Jim. You think he's done this kind of thing before? Killed kids, I mean."

"I do." That came from himself. Ali had said nothing to suggest the idea. Nothing concrete, that is.

"Me, too." Long nodded. "But he ain't armed, you think. You hope. Besides, he only goes after widows and orphans, right?" Reassured by his own logic, he settled back again, then swiveled. "That's New City, that was." He consulted the map. "It's supposed to be straight ahead," he added, as if he wouldn't put it past the place to move. "Then it's a left at Bonner's, that's a hunting-supply store. After that, we're in clover."

A cramp menaced Hackett's stomach. It's excitement, he told himself, and flexed his hands on the wheel. At a similar point in her journey, Junie would have been excited, too. And James . . .

"You ever wonder," Long said, "how come we have to go through New Jersey to get to New York? What kind of planning's that? I ask you."

Hackett smiled with relief. The old patroons, slaughtering the Indians like deer, had not worried their heads over such details. In his mind he saw the names on the map: Catskill, Peekskill, Sparkill. "Kill" must mean something in Dutch; a river crossing or a mountain, maybe. Something geographical, at any rate; harmless. Not like "kill" in English. "Kill" in English meant smothering a child who trusted you. Whose few good memories you wiped out in the terror of her final moments. Watch it, Hackett, he told himself. You'll be weeping at the wheel next. All those double-u's. Like an ad in the newspaper. Wallman's wonderful white sale. Wonderful winter white sale.

"Slow down. We don't wanna miss the turn," Long said, and consulted his pad. "After the turn, we go a couple of miles, past the Anderson place, you can tell which one that is by the new one being built across from it. Just before we get to the next crossroads, our place is on the right. Got it?"

Hackett, concentrating on the road, was slow on the uptake. "Anderson?"

"He's some sort of writer. Who lives next door to some sort of actor. The guy in Haverstraw told me all about them, like they was the Statue of Liberty and George Washington all rolled into one. Trying to make me out ignorant, this bastard that goes around hiring undesirables. A little knowledge goes a long way with some people, huh?"

Famous, too, he had told Ali. Maxwell or Sherwood; either one rich enough to have two houses. "Once you know who he is," Hackett said, "you see what a loose mouth he was."

"That's always the way. Once you know. Besides," Long added with rare generosity, "he had no way of knowing how quick she was. You know, how much she was gonna remember."

That still left him stupid; because he should have known. But that, Hackett saw, was a judgment which included Long. He kept his mouth shut.

"Okay. This is where we go left." Long pointed. "That's Bonner's."

A small hut boarded against the bears.

His mouth dry, Hackett negotiated the turn onto South Mountain Road. Don't let the rich folk be home in either of their houses. Don't let them turn on a light when we pass.

A few yards in, and a house appeared on the left. Impossible to tell in the dark if it was worthy of a rich man. A few more yards, then another house, this one set farther back from the road. You would have thought they would have bought more space, more privacy with their money. There seemed to be more houses on this one deer track . . .

Long was panting whiskey in his ear. "See that pile of stuff? That has to be the Anderson place, right?"

Hackett nodded. He was having trouble with his breathing again. If the rich folk are home, let them be asleep. He checked the time. How could it not be eight-thirty yet? They'd been in the car forever. Did country types go to bed this early? The noise of the motor was enough to wake the dead. If James was around, he would hear it and run. Rigid with tension, Hackett unclenched his aching jaws.

Long grabbed his arm. "That's the convent, ain't it? That light there?"

Hackett braked as gently as he could. His throat was now so dry it hurt.

"There it is," he breathed, and nodded at the little shack not ten feet from the front of the car. "There's the palace he promised Mary Stephens."

21

Once upon a time there was a baby girl who was fat and pink and who hardly ever cried. I say that last part only to give the tale a ring of tradition, for the truth is, from the cradle on, girls make more fuss than boys—if Matron can be believed. That's why she worked with boys. Girls, she used to tell us, need the authority of men to check their natural waywardness. Girls and women both, it has been my lot to discover, and poor little effect our presence seems to have, even then. But be that as it may.

Once upon a time there was a baby girl who was fat and pink and who hardly ever cried. Every morning the proud mother would wheel her baby to the river, where the mother would sit dreaming and the baby would lie cooing, protected by white netting from the flies. Now it chanced one day, as the mother was arranging the netting, that some fairies were hovering nearby, as fairies will—more in Mayo than in Manhattan, I grant you, but they are all over the place and especially do they congregate near water—and these fairies grew excited at the baby's beauty. Determined to have her for their own, they dazzled the mother's eyes with a beam of sunlight, and while she was thus blinded, they stole away the child. In her place they left a squalling fetch: a double.

Years passed. The changeling became a maiden, and though by this time she bore all the stigmata of her kind—she was wan and wizened and ugly as sin—the mother never once suspected that she was rearing a substitute. That's what happens when your mother doesn't come from Ireland, for your average Irish mother would have known right away that the child was an imp and would have gone through the rituals—burning off its nose or roasting it alive—that would have put an end to the whole sorry situation.

Not everyone, however, was as besotted as the mother. Ordinary mortals, who had no way of knowing the changeling's dark secret, would shun her for her lying tongue and spiteful tricks. Even the fairies kept their distance. Except for the company of the mother, the girl was left to fester more or less alone.

Now it comes to pass that the time draws near for the maiden to fulfill her destiny. For two days she has been hissing, conjuring a spell that will send a soul to Satan (changelings, being heathen, take delight in such things), and unless she is dealt with now, she will assume forever the mortal shape she has usurped. Behold her then, in her dank chamber, humming magic chants as she lies coiled within her rags. Her eyes are black with power, and her smile turns inward. She is bewitched.

She looks up. Perhaps she has heard something. But all she does is cross the room and touch the picture on the wall. There is red in the picture—red is the color of magic the world over; facts are weapons—and she is trying to absorb it, to add to her power. Her lips move. Now she is murmuring: a stronger spell, a pishogue. Suddenly she turns. This time she *has* heard something. The door is gliding slowly open.

Hate glows from her face. She steps back quickly; bumps into the picture. She has recognized her visitor, engorged with righteousness for his name's sake. Now in the form of a dragon, next in the shape of a goat, yet always with the gift of human speech, he is the one who comes to wicked children in their sleep. Nightmare to the unholy.

Her eyes, blue up close, are black again. Her face whitens; even her lips blanch. Save for the heaving of her chest, she is utterly still, immobile with the weight of her sins. Evil virgin. Chaste evil. Who knows that nothing now can help her. Not the red in the picture, not the red in the scarf around her neck. For the dragon has come to fight fire with fire. She has more than met her match this time: The day of judgment is at hand.

Sly as a serpent, she tries to wriggle out of it anyway. She slithers around the table, then darts back, out of reach. She seeks another route, but rescue is as likely as pity in the room that day, and fire blocks her escape. She is trying to slide under the table when words stronger than her spell make her falter. First one kicking leg, then the other, is snared.

Now at last the demon pleads. But it's late, more than late, and she knows this, too, for she is a snake again, writhing and repulsive and slimy to the touch; more like a sea serpent than a snake. She is deaf to her own moans, for the whispering in her ear rolls like thunder through the room. She is blind to her own tears, for a darkness descends as black as her eyes, as black as her soul, if she had one, which she never now will. There is a puff of smoke, a stench of burning, and the abomination is cast into hellfire. Burn, burn, burn. If of the devil, burn. But if of God and the saints, Be safe from harm.

It's what her mother should have said years ago.

There is enough red around the room at this point to bring magic to a whole troop of fairies, but the imp is beyond their aid. Her days of mischief are done: You can tell by the way her eyes have turned to blue again. (Don't worry. There's not going to be a color reprise here about her black soul or her white lips, though you have to understand that fairy stories go in for that sort of thing: Red Riding Hood, Snow White, Golden Bird.) Her days of mischief are over, and only just in time. The slender feet protruding are those of a real mortal. The change had already begun.

And so, his work accomplished, the dragon returns to the land of the blessed, away, far away, by the banks of a shining stream, and lives happily ever after.

Follow me, said Jesus, and let the dead bury their dead. That would be the Jesus striding around Capernaum, strong in the power of His glory. Not the frail stick of a man that is the fashion in churches nowadays. Not the feeble witness on the wall. For there is more red now in the picture than the devil's whore ever touched; more than the painter intended. Scarlet cataracts seal the vision of Our Lord. The Son of God is blind.

Yet can the children of the bridechamber mourn, as long as the bridegroom is with them?

22

Except for the solitary window gleaming from the convent opposite, the darkness was total. Mother Superior must be balancing the books and saving on the light bill, Hackett decided, and shivered. It was unnatural for people to live way in the back of beyond; especially women, especially at night. Cities were progress, everyone knew that; like forks over chopsticks. Hackett shivered again.

Standing beside him, Long pushed open the door. Gun in one hand, flashlight in the other, he probed the blackness. Nothing moved within the shack. No sounds.

It's the cold, Hackett told himself as the hair began to prick at the nape of his neck, along his arms. Shit, it's nerves. James could be lurking anywhere. Taking courage from Long's wariness —he was not, Hackett noticed, exactly rushing bold into the lion's den either—he forced himself to step forward and into the room.

"It's hot," he murmured, pulling his hand back from the stove. "And someone's just turned out the lamp." The whole place stank of kerosene.

Long entered slowly, and the beam of light found another door. Again nothing. The second room was empty, but for the sound of their joint breathing.

"He's gone," Hackett said, still speaking low. Whispers carry farther, not the words so much; the hissing. "He heard the car and ran."

There was no light in the convent's top window when they went back out. Together they crunched their way around to the rear of the cabin, stumbling on the uneven ground. Just as well there's no moon, Hackett was thinking when Long tugged at his arm. Hackett froze with fear.

Somewhere ahead a man's voice in falsetto began to sing. "Away in a Manger." They stood there spellbound. A shudder joined them, then they separated, circling toward the sound.

"Hide-and-seek. Peekaboo. Fainights. Fins." The voice, dead ahead, was light and playful. There was no trace of the famous accent.

Long's flashlight stabbed with accuracy. Not two yards from him stood a man, his arms held high.

Even in the dark, even in the heavy coat, it was certain that he was slight; small. A good two inches shorter than Long. An unprepossessing Judas, and Hackett was simultaneously ashamed of his fear and disappointed in his quarry. This was the man that had launched a thousand cops—well, several hundred, anyway; who had made romance bloom in Mary Stephens' arid heart.

"Is it only the two of you, then?" the man said, and smiled. "You were making noise enough for an army." And it wasn't any strangling of vowels that now gave his words a twang; rather, it was the inflection that was unfamiliar. A flavor of Orange.

Long waved the gun at him. "You're surrounded," he said, gruff but good-humored, and Hackett heard the relief in his voice. Long had noted, and welcomed, the two-inch difference.

"I give up," the man said. "That's what I'm supposed to say, isn't it?" When they stared at him in silence, he went on, "Can I put my hands down? I mean. You *are* the law, aren't you?" For the first time he seemed edgy.

"The nippers," Long said to Hackett with a trace of his former superciliousness.

The man dropped his arms. "Can you do it in front? It's just that my foot is acting up right now, so it'd be better in front. It'll help with the balance." He held out his wrists, and Hackett, resisting the urge to look to Long for guidance, snapped on the handcuffs. "It isn't as if," the man added, "as if I tried to run away, is it?"

Leaving Hackett to wonder why he had not.

A partial answer, perhaps, was the lameness. On the walk back to the cabin, the limp that Greene Street had been blind to was making the man stumble; every other step he was clutching at Hackett. Then, too, there was the matter of the noise. Even if the man were running free, without handcuffs, there would still have been that. The night was full of sounds, of trees sighing and strange rustlings that were making Long as nervous as the man's erratic pitches, but the noise of the man's feet ricocheted much more loudly than did theirs on the frozen ground. For all his talk of armies.

A more complete answer, perhaps, was the old tried-and-true: Wallace, however unwittingly, had wanted to be caught. That would explain the sending of the doll, would account for the man's not hiding, silent in the bushes, waiting for the city slickers to cower in the rural dark, then take their leave as soon as decency allowed. That would also make Long right, yet again.

"No one wants a bullet in the back," Long was saying. "That's why you didn't run, shitface."

The closer he got to the cabin, Hackett saw, the closer Long got to his real self.

When, under the glow of the lamp inside—which the man had lighted at Long's bidding, Long watching the process through narrowed eyes, as at some arcane ritual—they got their first good look at him, Hackett at least was surprised. The man's appearance was positively bucolic. With his ruddy cheeks and his soiled hands, he looked like nothing so much as a healthy, if diminutive farm worker. His face was broader, less rat-like than

Hackett had imagined, and the eyes staring back at his were steady; blue or gray, it was hard to tell in the bad light.

There was no resemblance to Hauptmann. Except that both were immigrant carpenters. Murderers.

The man broke the speculative silence.

"Won't you sit down?" he said, host to unforeseen but by no means unwelcome guests. He indicated the two stools as if they were thrones. "I'm sorry about the mess, but I only just got back here myself. An hour ago."

Hackett shot him a look, but there was no sarcasm visible.

It was the lack of clutter that caught the eye, that gave to the place a look of austerity rather than poverty. A narrow bed stood too close to the stove. Behind the bed, a wall of tools hanging neat: planes, knives, saws, arranged according to size, the smallest at the top. An empty sink on the window wall, and a scarred table more or less in the center of the room. That, together with the two stools, was all that the room contained. The only mess, if you could call it that, was a book open on the table.

"You sit down," Long barked, his out-of-doors bonhomie now utterly vanished.

Hackett was working it out too slowly, but he guessed that Long was reacting to the man's composure, to the subtle assumption of equality, perhaps of superiority, that the man's air of calm gave him.

"I'll sit on the bed then, shall I?" And again there was the alien inflection. "The warmest seat in the house."

"It's not as hot as the seat we've got in mind," Long said.

The man shrugged within his outsize coat, a dark tweed with frayed cuffs, and Hackett was reminded of a small, loose-skinned dog; remembered, too, that in spite of the man's seeming frailness, there had been a hardness in the man's body when he had searched him, a mongrel toughness that matched the steely eyes. But his forehead was drenched in sweat.

"I know who you are," the man said as he perched himself on the bed. "You're Detective Long, aren't you? I've seen your picture in the papers."

Long played deaf. "Your name Robert Wallace?" he said, leaning back against the table.

"Ask me no questions, I'll tell you no lies," the man said.

As if he hadn't heard, Long asked, "You Robert Wallace?"

Taking his time about it, the man gave a slow nod.

Hackett found his voice. "Say yes," he ordered.

"Yes." No change of expression.

"Are you also known as Robert Wall, Robert James, John James? Hackett was reciting from memory, in the correct chronology.

The man frowned at the floor. "Who are you?" he said finally.

"I'm the one's gonna hurt you, you don't answer right," Hackett said, pleasantly enough, considering his picture wasn't in the papers. "Robert Wallace, John James," he pressed. "Any others you can think of?"

"I was James Wallace once," the man said after another pause that had Long drumming his fingers on the table. "But that doesn't count. That was in Pennsylvania."

"But Robert Wallace is your true name?" Long again, determined to go through the whole ritual. There was none of the flamboyance in his manner that Hackett had anticipated.

Wallace nodded, then looked at Hackett. "Yes."

"You live here?"

"Yes."

"This ain't your only abode?"

As if he had come to some private decision, Wallace took a deep breath. "My name is Robert Wallace," he chanted in a rapid singsong, "and under that name I maintain a room at 713 Amsterdam Avenue in New York City."

They were neighbors, Hackett realized with dull surprise. They could have passed each other umpteen times in the last six months.

"How old are you?"

Fifty, Hackett told himself. If he's a day.

"Fifty," Wallace said, and lapsed without warning into a full brogue. "I was born in Belfast, Northern Ireland, on March 26, the same day as Beethoven the composer, though not the same year at all." He looked from one to the other, checking their reaction, and they stared back, stony-faced.

"What's your occupation? Your job?"

"I'm a shipwright by trade."

"Carpenter," Hackett translated for Long's benefit, and Wallace favored him with another look.

"Sometime in March of this year, did you place a notice in the personals column of the *Police Gazette*, and did you, in response to a letter . . ."

Separating himself from Long's endless prologue, Hackett wandered over to the table. It was a school exercise book open there, the kind that had sums on the back. Checking and confirming, Hackett turned it over. $11 \times 11 = 121$; 8 pints $= 1$ gal. Inside, the ruled sheets were covered with Wallace's even handwriting. Lacking a live audience, Wallace had taken to putting his fairy stories down on paper. Consistent, truncated man.

Hackett looked up to see Wallace studying him, and in the second before the man's eyes settled into blandness, Hackett caught again the cold appraisal of their opening stare.

Watch for his moments, then, Hackett told himself. Smiling and lying, he is used to taking care of the minutes.

"Sure and you haven't cautioned me yet," Wallace said to him. "Aren't you supposed to do that first?" The brogue was back. He used it, Hackett guessed, as a device to distance them. Language as barrier, he knew all about that.

Hackett swung on Long. "Hark at the man, all rules and regulations." He turned back to Wallace. "Is that what they taught you at Sing Sing?"

"He's enough to make a saint swear," Wallace said, shaking his head at the floor. Fresh sweat broke out on his brow. "Things have come to a pretty pass when you can't trust the law to keep the law. A pretty pass, I must say."

Under other circumstances, Hackett could see that he might have found the self-righteous tone amusing.

Long, impatient with the sidetracking, leaped in.

"I am going to ask you some questions about the disappearance of one Frances June Stephens—"

"Why didn't you say so?" And now it was Wallace's turn to find something amusing in the situation. "I know where she is. She's with the fairies at the bottom of my garden. A little bird

told me." The smile broadened. "That would be the early bird.
The one that catches the worm."

"She's dead, you mean." Long was still going by the book.

"She's alive in my heart, and that's what counts. Memory is
immortality, look it up."

"You're gonna be looking up at the fucking ceiling, you
don't get on with it," Long said. Without glancing at one another, he and Hackett approached the bed together, making a
threat of their size above him. "She's dead," Long insisted.

Another maddening pause, another private decision; more
sweat. Wallace lifted shackled hands and wiped his forehead.
Dirt streaked his face, increasing the laborer look.

"December is an unlucky month for me," he said finally.
"This'll be my fourth Christmas in jail, my second in Bellevue.
Because that's where I'll end up now. I know the rules." He
shifted farther back on the bed, away from them. "It was irresistible impulse. You know, like Leopold and Loeb. I knew what
I was doing, I always know that. Nobody's ever been able to say I
didn't know what I was doing. It's just that I'm not responsible.
Look it up. I've been in Bellevue, I don't know right from wrong,
it's all there in black and white. I can sit here and talk rubbish all
night long, I can sit here and talk about the weather or Jesus or
whatever else takes my fancy, and there's nothing you can do
about it. For the sins of the father shall be visited upon the children unto the seventh generation. In the year of Our Lord 1935.
No, '34. Bellevue, I'm talking about."

"Irresistible impulse," Long said, flat, as if it was all he had
heard of the speech. "You killed her."

"Let's talk about the weather," Hackett said after a while.
"About what a cold winter we've been having. That's because
we're in New York State, where we have hot summers and cold
winters, have you noticed that fact, Mr. Wallace? You should
have done her in California. They're not so sharp out there about
hot and cold, right and wrong, stuff like that. All that sun, it
blurs the distinctions. Makes them more generous about sharing
their air with slime like you. And more religious," he added.
"They would've liked your line of rubbish more. The electric
chair, I'm talking about."

Without moving his head, Wallace slid his eyes around to look at Hackett. It's something he's seen done in a movie, Hackett thought, but the hair stirred on his neck. Like a snake about to strike, that's what he looked like.

All that Wallace said, however, was "Fools rush in where wise men fear to tread."

"You live with a lame man, you learn to limp," Hackett retorted, and they were both still, staring at one another.

"At the bottom of the garden." Long was reading from his notebook. He nudged Wallace's knee with his gun, produced again for the purpose. "Show us."

"I'm not hiding anything," Wallace said, and edged clumsily off the bed. "I stand here with clean hands and a pure heart. As the psalmist says," he added, for Hackett.

"Not such clean hands," Hackett pointed out.

Wallace looked down at them. "Ah, that. That was a little obfuscation." Again he glinted at Hackett.

Long picked up the lamp. "What's he talking about now?" Out of his depth, but with the confidence of an expert in the shallows.

"Sugar and spice and everything nice," Wallace said before Hackett could answer. "Not so nice anymore, actually. She's in pieces, you see, and they always go faster when they're in pieces, don't they?"

The time had come to resurrect Junie Stephens. The resurrection and the death, Hackett thought, closing the door behind him. She would be buried at last in a proper grave, and Long would lead Mary Stephens from the church, pausing on the steps to make life easier for the photographers.

Ignoring Hackett, Wallace was sticking close to Long. He was limping badly again, but keeping up with Long's hurried pace. From behind, you couldn't tell that one was a cop, one a killer. Sharing the lamp like an equal, Wallace looked like a disabled but dedicated member of the team. Certainly not as anyone responsible for the grisly business ahead. Hanging back in the dark, Hackett could be taken for the perpetrator.

Wallace stumbled and clutched at Long. Long stopped short.

"There's a hole here," he warned. "And stones."

"That's it," Wallace said. He crouched down. "I'll find it for you, shall I? I just had it, just before," he explained, all helpfulness, and Hackett hoped it was the stones that were clunking against the handcuffs. Find what? he wondered, half knowing.

A gust of wind struck them, and Long shivered openly. "It's cold as a witch's tit out here," he said, but neither he nor Hackett made any move to hurry things along.

There was a dank smell of newly turned earth; more clanking. Hackett began breathing through his mouth. Six months was a long time, but he didn't want to put it to the test. He did not trust the wind not to turn.

"I know it's here somewhere," Wallace said, still fishing. "I had it just before. And here it is." Two-handed, he held it up to Long.

It's the graveyard scene from *Hamlet*, Hackett thought in despair and turned away. Long, taken unawares by the coroner role, stepped back hurriedly. Too late, he swung the lamp wide.

Wallace straightened, wobbling. "You ought to take it," he urged in the same spirit of mutual help. "After all, it's the most important part. There's not a dentist around who wouldn't give his eyeteeth for—" He stopped and smiled. "Besides, it's very mucky down there."

Oh God, Hackett thought, did I touch his hands when I put on the bracelets? Yes, he had touched them. Fresh from Junie.

Relishing their squeamishness and the authority it gave him, Wallace slowly turned the skull, appraising. "The lower jaw is broken, that's why it looks so small. It broke off as you arrived. Because you arrived, actually. I should've got rid of it before, but I wanted her to stay together." He crouched again. "There. It's back where it belongs. With the rest of her." There was a soft clink.

As Wallace stood up, Long barked: "Stay where you are." He stooped. "What's this?"

"Tools of the trade, tools of the trade. I forgot all about them. They really let the cat out of the bag, don't they?"

"Obfuscation," Hackett reminded Long. "Our carpenter fancies himself a dentist."

"Sweet fucking Virgin," Long said, though whether it was the idea or the pliers in his hand that upset him was hard to tell.

"There's more than one way to skin a cat, if you know what's what," Wallace said.

Skin a cat. Fools rush in. Ali had not told him about the tag lines.

Wallace was still jumping from role to role; from host to comrade-in-arms. At the moment he was playing teacher. Like an on-site archaeologist, he was pointing out to Long the original position of the body, the reasons for its rapid deterioration, the placement of the boulders. At intervals Long would nod. He was keeping well away from Wallace's clutchings this time around.

The sounds went on behind them—twigs walking, bushes crashing into one another—but for all the other signs of life, they could be three men alone on the moon. Where it would make sense, Hackett reasoned, that one of them was a lunatic. Because, he saw, the man was raving. An undernourished troll in an outsize coat who happened to be crazy.

It was not the religious ranting. For all Hackett knew or cared, the ranting could be—probably was—a sham calculated to land Wallace safe in Bellevue. It was the realization that Wallace did not know—and he did not; Hackett would go bail on it—that it was crazy to dig unmoved through the bones of a child you have murdered, then discuss her dismemberment as if it were a cold spell or some other topic that sprang as casually to mind.

Crazy or not, whichever; either way, he should die. After what he had done, it was unthinkable that he not die. After that, he could never be as other men were, could never, should never, belong anywhere. He had in fact never belonged anywhere, and Hackett for a moment felt the man's terrible isolation. Something close to pity stirred, but only for a moment. It made him feel disloyal to Ali, this lack of hate for Wallace. Then, too, the gods might be listening.

On the way back to the cabin, Wallace, repeating himself, described Junie's death again, but incidentally now; as a detail in a more elaborate rite. He had smothered her. "A gentle death," he threw off into the darkness. He seemed most proud of the care he had taken not to spill any blood. On the floor, he meant.

It was a buoyant performance, shifting effortlessly from the macabre to the matter-of-fact, then back again.

But get him on the stand, Hackett reflected, and there'll be no Bellevue for him. He'll talk himself to death. It was the cheerfulness that would fry him.

Hackett stumbled into Wallace, who had stopped.

"You came here in that?" Wallace was noticing the car for the first time. "That's not a police car."

Long pushed him into the hut. The stove had smoked up the place in their absence, but at least it was warm in there.

Why don't I feel more? Hackett wondered. He tried to picture Junie Stephens in the shack. It would have been warm then, too, from the sun, and she would have been trapped, and he . . . But Hackett's mind blanked and his head began to ache.

"So you don't know right from root beer, you said," Long was saying. "So how come you run away? After you killed her. How come you hid, you didn't know it was wrong?"

"I didn't hide," Wallace objected, apparently serious. "I went into retreat. For the sake of her soul."

"For the sake of her body, you mean," Long said. "You do it to her before or after?"

Wallace's smile slipped. "Do what?"

"You rape her before or after?"

There was a place in the world for people like Long. You didn't have to like it, but you had to admit it: They belonged. They were more useful than most: They cleaned the streets of bodies in the plague, they ferreted out the potatoes in the famine and asked the questions too dirty for the squeamish to deal with. He wasn't a bad guy, Long.

Wallace suddenly did not care for people like Long. He wrinkled his nose fastidiously. "It wasn't like that," he said, and cleared his throat. "I had no wish to make her suffer."

"It was after, you're saying."

Let us pray, Hackett thought. He wandered over to the smoking stove.

"It's always going wrong, that stove," Wallace offered. He

seemed glad of the distraction. "I'm always having to fix it. It's just that I haven't had time . . ."

Hackett swung on him. "What's been keeping you so busy? Killing little girls?"

Wallace retreated to the bed. "I know who you are," he said when he had settled there. "You're the one's been seeing our Alice. Alice Blue Gown, I called her, did she tell you that? Not that you can believe a word she says. Lady Muck, I call her, but just to myself, you understand. Did she tell you how she never once thanked me, and me putting the food in her mouth for a month? Lying to her elders and betters, she didn't tell you that part." He seemed to have worked himself up to genuine anger. "Her lying tongue and her spiteful tricks. She was always too big for her boots, that one."

"This one?" Long said at the wall. The lowest, the largest knife.

"What?" Wallace turned. "Yes," he said, almost absently, as if, Hackett thought, as if he was having trouble concentrating on anything so trivial. "And the saw next to it as well. I didn't really need the saw, she was so fine-boned. But I didn't want to make a mess of her."

"Course you didn't." Hackett up close was savage. "Any more than you wanted her to suffer, right?"

"Why'd you send the doll?" Long asked then.

Wallace stared thoughtfully at Hackett. He moved back on the bed, away from Hackett, and his face was in shadow, unreadable.

"It was God's will," he said finally. "I'd planned on doing it all along. I used to lie on this bed here, thinking about how I'd do it. I'm not sure when the idea first came to me, but once it came, I knew it had to be done. It was ordained, you could say."

"Shades of Bellevue, it's our religious nut again." Hackett was belittling on purpose, to dispel a sudden queasiness in his gut. In the smoke-filled room, Wallace was beginning to look more and more like an evil gnome squatting on the bed. "You've got to watch out when he starts invoking the Almighty. Who's got nothing better to do with His time, mind you, than guide our specimen here to the Post Office."

"I don't have to take his guff," Wallace told Long. "It was God's will. He sent me a vision."

"It was God's way," Hackett corrected. "His way of getting you collared. He sent you us."

"Otherwise she would have sent my soul to Satan. She was bewitched."

"You pathetic piece of shit," Hackett began softly, then stopped, halted by some distraction, some inconsistency in the man's manner. It was the look on his face, perhaps. In shadow, his eyes looked like black holes. Skull sockets; and teeth. Wallace was smiling at him.

"Do you know he's been seeing her on the sly?" Wallace said, soft as Hackett. "Courting her? Did you know that about him? I'm not the only pebble on the beach around here."

Hackett loomed, threatening, but Wallace went on, still soft, still smiling; as if he knew about the state of Hackett's insides. "I know who you are all right. You're the one who's been whispering to her in the car. Stroking her hair. I'm not blind, I knew what you were up to."

Congestion, smoke, was affecting Hackett's vision. He hit Wallace hard across the cheek.

"Not the face, Jim," Long said. Then: "Who? Seeing who?"

Wallace held his cheek. "Tell him he'd better not hurt me," he said, speaking to Long but staring straight at Hackett. "Tell him if he hurts me again, I'm going to hurt him back. Two can play at that game, an eye for an eye, tell him. Two eyes for two eyes, more like, only I'm not the blind one. I'm the one with eyes. I've seen what he'll never get to see, tell him. I've been where he'll never get to go. God's will be done. He's not the only one to whisper in her ear."

There was a sound like pencils snapping. Hackett had hit him again.

"Christ, it'll show, Jim."

But the sound had snapped something in Hackett's head, he fancied he could hear brain cells shuddering into life; catching up, finally, with his gut. God's will be done. It was ordained: Wallace's words. He had not been talking about the sending of the doll. Squatting on the bed, he had been describing, savoring, a different vision entirely. Breathless with dread, Hackett was drowning in a sea of poison. Whispering in her ear.

"You've asked for it now." Wallace's mouth hung slack but his eyes were steady. "You need another doll to play with. Because Alice Blue Gown has changed her color. She's black by now. Black is her body—"

And then Hackett was on him. "Oh God, make him dead," he was yelling above the stream of obscenity. "Make him dead." Over and over, his voice vibrating with the shock. He was smashing Wallace's head, rhythmically, against the iron bedpost.

"Let him go, for Chrissake, Jim." Urgent yet distant.

But Hackett could not let him go. Not until the legs stopped thrashing and the hands stopped clawing and the tongue protruded, silent.

Yet even then there was not silence. Even then the words were crashing through Hackett's head.

In the part of his brain that was not frozen, the thought rose unbidden: Long had been wrong. They're always shy about the sex part, Long had said, and he was wrong.

Hackett looked down and saw that his hands were shackled with blood.

After a while—ten seconds, ten minutes, Hackett never found out—Long said shakily, "Let him go, Jim," and Hackett let him go. He turned wonderingly to Long, and after another pause, Long in the same faraway voice said, "You're a lot of things before you're smart, Hackett. You've fucking well killed the bastard."

Hackett began to cough, and Long led him like a blind man to the sink. Backing off discreetly, Long bumped into the bed.

"We won't have any trouble with the county boys now," Long said, sounding a lot more normal. He dropped Wallace's wrists carelessly, so that they dangled over the bed. "There's no glory in a dead man."

Hackett closed his eyes and retched. When he opened them again, the room seemed very bright, and he wondered if Long had turned up the lamp. He washed his hands; then, to avoid looking at the pile of tweed on the bed, he washed them again. The shaking will stop, he told himself, studying them. Other things won't go away, but the shaking will stop. The shredded cuticle had been there before. I should paint it with bitter aloes, he thought. Like a kid.

Still examining his hands, he said, "Evil be to he who evil thinks."

Long pulled out his flask and waited until Hackett had taken a draught before saying, "We'll call it restraint. Momentary restraint without intent, right?"

With intent. And unrestrained, Hackett emended silently. He took another swig and looked. There was little left of the back of Wallace's head. Long had heard it crack, too, and anyway, there was the blood to prove it.

"Maybe he was lying. Maybe he didn't," Long said, and Hackett felt excluded from a world that could muster such vain optimism.

"That convent's gotta have a phone," Long said after another while.

"Pay as you go," Hackett said. "Though gambling is still the main source of police graft. A little off-the-cuff killing don't even rate, statistically. They're poor," he explained wearily. "The sisters. They're saying their prayers in the dark. We don't want to make them any poorer, do we?"

Long opened his mouth, then closed it. "You keep the lamp," he said finally.

Leaving the lamp where it was, Hackett followed Long out and climbed into the car. It's true what they say about the heart, he reasoned. Cut off from the night sounds beyond the car, he could hear it thundering.

The halo of Long's flashlight wheeled, and he stuck his head through the door. "What's the name of that guy you know at the morgue? The hebe?"

"Schnitzer." Hackett coughed to cover the hoarseness. "Larry Schnitzer. But he's not working tonight." He's having a party for his daughter.

"You got his number, then?" Long said with a noble show of patience. "His home number?"

Hackett told him. "He doesn't believe in the death penalty," he added. He meant to smile, but it came out a grimace.

"No embarrassing personal stuff, Jim," Long said heartily, and laughed in place of Hackett. He recrossed the road, his footsteps arrogant on the convent's tarmac apron.

He's making noise so he won't startle them, Hackett guessed. Off your knees, Angels of Mercy, there's a cop in sheep's clothing at your door. A wolf in cop's clothing, come to growl lies down your phone.

Time was still playing tricks, and Hackett was not sure how long he sat there in the dark. All he knew was that he was freezing, that he could shiver with cause, and the cold would seep up his spine and numb his brain. Hot or cold, neither condition was good for the brain. That's why he'd been so slow; why he hadn't picked up sooner.

I did it too fast, he thought then. Wallace had not had time to suffer.

Footsteps heralded the return of Long. Hark! the Herald Angels, and where's the cold, where's nature's fucking anesthesia? Furious, Hackett rolled down the window.

"That's done," Long said, sliding in. He did not look at Hackett.

Because New York had confirmed. Long had spoken to someone, probably Ryan, and it had been confirmed.

"Got a bit tricky back there," Long said. "Mother Superior wouldn't let the phone out of her sight, like I might walk off with it or something. But I got Cawley at the other end, I forgot he moved up here, and Cawley can figure out a whole case from a couple of grunts, so it all got done. Jesus, close that window, will ya?" When Hackett didn't move, Long leaned across him and rolled it up. "Me, I don't plan to die of pneumonia. I'm getting me a medal to shine."

Lights grew brighter on the road alongside. More lights sprang on in the convent. The car drew up next to them.

"Here they are," Long said, as if Hackett were deaf as well as blind. "You stay put, Jim." He climbed out.

Grunts and handshakes. Cawley the local law and friend.

Neither looked in Hackett's direction, and he ignored them to- tally. He heard them crunch their way to the back: Long showing off the bones. He heard them enter the cabin, heard their foot- steps when they emerged, uneven under the weight of their bur- den. They had wrapped him in a blanket from the bed.

"Simple is best," Long said, back in the car. "They get to keep the tools. Get to share in the glory, too, what's left of it. You driving?" When Hackett didn't answer, Long said carefully, "Because if you are, the idea is to follow them to Bellevue, okay?"

Hackett kept a three-car length between himself and Wal- lace's body, slowing down when necessary to preserve the proper distance. By the time they passed through New City, he was maintaining as well a two-foot margin between the car and the white line, where there was one. When the line vanished, Hack- ett did it by guesswork, his eyes flicking between the two points. Long's chatter was the only threat to his concentration.

"Simple is best," Long was saying again. He took a self- congratulatory swallow, but this time did not hand the flask to Hackett. "He died while attempting. We jumped him and his heart stopped. Schlitzer'll be there to fix the face."

"Schnitzer." Hackett made the effort out of loyalty to Long's "we": We jumped him. "With an 'n.'"

"With a pot of paint. Color him normal and stick his tongue back in. One shot for the file, and we can sew him up and throw him away. Maybe one for the papers, too, Schlitzer does his job right. You broke his jaw, too." He took another turn with the whiskey.

"That Cawley," Long went on, nodding at the car ahead. They were too close, and Hackett slowed. "I forgot he moved up here," Long said, smiling, "but I didn't forget why. A couple of grunts along those lines worked wonders, poor bastard. Before your time, those particular shenanigans, but it's just as well he quit. Valentine would've had his ass by now. What I'm saying, Jim, you don't have nothing to worry about. Cawley's one of the best."

There was no chance of getting lost on the way back, but still; sooner than Hackett would have believed possible, the bridge lights streamed across the sky. In thirty minutes Long would be saying out loud the words that were clinging like tendrils to Hackett's mind.

There was a sudden flow of traffic as they crossed the bridge, and a larger car forced Hackett over too far. He broke into a sweat as his wheel barely missed the white line. He slowed down, cursing, then had to accelerate to correct the distance with the lead car. He could not think how, on the way up, he had seen the bridge lights as a Christmas garland looping the river. Close up, they were ugly.

"They're the first real lights we've come to, you aware of that?" Long said. He had noticed Hackett peering. "Traffic lights, any kind of lights. Who in their right minds would wanna live out there? You tell me that."

Purple for Good Friday, candles for Easter. Dark is death; light is life. Life of light, Light of Light, Light of the World: It was something the Church had always known.

Long was looking at him. "Too bad about the kid," he said, safe in the light.

Adjusting to city conditions, Hackett on a whim reversed the distances: two car lengths behind, three feet from the white line. Flexible.

"How'd you figure it?" Long asked.

Hackett turned east on Forty-second Street. Follow my leader.

"I didn't figure it," Long added generously. "Most of the time I didn't know what the fuck he was talking about."

A moment of warning, that was all Hackett had been given. Had allowed himself.

The wheels of the car in front shrieked at the turn into Bellevue, and Wallace's scream echoed through Hackett's head.

Whisper in her ear, Wallace had said for the second time, and only then had Hackett known: the fact, not the words.

Black is her body to match her soul. I shaved her and I fucked her, fucked her to Kingdom Come. And the smoke went up the chimney just the same.

23

They were all being very nice to Hackett. Schnitzer, Cassidy, all of them; then inching away as they ran out of the right words.

This must be the way the fighter with the unpronounceable name was feeling now. Louis had won, of course. The stretcher bearers, not giving Wallace a second look, had hung around for a while to give a blow-by-blow on the fight; Long, strutting from his own sense of victory, had urged them on. From time to time he had batted an eye at Hackett, to see if he was interested.

Schnitzer and Long had inched their way to the door. Any minute now Hackett expected them to run off, leaving him alone. Schnitzer was making washing motions with his dry hands as he listened to Long. The stench of formaldehyde was strong in the little room.

Somewhere a door banged, and Long's head jerked. He was edgy, but the noise, Hackett knew, could not have come from the morgue. The autopsy room had swinging doors and they would have opened, silent, as she was passed through on the stretcher. He and Long would have been approaching New City around then.

"Crazy's no defense for what he did," Long was saying, not low enough. It was an argument going on over there. "Nothing's a defense, you listen to Ryan. He's the one brought her in."

Schnitzer, not looking at Hackett, murmured something.

Long nodded. "Sure, he's crazy. Crazy as a bedbug, so what? Tell me, Larry"—it was a discussion then, not an argument—"if you had a mad dog, you'd put him in a kennel? Like hell, you would. You'd put him out of his misery, right?"

The dog was being maligned by the comparison, but Hackett was too weary to ally himself with Long.

Long didn't need help anyway. Like a priest confident of conversion, he spun back to Schnitzer. "This way, we're all out of his misery. Did you see her? What he did to her?"

Cassidy, even now, was cutting her open. Finishing the job Wallace had started. Hackett shuddered.

Schnitzer came over and sat down next to him on the bench.

"It was only when she didn't show up after the CYO that Sol thought to look for her," Long said, joining them. "Around six-fifteen, according to Ryan. It was only when Sol got to the house and heard the neighbor that he knew anything for sure was wrong. Ryan says that Sol thought—" Long stopped.

"Lumps on your arm and spots on the sheets. Spots of blood," Hackett said, sounding loud in the quiet room. "That's how you know. People think they breed in mattresses, but they don't. They breed in wood. In baseboards, furniture, wood. There's an odor, too, so I'm told, but all I can remember is the smell of kerosene."

He was attempting to join in, too, but they stared at him, uncomprehending. They had forgotten what they were talking about. "Bedbugs," he reminded them. "They can hole up a full year without food. An entire year. They only come out when there's blood around." Forcing himself to gulp down the awful air, he battled sudden tears.

At six-fifteen he had been playing boy's games with a stupid truck, and she was already dead, waiting to be carried like a sack of coal to the morgue. A lump of coal is all you'll be getting in your stocking, Christmas, his mother would threaten. He and Long had still been in Manhattan when the call came through.

"It was all over in fifteen, twenty seconds," Schnitzer said.

"Save your fucking lies for your report. I'll save mine for mine. And while you're at it, put in a plea for mercy, why don't you, you soft-minded shithead." Mercy for Wallace's soul, Hackett meant. Clement kike, he'd called Schnitzer in better times. Did Jews believe in souls?

But all Schnitzer did was pat his arm. He never knew how close Hackett came to clubbing him.

"Ryan," Long began.

"Ryan?" Hackett looked around as if he had somehow missed noticing him. "Where's Ryan?"

"He's still in with Cassidy," Long said.

"Sol thought she was with me. Safe with me."

"He thought she was at the play, Jim."

"What I did wrong," Hackett said slowly, "was I didn't meet her at school. She would've been safe then."

"No. Because then he wouldn't't've been up there for us to grab tonight, he would've been hanging around here, waiting. And tomorrow, next week, he'd have reached her. Before we'd have reached him. Talk sense, Jim."

"What I did wrong," Hackett said after a while, and even Long was still. "What I did wrong, was I did it too quick. I should've stopped to think, and I should've hurt him more. He mutilated her."

When it became clear that Schnitzer was not going to say anything, Hackett turned to him. "How?" he asked.

Schnitzer was washing his hands with air again. "He smothered her. With her scarf. Twenty seconds at most."

"I don't mean that how," Hackett said, furious. "You know I don't mean that how."

Schnitzer ignored Long's gesturing. "He cut her throat," he said reluctantly. "But that was afterward. Cassidy says she was already dead by then."

"Was everything—afterward?" Schnitzer's smell was making Hackett nauseous, and he spoke between gulps.

Schnitzer closed his eyes. "Why are you doing this, Jim?"

"No." Watching Schnitzer, Hackett answered himself. "Everything was before."

"She would have been in shock, Jim. Almost from the beginning. Cassidy says—"

"Cassidy says, Cassidy says. What's Cassidy know about slime like Wallace? Or you either? He was talking to her, *talking* to her, telling her what he was gonna do to her. That was part of it for him. He would've made sure she could hear. That she didn't go into shock."

Ryan appeared. Hackett had not heard him come in.

"Cassidy's through," Ryan said as he struggled into his coat. "Cause of death, her death, asphyxia." He looked from Long to Schnitzer to Hackett, then nodded at Hackett. "You did good, what I saw. The blows to the head did it, but a few more seconds, Cassidy says, and his would have been asphyxia, too."

"One blow to the head. One single blow," Long said. "He fell, remember? Jesus."

"He said she was black," Hackett said to Ryan.

Ryan screwed up his face judiciously. "Not really black. What we figured, he must've been trying to burn off her hair or something. He shoved her head in the stove, see, and her face got scorched. Near as we can figure, something must've scared him off. She'd been dead maybe an hour when we found her, draped over the stove. Shameful. He used whatever was around. You know, the poker, the kitchen knife. Jesus, you should've seen the blood."

"That's enough," Long said.

The Romans had a word for it, Hackett was thinking. Several words. They had one for life's blood, another for blood flowing from a wound, another for the blood . . . Words or aqueducts, they were a people who knew the value of precision.

"Martha Butler found her," he told Ryan.

Ryan brought out his notebook. "Yeah. Martha Butler the neighbor. She's downstairs in Emergency. With the mother."

Hackett, veering from the image of Mary Stephens, said, "Nobody scared him off. He had the six-ten train to catch. He was that sort of person. Precise." Downgrading the Romans.

"Could be," Ryan said, then his eyes moved on; briefly he looked like a man with something on his mind. "Though that ain't all I'd call him, by Christ." He snapped his notebook shut. "Don't you worry none, Jim. You did real good," and as silently as he had arrived, he vanished down the hall. Rubber soles, Hackett told himself, wise.

Afterward, when Hackett tried to reconstruct the next hour, his clearest memory was of Cassidy stooping to lock the door of the little room with steady hands; hands that could always be counted on. Cassidy looked like your average bald man, your everyday human being—yuman bean, Cassidy pronounced it, Brooklyn, making it sound like a Mexican vegetable—yet he could witness the awfulness of the world and still remember to lock the door. He was like Long, which made sense. He had come on the double at Long's bidding.

Perhaps it was the formaldehyde, Hackett remembered thinking as he looked from Cassidy to Schnitzer. Which made the hair fall out. Then remembered thinking he didn't want to think about hair.

Hackett was conscious, too, of everybody going out of their way to call him Jim. For the rest, he could recall some of the things they said, but he was not always sure who it was they were talking about, nor the order in which they said those things.

Cassidy had entered with a uniformed cop Hackett didn't recognize. That had happened at the beginning, that part was easy. Schnitzer and Long, communicating by high-pitched frequencies that he couldn't hear, crossed together to join the other two, but not so close to the door. It's a cabal, Hackett decided. In a sealed tomb.

For secret plotters, though, they were growing pretty noisy. Why don't they keep their voices down? he wondered at one point. Their murmurs were echoing in the small room as if it were a hall. Someone will hear them. He covered his ears with his hands and listened to the sea in his head and thought of Coney Island, which was all right; but then he thought of the Aquarium and that led to the Automat. Feeling dizzy, he shoved his hands in his pockets. He was almost out of cigarettes.

"How'd he get in without being spotted?" Long was asking none too quietly. The question had not yet occurred to Hackett.

"He could've got in by the top stairs maybe. When a truck was blocking my view, or something. He must've planned it that way. Or maybe he climbed in through the back?"

Which explained the presence of the unknown cop. He was the blind and useless sentinel. The Apaches would have smeared him with honey and left him for the ants.

Cassidy talked on and on about blood. Blood under his nails, blood on his genitals. But his clothing was clean: Wallace.

"Naked," Long said, nodding. He was reading from the school exercise book. He must have brought it back with them: something else Hackett had not thought of.

Long took the book with him when he was called away to the phone, though Hackett would not have touched it with a barge pole.

"Cawley," Long said, re-entering. "He's back up there. He's called in the smoke eaters." By the light of New City's only fire truck, Cawley was at that moment digging up Junie Stephens' bones.

Hackett had forgotten her existence, let alone her death.

They were discussing her death now. At least he was fairly sure it was Junie they were talking about. The last time I was listening to this was when Wallace . . .

He had not known then.

"She was gagged," he said, but he could not say her name and they thought he was talking about Junie. "Otherwise," he clarified, "Martha Butler would have heard something."

"Now you're talking sense," Long said. "Jim."

"Saliva on the scarf," Cassidy said, but Hackett ignored the rest of what Cassidy tried to feed him.

Hackett knew that she had been conscious for the worst part. She had not been stupefied by fear, though he would have liked to pray so. She had never been made senseless by anything; not by grief, not by anything. He was unable to console himself, or unwilling.

Some part of his brain must have stirred, for he stood up, shaking, not caring that his voice was as unsteady as his legs. "Because she was gagged. So don't tell me she was out. Don't tell me that, okay? Just don't keep telling me that." Gulping in air to block the tears, not caring that he was making a public spectacle of himself.

He fumbled with the key. Cassidy took over and unlocked the door.

"The press is downstairs," Long called in warning, and as usual he was right. The lobby was alive with reporters, and one who came too close got bashed. At least, Hackett thought he might have hit someone, or maybe fell against someone. He was altogether vague about the entire last hour.

Somewhere along the line he remembered Cassidy stooping to lock the door. Or to unlock it. He was vague about the last part altogether.

Somewhere along the line he had made a public spectacle of himself. In front of Schnitzer and Long and Cassidy. And the cop who should or should not be eaten alive. It didn't matter, in front of Schnitzer. It didn't matter, in fact, in front of any of them; for the first time in his life.

A final thought as he drove off: It had not been Schnitzer, after all. It was Hackett's own sweat that was stinking up the car.

24

Hackett went through a red light at Fourteenth Street. He could have killed someone right then, who would be just as dead, just as bloody.

She could have been run down by a car anytime.

Except that the safety campaign was working. Predictions so far this year had the fatality rate the lowest in years. Say the numbers stayed around 190 dead, and say preschoolers made up 78 percent of that figure, as they did, then she could have been one of . . . Concentrating on the arithmetic, he went through another red light.

Except that she was smart. And wary. She would have anticipated.

Except that she had not. She had been stupid and careless. He had given her credit where none was due, and she had been stupid.

He passed a girl who looked just like— But from the front, she was a woman; elderly, not yet old. Will this keep happening?

he wondered then. For months after the funeral, he had heard his father's cough through the wall; had seen him in the hat of a stranger.

She was just a child, not yet grown. Ah Christ.

Familiar and beautiful to him at that moment, the Williamsburg Bridge took shape.

Ceil was home. The house was silent, but there were lights on upstairs as well as down. A Christmas wreath hung behind the window in the door.

He hammered on the ornamental knocker. Too late, he noticed the bell to the side.

"Who is it?" A face appeared within the wreath: Con, unlikely satyr. Too late again, Hackett remembered Con's Friday arrival.

"What the hell are you doing here?" Con said, belligerent, but even in silhouette his bulk looked soft, unthreatening. "You any idea what time it is?" As if the hour alone made peculiar Hackett's presence on his doorstep.

"It's past midnight, Con," Hackett said, almost gently. He was looking beyond Con at the wallpaper: cream with tan and maroon stripes. Ceil had described it to him the week she'd had it put up. It was prettier than it sounded, she had told him; she was right.

Ceil in her topcoat came down the narrow stairs. As the light hit her face, he saw that she was not wearing makeup. She has almond-shaped eyes, too, he thought, shocked that he had not noticed it before. That's why they reminded me of one another.

"Larry called," she said, as though Con were not standing between them. Her eyes were glittering, but a shadow distorted her chin. She looked like someone who resembled Ceil, but who was not her. Not she. She has done something with her hair, Hackett decided. Schnitzer had called, and she looked like death.

"Who's Larry?" Con said, of course.

"You've done something with your hair," Hackett said, and his voice cracked. Women pulled out their hair or cut it off; in mourning.

"You think I don't know what's going on here?" Con looked from one to the other, sharp for a soft man. Scorn pulled Hackett upright. Con resumed, "The whole fucking borough knows what's going on here." His genius for the obvious had expanded since his twenties; along with his waistline.

Considering the state of his muscles, Hackett managed a creditable smile. "You're a ten-day wonder in these parts yourself, Con, you know that. The whole fucking borough wants to know the names of your kids, Con, and why not? You're free enough with the rest of the shit."

Ceil turned abruptly and picked up the new cloche.

Con grabbed her arm. "And just where do you think you're going?"

"You're no slouch, Con, I'll give you that," Hackett said. He advanced into the hall, but Ceil had already shaken herself free.

She went behind the stairwell and returned with a small suitcase. "Whether you came or not," she said. "Either way, I was leaving."

She deserves better, Hackett was thinking. A little reassurance at least. He took the case from her.

"You won't get away with this, Hackett, I'll see to that," Con said like a schoolboy. "This is gonna cost you, maybe your job even."

"Is that a threat or a promise?" You would be surprised, Cornelius, what I can get away with. "Nothing goes on forever, you dumb bastard, don't you know that yet? Nothing's safe." Then remembered it was wasted on Con. Deliberately slow, Hackett turned his back.

He staggered once on the way out, nearly ruining the effect. Con was watching through the door.

"You knew I'd be back," he said in the car, but she didn't answer. Because she had not known, any more than he had. She would have curled her hair.

He got as far as the corner, then braked.

"She thought she was safe," he blurted. "I told her he was in the bag. I wanted her to feel safe. And I let her die."

He covered his ears, not his face, and the harsh, unlovely sounds seemed so removed it could have been Ceil crying. Or so he imagined.

25

The next morning, Saturday, Ceil called Hackett in sick for work. He failed to appear at the scheduled news conference that afternoon, too, and Long, pleased with the coverage, gave Hackett's photo to the papers. It was an old one, from the files, that made him look like a choirboy. Ceil saved it.

Mary Stephens was still under sedation at Bellevue. Sol, presumably on her behalf, made a faltering statement to the *News*, and some of his conjectures were so close to the mark that only pressure from Valentine himself prevented their publication; or so it was rumored. (This from Long, on the phone to Ceil.)

"Good Riddance to Bad Rubbish," the *News* bannered instead. The headline was Long's. ("And, oh yeah," Long threw in on the next call. He phoned daily. "Tell Jim we got a list here for him. From Washington. You can tell the country's going to the dogs, the paper it come on. Thin like a roll of—well, anyway. Our man's name on the list, ain't that something? And he's maybe on somebody else's list, too. We got a real interesting call from someplace in Iowa. No, Ohio. If our man was ever in Ohio. I'm saving that for him, too, tell him.")

Hackett continued to stay away from the bureau, and on the day of the joint funeral, his legs gave out completely. Ceil, who had seen it coming, sent flowers and Mass cards in his name to West Seventeenth Street, then called in a departmental doctor. Two weeks' sick leave was prescribed. A well-earned rest it was called in the personal note that arrived from the commissioner. Hackett's fortitude and perseverance were commended, and he was, further, an inspiration to all the city's bluecoats. Once upon a time the language would have made Hackett smile. Now he merely crumpled the paper and went back to studying the still lifes in the park. Once upon a time, he thought. Oh God.

Ceil handed him another whiskey. Ceil, whose almond-shaped eyes he could not meet, still looking like death. Death, which had been reduced to whiskey and remorse. Not death: Life.

At the beginning of Christmas week, a letter arrived from Mary Stephens. He refused to open it at first. He did read it, finally, on the day he received, and finished, the bottle of Chivas that Long—still generous—had sent him for Christmas.

"Then he went into the bedroom and just lay there," Ceil told her sister Nora on the phone next day. "Not even drinking. He seems better this morning. He's stopped waiting for the worst to hit him, I think. He walked around a bit, and he read the paper, at least. But he's still not talking." Ceil kept her voice down. There always seemed to be a reason for her, and her sisters, to discuss men in lowered tones.

By Christmas Eve, though, Ceil had had her fill of silence. She summoned Brennan, and the next day they escorted Hackett to the Blakes' Christmas dinner.

"You can like it or lump it," Ceil said flatly when her mother stared at him in disbelief. Back on her home ground, Ceil moved with an assurance she had almost forgotten she could call on. And now had a right to, she thought, and caught Jim smiling at her. He had read her mind.

Her mother, seeing confrontation in her daughter's face and

conciliation in his, said mournfully, "I don't understand the world anymore."

He cleared his throat carefully, like a man not used to speech. "I never did," he said, taking his turn with the white flag.

Under the table, Ceil took his hand. He leaned slightly, and both Ceil's sisters stared at him. He leaned away, and Ceil with lifted chin stood and followed her mother into the kitchen.

He thinks I tell them everything, she thought resentfully.

Outspoken with him, she was in fact reticent with them, even with Nora. ("It wouldn't be fair," she had told them once when both sisters were teasing her. "After all, it's Jim's love life, too. I'll tell you this much, though. If Jim were here, and we . . . Well, you'd both be in the confessional for a month." They had jeered then, and now they were staring, and he would never believe it was their own minds at work.

(In this, however, she wronged him. "They don't need any help along those lines. They're your sisters, right?" he told her, and Ceil stroked him. But that was a long time later.)

"He's very quiet, isn't he?" her mother said at the stove.

Ceil smiled. "Not once you get to know him," she said, and watched her mother put extra stuffing on his plate.

Truce of a more temporary nature took place the day after Christmas. That was when Brennan, still operating under Ceil's orders, showed up with Hackett's mother in tow. She was clean and relatively sober, and not only because of her awe of Ceil. Until Brennan had arrived to collect her, Walter, it turned out, had sat vigil with her.

"A lovely black lace he had on, Walter," she said in one of the silences. Behind her, Brennan choked. "He gave it to himself as a Christmas present. I only hope he doesn't catch his death wearing it. I only hope he doesn't have to go back to that hospital, is all. They're places to die in, hospitals."

She was trying, Hackett had to concede that. She was even trying to follow Brennan's banter, and out of deference to Ceil—whom she stared at without knowing that she did so—she was making each drink last longer. Ceil, as relaxed as Hackett had ever seen her, was fielding gracefully the abrupt non sequiturs that passed in his mother's mind for conversation. All in all, the time went faster than he had any right to expect.

On New Year's Day 1936, Detectives Long and Hackett were among the half-frozen police officers honored by Mayor La Guardia on the steps of City Hall. In spite of the weather, Hizzoner insisted on a long and flowery speech, and Hackett passed the time counting the number of "grands" the mayor managed to include. La Guardia always played best to an audience of specific composition. Hackett had once heard him speak to some immigrant group, and no word then had been longer than two syllables.

Ceil, looking too tall in a hat that didn't suit her, was standing between Brennan and Schnitzer. She had moved back to Brooklyn temporarily (she had stressed the word to her mother, who took exception to her tone, Ceil told Hackett). Until Brennan did his stuff. The plan called for Ceil to stand up and be counted among the virgins. Straight-faced, she was going to swear that she and Con had never; and Con and a couple of Brennan-supplied doctors were going to nod and say she spoke true. Ceil was looking forward to it; joking. But Hackett knew she was relieved to stay within the Church, and not only for her mother's sake either.

Hackett caught Brennan's eye and winked. Brennan, who should have been a politician. He was wittier, and briefer, than La Guardia. Briefer, anyway. It must be his own hot air that was keeping Fiorello warm.

In the pocket of Hackett's dress uniform was a crumpled Christmas card. Its design was an embarrassment—a crèche scene: unlikely beasts leering at a wistful Virgin—and Hackett had not yet shown it to Ceil.

Brother Gregory must have dashed it off while marking homework; the message inside was in the old red ink. "God bless you, my son. And a good year for our side, after all. Sir Thomas More is now officially St. Thomas More. *Slainté.*"

La Guardia stopped talking, and the crowd clapped in relief.

Long, predictably in front, for reasons of height and pushiness, was tugging at him. "It's us, Jim," he hissed. Anxious for his medal.

Slainté, Hackett thought, stepping forward. Cheers to you, too.